To Jack and Tom:
may you have adventures
to come in books and elsewhere,
and always come home safely

PIRATE BOY of SYDNEY TOWN

JACKIE FRENCH

Angus&Robertson
An imprint of HarperCollinsChildren'sBooks

Angus&Robertson
An imprint of HarperCollins*Children'sBooks*, Australia

First published in Australia in 2019
by HarperCollins*Publishers* Australia Pty Limited
ABN 36 009 913 517
harpercollins.com.au

HarperCollins*Publishers*
Level 13, 201 Elizabeth Street, Sydney NSW 2000, Australia
Unit D1, 63 Apollo Drive, Rosedale, Auckland 0632, New Zealand
A 53, Sector 57, Noida, UP, India
1 London Bridge Street, London SE1 9GF, United Kingdom
2 Bloor Street East, 20th floor, Toronto, Ontario M4W 1A8, Canada
195 Broadway, New York NY 10007, USA

A catalogue record for this book is available
from the National Library of Australia

ISBN 978 1 4607 5479 5 (paperback)
ISBN 978 1 4607 0918 4 (ebook)

Cover design by Lisa White
Cover images: Boy by Clayton Bastiani / Trevillion Images; map courtesy of the National Library of Australia [nla.obj-232400081]; all other images by shutterstock.com
Author photograph by Kelly Sturgiss
Typeset in Sabon LT Std by Kirby Jones
Printed and bound in Australia by McPherson's Printing Group
The papers used by HarperCollins in the manufacture of this book are a natural, recyclable product made from wood grown in sustainable plantation forests. The fibre source and manufacturing processes meet recognised international environmental standards, and carry certification.

CHAPTER 1

ENGLAND, 1809

The land was gold: fields of wheat that met the pale midsummer sky, the stalks rippling as the men moved through the crop, cutting with their scythes or bending to gather it into stooks. Ben ran from group to group with the other boys, taking the workers flasks of cold tea or doorstops of bread and cheese. Mama had taught him that a good landlord worked alongside his men. He glanced at the stooks of wheat, the sweating men and his excited friends — Tugger, Lugs, Young Lon. This was the most important work in all the world. This was their harvest, all of Badger's Hill working together. This wheat would become sacks of flour, and the flour would become bread to feed each person here, as well as distant others.

Old Barney took the flask from Ben, drained it, then gazed at the final, shrinking stand of wheat. 'Thank thee, Master Ebenezer. We's nearly done, I'm thinking.' He grinned. 'The good bit comes now.'

Ben grinned back. He returned to the carts with the empty flask, then raced back to form a wide circle around the last stand of wheat with the other boys. The men moved in, closer, closer, their scythes slashing. The stand of wheat was only three yards wide now.

A rabbit dashed out under Tugger's feet. 'Get 'im!' he yelled.

Young Lon and Lugs grabbed at it, but Ben had it first. He raised the rabbit triumphantly as it wriggled to get free, then quickly dislocated its neck and dropped it. More animals fled from the final cover in the field — rabbits, a scatter of mice, a hare. The boys darted, grabbing, cheering, adding to the pile of furry animals.

And the last of the wheat was cut.

Ben glanced at the pile of small animals. Their meat belonged to the boys who'd worked the harvest, even the rabbit he'd caught. But his catch had been the first! For a moment he thought he would float away with happiness.

He looked up to find Old Barney beaming at him, his six remaining teeth long and yellow. 'Harvest Home feast tomorrow night, eh, young master? The mistress got them puddins boilin'?'

Ben laughed. 'Puddings by the dozen, and jam tarts and apple pies.'

This was the tradition. A year of hard work, and then master and workmen feasted together, sang together, laughed together. This was the way it had been for the six hundred years Mama's family had owned Badger's Hill; since Ben's ancestor, Sir Roderick Montclaire, had tripped on a badger's hole, laughed, then claimed the land around it as his own.

Tugger nudged Ben. 'Ain't fair that boys is left out of the feast,' he muttered, too low for Old Barney to hear. 'We worked too.'

'Aye,' said Lugs indignantly. 'We should have our own feast.'

Ben glanced at the men clambering onto the carts with the scythes. He grinned again. 'All right. I'll see to it.'

'How?' demanded Lugs.

'You'll see. Meet me at moonrise at the oak tree behind the barn tomorrow night,' said Ben softly. 'Tell the other boys.'

'Girls too?' suggested Tugger.

'Course not,' said Lugs. 'And anyhow, girls can't climb trees.'

They ran to get their share of the harvest animals. Ben watched them go, the boys he had grown up with: tenant farmers' sons, workmen's sons. Then he looked across the spreading fields fenced with hawthorn hedges, and up to the tall honey-coloured stone of the house he lived in on the crest of the hill, with its orchards, its outbuildings, and the clustered cottages of the workers, each with its rose bush and neat lines of cabbages and potato plants. Badger's Hill. Home.

The barn smelled of the roasted ox on its spit outside, of cider, smoke and sweat. Faces gleamed in the lamplight, their plates piled high with meat. The giant platters of roast potatoes, parsnips and buttered cabbage were almost untouched. A man could eat cabbage from his garden any day, but only on this one night of the year could he eat all the meat he could scoff, then take a parcel of beef home to the wife and little'uns too, along with a head cheese maybe for the toothless old folk.

Mama sat at the head of the table, Old Barney at her left hand and Sidney, the head groom, at her right. Ben sat at the other end, where Father would have been if business didn't keep him in London most of the year.

When at last everyone had eaten their fill of meat, Mama nodded to the servants. The platters were replaced with apple pies, plum puddings, great wheels of cheese — for who'd want apple pie without a hunk of cheese? — jugs of clotted cream and custard. There were spoons for those who preferred them to Adam's cutlery, their fingers; and fresh jugs of cider lined the table.

Old Barney stood. 'And now, folks, it be time to lift your glasses to the mistress and to Master Ebenezer, to thank 'em for another Harvest Home!'

Ben flushed with pleasure. This was the first time he had been publicly thanked as well as Mama. He remained seated as the men all stood and drank their health.

More toasts came, and the pies and puddings shrank to crumbs. At last Old Barney rose again. It was time to sing.

''Twas in the spring when young Jed Brown
Thought he might walk to Lunnon Town
For there he might just find a mart
To buy himself a true sweetheart ...'

Ben had heard the song a dozen times. Knew how Jed Brown would find a guinea, lose it to highwaymen, follow them to their lair, rescue the fair maiden held captive there, carry off the stolen gold and walk back home triumphant, never having been to 'Lunnon Town' at all. But he still enjoyed it. Loved the laughter, loved joining in at the chorus: '*Derry down, derry down ...*'

The song finished to cheers and applause. Someone began 'John Barleycorn'. Ben glanced out of the barn door. The moon was a sliver of cheese on the horizon. The men would sing for hours. No one would notice if he left now.

He slipped out the back door, grabbed the sack he'd left there and made for the big oak that stood at the edge of the park. Some said it had stood there since Sir Roderick's time.

Ben peered up into the branches. Faces looked down at him. 'Here, take this,' he hissed, holding up the sack.

'What you got?'

'You'll see.'

He waited till Tugger had hauled up the sack, then shinned up the giant trunk, gripping with his knees and elbows till he reached the first broad branch. Three boys sat there already, with others above them. Ben opened the sack and pulled out a huge sirloin of cold roast beef.

'Cor, look at that,' said Young Lon appreciatively. 'Anyone got a knife?'

'Me,' said Lugs.

'Chop it up, will you?' asked Ben.

Tugger peered into the dimness of the sack. 'What else you got in there?'

'Two apple pies, half a cheese, a plum pudding, a roast chicken … sorry, it's squashed the pies a bit … half a game pie, and this!' Ben held up the flagon of cider in triumph.

'How'd you get it all?' demanded Tugger, his mouth already full of cold roast beef.

'Waited till the servants were having dinner. Cookie made so much she won't miss this.'

She probably would. But Cookie also snuck Ben gingerbread between meals and made him extra-large ham pies when he went egging with the other boys so he could share with them.

'Three cheers for Ben,' said Lugs softly. He took a gulp of cider and passed it on.

Ben broke off a hunk of apple pie, slightly chicken-flavoured, and passed the rest up to the boys on the branch above. The tree filled with the sounds of eating, while the moon floated lily-like in the vast pond of the sky.

We must do this every year, thought Ben. Even when I am an old man, I will make sure there is a feast for the boys in the oak tree.

Happiness filled him, as fizzy as the cider in the jug.

Ben slept late the next morning. He woke to find his clothes had been left warming for him by the fire. He dressed quickly, then ran downstairs to the morning room. Breakfast was still laid out on the sideboard, though Mama must have eaten hours ago. He helped himself to kidneys and bacon, kept hot in the silver chafing dishes.

'Fresh toast, Master Ebenezer,' said Filkinghorn, placing the toast rack before Ben. The butler had been at Badger's Hill ever since Mama was a girl. 'And tea,' he added disapprovingly.

Ale had been served at breakfast until Mama had brought the tea-drinking habit back from school. That had been twenty years ago, but Filkinghorn still wasn't used to it.

'Thank you, Filkinghorn,' said Ben, spreading marmalade thickly on his toast.

He looked up at a clatter in the yard. Filkinghorn vanished to open the front door. Ben wished he could follow, but only urchins peered around front doors. Voices … Mama's and a stranger's, and Father's too! Why hadn't Father sent word to expect him?

Ben ran out to the hall just as Filkinghorn shut the library door. 'What's happening?' he demanded. 'Was that Father?'

The butler's expression was impossible to read. 'Yes, Master Ebenezer. The mistress said she'd send for you when they need you.'

'Thank you, Filkinghorn.'

What was happening? Why shouldn't he go in to greet his father straight away? Father only visited Badger's Hill for a few weeks in midsummer when London was full of diseases and smells. He should have been here weeks ago, but there had been no letter saying when he'd arrive. He always came with exotic gifts carried back by his ships: bright-coloured silks, fireworks from China that had astounded everybody, and once a parrot that really talked, though only in French, which Mama had said was a good thing because of the sailors' swearwords it shouted out.

Ben walked back to the morning room, finished his tea and toast after his kidneys and bacon, then nodded to Elsie to clear the sideboard. The hall clock chimed ten. It was time for his Latin lesson down at the rectory.

'Master Ebenezer? The master wishes to see you in the library.' Filkinghorn's voice sounded ... odd.

'Is ... is something the matter, Filkinghorn?'

The butler's gaze seemed to drink in the ordered morning room, the polished table and sideboard, the blue silk curtains at the window. At last he said, 'That is for the master to say, Master Ebenezer.'

Ben checked that his cuffs didn't have marmalade on them, then crossed the room into the hallway. Filkinghorn opened the library door for him, and Ben stepped into the scent of old books, neatsfoot oil and lavender polish. His father stood by the window, stiff and silent. Mama sat on the sofa, her body rigid, as though all life had been squeezed from it. The stranger sat next to her, gazing at the books as if counting them. He looked around as Ben came in.

'Father!' Ben said.

Mr Huntsmore gave him a brief nod.

Ben had been about to run to him, but stopped as Mama said shakily, 'Mr Nattisville, this is our son, Ebenezer. Ben, this is Mr Nattisville, the new ... owner ... of Badger's Hill.'

The library seemed to fade, as if the summer sun had flickered. Ben stared at the man sitting next to Mama. He was stout, pale, a city man. No. This was impossible.

'I ... I don't understand,' he said. 'Badger's Hill is ours. It's always been ours.'

The stranger smiled at him, not unkindly. 'No longer, I'm afraid. Your father mortgaged the land to me two years ago to fund his shipping venture to China. The ships sank and the mortgage is due.'

'But Badger's Hill belongs to Mama.'

'A woman's property becomes her husband's on her marriage,' said Mama, her voice carefully emptied of emotion. She did not look at Father.

Badger's Hill isn't 'property', thought Ben. It's land and people. It's Lugs and Tugger and Old Barney and Filkinghorn. It's our life.

Mama stood, her face pale, her fingers clenched. She still didn't look at her husband, but her voice was steady as she said, 'Mr Nattisville, please let me show you the accounts. You will wish to see the property too, and be introduced to the household.'

'Thank you, Mrs Huntsmore,' said Mr Nattisville, rising and bowing politely. He followed her into the hall.

Ben ran after them. 'Mama —' he began.

Mama smiled that empty, polite smile at Mr Nattisville. 'If you will excuse us, I will change into something more suitable. Ben, if you would come with me.'

Ben waited till they had turned the corner of the staircase. 'Mama, it ... it can't be true.'

His mother kept climbing, step by step, as evenly as if she had been wound up, like a clock, and could not stop. 'It is,' she said briefly.

'But Father couldn't … he wouldn't …'

'Of course he would.' For the first time anger seeped into her words. 'He married me for my money. Once he had that and a son, he no longer needed me or Badger's Hill. And now he has lost both the money and the land.'

Ben stared at her. Why had she never told him? He'd never guessed. 'But what will we do?' he asked her.

Mama stopped at that and held out her arms to him. 'Ben …' He fell into her embrace, felt her warmth about him. 'We have no choice,' she whispered. 'A wife belongs to her husband. A son belongs to his father. He can do what he wants with us.'

Ben longed to comfort her, to say, 'When I grow up, I will win Badger's Hill back for you.' But how could he promise that? This was the only world he knew.

At last she pushed him gently away. 'I need to persuade Mr Nattisville to do well by our people,' she said quietly. 'Go to your father. I don't know what he intends for us now, but perhaps he will tell his son.' She gave a bitter smile.

Ben returned to the library and opened the door quietly. The room's scent seemed to have changed. Now it smelled of betrayal. His father still stood by the window, gazing at the gardens that were no longer theirs.

Ben had thought his father a brave man who rode the wave-lashed trade routes from England to Calcutta and

Shanghai. A man who loved his son, his wife, his land. But Ben realised he had made that man from his own imagination, like Cookie fashioned gingerbread men from dough.

'How could you lose Badger's Hill, sir?' he demanded.

His father turned to look at him. 'It's land, son. No more, no less,' he said flatly. 'It hardly makes a profit.'

Ben stared at him. Profit? How could anyone reduce Badger's Hill to mere money? Was this truly all his father had thought when he visited the place? And yet it seemed Badger's Hill *was* just money, in the eyes of his father and of the law.

'What about the servants?' he asked. 'The men? The tenant farmers?'

'Nattisville will keep some of the servants, or whoever rents the place will. I doubt Nattisville wants to live so far from society. And if the men and tenants are hardworking, he'll keep them on too.'

What of those who could no longer work, like old Mr Porter, or the widow Jeffries and her children? Ben wanted to strike this man who called himself his father; he wanted to defend his home and people.

He met his father's eyes. 'And us, sir — Mama and me? Do you expect us to go to London with you?'

He had only been to the capital once, with its choking fogs and foulness, its creeping filthy river and houses as far as you could see.

'London? No, I'm through with London for a while. I've had a run of bad luck at the gaming tables. If I don't make good on my promises,' Mr Huntsmore shrugged, 'there won't be a club in London that will open its doors to me. But I've found a way to turn our fortunes around.' He glanced at the door, as if to make sure no servants were lurking, then drew an envelope from his pocket. 'Look!' His voice grew eager. 'Do you know what these are, son?'

'No, sir,' said Ben, holding his politeness like a shield. Like Mama had done, he thought.

'They are letters of marque, signed by the Prince of Wales himself a week ago when we were playing cards.' His father's voice dropped low. 'These letters give me permission to sail against any enemies of the Crown. That means the Frenchies, boy. I have one ship left, and even she is mortgaged, but one ship is all I need to rebuild our fortunes. Riches unlimited!'

'How, sir?' asked Ben, because his father seemed to want him to.

'You know the Port Jackson colony?'

Ben nodded. A prison colony at the end of the world, on the east coast of New Holland, or New South Wales as some now called it, filled with criminals and poisonous snakes, and where nothing grew the way it should. The rector had lent him William Tench's account of the colony's terror of starvation a decade or two before.

'And you know where it is near, son?'

Ben forced himself to answer. 'It's south of India and China, sir.'

'Ha! Ships that ply the India and China trade routes are too well-armed to attack. We'll have no truck with them. No, boy, Port Jackson is south of the richest port in all the world: Batavia. Used to be a Dutch port, but the French control Holland now Napoleon has put his brother on the throne there.'

'So now the Dutch are our enemies too?'

'Exactly. Napoleon would take England too if he could, just like he's invaded half of Europe. But we will beat him — and as we do, men like me will make our fortunes. And you will be at my side.'

'I don't understand, sir.' Ben's lips felt numb, his mind as thick as treacle.

His father lowered his voice even further. 'No more plodding among the country clods for my son. We're going to capture a Dutch ship, lad. Not a warship like the Navy fights, but an enemy's trading ship. Ships laden with gold that sail far south to catch the world's fastest winds, then up the west coast of New Holland to Batavia to buy their pepper, nutmeg and cinnamon. Not one of them will suspect they might be attacked so far south.' Mr Huntsmore's face had fallen into what Ben suspected was his true expression: the bright face of a gambler dreaming of gold. 'Capturing just one of those ships will pay my debts a hundred times over, make us rich as nabobs. And these …' He lifted the letters and kissed them. 'These give me, Branwell Huntsmore, the right to take any enemy ship, lock, stock, gold and spices.'

The clock seemed to stop ticking. Time stretched, so it felt like minutes before Ben managed to whisper, 'We'll be pirates?'

Pirates were thieves. Murderers.

His father grinned. 'Privateers, because we have the blessing of the Prince of Wales. We'll take a load of convicts out there and cargo too, to get some ready cash and so nobody suspects what we plan to do. We don't want others joining in our game. Once two or three Dutch ships have been taken, other captains will get wary and arm their ships. We want them just sitting there, ripe for the plucking. The *Golden Girl*'s decks are being reinforced even as we speak, and Captain Danvers has set about hiring the right crew. There'll be cast-iron cannons and muskets down in the hold and barrels of gunpowder. Just one ship, son, to turn our fortunes right!'

Ben couldn't seem to move or speak. It was too much to take in. He had lost his home, his life. And this was what his father was offering to replace it.

'Well, son? Are you with me? Or have you been turned into a mouse by too much petticoat rule?'

Ben met his father's eyes. 'What if I say no, sir?'

Mr Huntsmore gazed at him. 'Lily-livered, eh?'

'I am not lily-livered!'

'This is for your sake too,' his father said. 'I'm offering you adventure! But if you are afraid to join me, you can stay with your mother in Sydney Town. I'll rent a house there.'

'Mama is coming too? But ... but it's a dangerous voyage to Port Jackson, sir!'

Ben knew enough about shipping to understand that one in four ships sank — wrecked on rocks or icebergs, or lashed with giant waves in storms; or were blown off course, or lost in the doldrums when no wind blew to fill their sails so all on board starved or died of thirst.

'Anything I leave here with your mother could be confiscated to pay my debts,' Mr Huntsmore said. 'She has to come. Well? Are you scared to leave your little badger's burrow? Frightened to face the world?'

Ben met his father's eyes again. 'I'm not scared, sir.' Mama's words came back to him: *We have no choice.* And this at least was a way he might be able to buy back their home. 'I'll fight with you,' he added quietly. 'If that will get our fortune back.'

His father laughed and clapped Ben on the back. He stank of rum toddy, Ben realised. Even his skin smelled of it.

'Losing this place may be the best thing that ever happened to you!' he said. 'Should have been sent to school long ago. But you mustn't breathe a word, eh?'

Mr Huntsmore tapped his nose. 'Not even to your mother. Especially not to her. Women don't understand business. Or the difference between being a privateer and a pirate.'

Yes, my father is a pirate, Ben thought. He is looting his wife's life and his son's.

He lifted his chin. 'When we have made our fortune, I will buy Badger's Hill back.'

His father shrugged. 'I doubt you'll still want this old place when you've seen more of the world. No, we'll have something much grander, boy. A castle maybe. And a proper heiress for you to marry, not a Friday face from a backwater where there are scarce three families fit to dine with.'

Anger seethed, but Ben kept his voice calm, as Mama had done. 'I want Badger's Hill, sir.'

'Well, I expect Nattisville will be willing enough to sell to you when the time comes. There's no decent hunting here, and tuppence in the bank at the end of the year.' He rang the bell. 'Another rum toddy,' he ordered Filkinghorn when the butler opened the library door.

Mr Huntsmore waited till the old man had left, then smiled at Ben, his eyes gleaming. 'They think Branwell Huntsmore is finished in the city, but we'll show them, won't we, son? We'll come sailing back with a fortune.'

'Yes, sir,' said Ben, but inside he was thinking that he no longer had a home. He must leave his friends as well as all the people he held dear. All he had now was a ship, a distant colony, and his father's dreams of riches and adventure — all dependent on the words he must not say.

Privateer. Pirate.

CHAPTER 2

1810

The *Golden Girl* sat off the heads of Sydney Harbour. The cold wind from the freezing Southern Ocean they had just left spat and buffeted them, and waves slapped at her sides. No man on board knew how to navigate the narrow passage between the headlands, or what treachery the harbour rocks might bring. Captain Danvers had sent two men in the ship's pinnace to fetch the pilot to bring the *Golden Girl* safely into port.

Ben sat numbly on a coil of rope on deck. He knew he should be excited, so near a strange new land and the enterprise that would make them rich. But he just felt numb, as if every bone had been leached of strength and his mind too.

The ship stank of death. Typhoid had come on board with the casks of water at Rio de Janeiro, and Ben had been one of the first to come down with it. Days and nights had merged as he lay there sweating, delirious, seeing Mama's face swimming in the dimness of the cabin as she bathed his skin to try to lower his fever. Then Mama had vanished, and the Scottish steward, McStewart, had tended him instead. Then he, too, disappeared.

Ben had been delirious for two weeks, and too weak for three weeks after that even to sit up. By the time he could eat the broth one of the sailors brought him, made from the jellied portable soup Mama had prepared so many months before at Badger's Hill, they had already sailed into the freezing gales of the Southern Ocean. And that was when he learned that Mama, and McStewart too, had died of the fever.

Mama's body had long since been wrapped in canvas and slipped overboard. His father told him there had been prayers.

Ben felt like yelling at the wind, 'It isn't fair!'

It wasn't fair that Mama should die, or that she should do so far from the soil and people that she loved. It wasn't fair that Ben hadn't been there to hold her hand, to whisper that he loved her, that one day he'd get back Badger's Hill. And it wasn't fair that now he was alone with the man he must call Father.

Life isn't fair, whispered the wind. *Only the scraps that we make fair.*

Mr Huntsmore and Captain Danvers were among the few who had escaped illness. Over half the ship's crew were dead, their corpses left, like Mama's, among the green water and the icebergs. But the fever had finally burned itself out. The ship no longer flew the yellow flag that warned other ships to keep clear in case the sickness was passed to them.

Up on the foredeck, Ben's father paced with Captain Danvers, watching for the pilot. A few sailors trimmed the sails just enough to keep the ship steady. The rest of the crew were below, weakened by fever and by scurvy. The waves sloshed against the hull, the seagulls screamed, the timbers creaked, and the sails slapped. But the ship was strangely quiet. Even the yells and curses from the convicts down below in the hold had ceased.

How many of them had died? Ben wondered. No one knew. It seemed that no one cared. Some must still be alive, because the buckets of food and water that were lowered twice a day into the hold returned empty. Other than that, no one opened the hatch except on the captain's orders.

When they had first sailed, the hundred and twenty men down there had seemed like a vast beehive below the decks. Ben had heard moans and sometimes screams; and laughter that was even worse, on and on until it became a shriek.

Mama had cried for the convicts in those first weeks at sea. Late at night, when his parents had thought him sleeping, Ben had heard her plead, 'For God's sake, Branwell! They are people, not just cargo.'

His father had just laughed. 'Of course they are cargo, Margaret. The best kind. I get paid for each man I take from Plymouth, not each one I deliver to Port Jackson. The fewer who survive the better. What they don't eat on the voyage, I can sell when we arrive.'

'You are a monster!'

'Then you are a monster's wife. Get used to it. Perhaps it's best things turned out the way they have before you make my son a lily-hearted weakling like yourself.'

His mother didn't answer. Later, he heard her sobs. Ben wished that he had risen from his trundle bed to comfort her and tell her that he loved her, and that his father was going to make their fortune once again and they would return to Badger's Hill, and be happy. But he had not. And now Mama was gone.

Something thudded against the deck below his feet. It sounded like a broom handle. A hoarse voice called, 'Anyone alive up there? For pity's sake, help us! We're half-dead down here, those of us who ain't corpses already. If there's anyone alive up there, help us!'

The surviving convicts must have realised the ship had stopped but was still at sea, buffeted by ocean waves and wind, not bobbing gently in the harbour. They must also have guessed that typhoid had thinned the crew, and perhaps wondered if enough remained to sail the ship to safety. How long would the convicts have to wait down there? And what if there was no spare pilot at the tiny port to sail the *Golden Girl* into safe harbour? How many more would die? And Ben could do nothing to help.

Or could he? He looked at the rope that let down the food and water buckets, the wheel that rolled the rope out and back. It took only one man to turn it. Ben was only a boy, still weak from the fever, but he could try.

He looked around. No one paid him any notice. He stepped over to the hatch and lifted. Nothing happened. He was too weak. Lily-hearted ... He was not!

He pulled again, and the hatch shifted. A stench wafted up, thick as toast. It knocked him backwards, almost blinded as the filthy air stung his eyes, and crawled down his nose, his throat.

A scurvy-weakened sailor, his bare feet swollen, stumbled towards him. 'What you doin'? You can't do that!'

'I'm the owner's son,' said Ben. 'I can do whatever I like.'

'We'll see about that.' The sailor limped away towards the foredeck.

Screams and mutters rose from below as the piercing ocean light blinded those who had lived for five months in darkness. If they could survive down there, then Ben could bear the stench. He lifted the bucket on its rope and swung it down into the filth and darkness of the hold.

'What's goin' on? The cursed bucket's empty!' It was the same voice as before, hoarse and angry.

Ben forced himself to peer through the hatch. Darkness moved within darkness. 'Can you cling onto the bucket?' he called. 'I'll haul you up.'

Silence. Was it hope or calculation?

'Let down the ladder, boy.' The tone was wheedling now.

'I can't do that.'

Wouldn't do that. Could a band of convicts take over the ship? Surely not, weak and starved as they must be. But Ben couldn't risk it. He might save just one or two though — bring them up into the light, feed them plum cake and portable soup.

The rope rocked. Someone screamed below. He heard a snarl, a gust of foul language, then the order: 'Heave away!'

Ben anchored himself against the rail and pulled at the rope, sweating, his arms trembling. Suddenly the rope moved easily and he heard a scrambling sound. Two claws grabbed the edge of the hatch and hauled up a heap of bones and rags and filth. It collapsed on the deck, hiding its face from the light.

It wasn't human. It couldn't be human.

'Water!' the creature muttered, still face down on the deck.

Ben grabbed the mug tied to one of the water barrels, filled it, unfastened it, then slid it towards the figure on the deck. A claw scrabbled blindly, found the mug, drank.

'More,' it muttered.

Ben ventured closer. He grabbed the mug before the claws could reach for him and filled it again. Again the figure drained it. The stench was unbelievable. Were those maggots in its hair? But the creature was human, and a human Ben had saved. Out of all the misery of the past year, he had done this at least — brought a suffering person up into the sunlight.

Ben waited for the convict to say, 'Bless you, young master.' Instead he muttered a string of words, so hoarsely that Ben had to struggle to make them out. They were filthy words, angry words, some of which he didn't know.

'Murtherin' buzzards … Heartless fevermongers … Puffguts stuffin' 'emselves while poor folk die …'

Ben recognised those words. And he deserved them, sailing in the comfort of the owner's cabin, with barrels of plum puddings stored in bran, and hams and soup to eat on their journey. But I had no choice, he thought. Except, of course, he had. He could have argued with his father, fought to send more food down to the convicts. He had been swallowed up by his misery and loss even before the fever.

'I'm sorry,' he said to the creature huddled on the deck. It was not enough. But it was all he had.

At last the muttering stopped and the thing began to sit up. Suddenly it became a man. A man in rags, dripping with filth, rusty shreds of what had once been hair now crawling with lice, face worm-white, red-rimmed eyes shut against the light.

'Water,' he murmured.

'I'll get you another drink,' Ben said.

'Water to wash, you widgeon.'

Of course. A bucket of seawater. As he turned to get it, Ben became aware that the sailor who had shouted at him earlier was coming back, and Father with him.

'What in the name of all that's holy are you doing, boy?' yelled Mr Huntsmore. Then to the sailor, 'Throw that thing back below.'

'No!' Ben forced his body between the convict and the sailor. 'You can't send him back down there!'

His father looked at the bundle of rags in disgust. 'I can send him anywhere I wish. Do you realise that typhoid may still be raging down there? They won't let us dock if they think we carry fever.'

'Ain't no fever,' said the man, still sitting with his eyes closed. 'There's scurvy, and a few gone mad. But the fever's gone.'

'Good.' Mr Huntsmore gestured to the sailor. 'What are you waiting for, man?'

'No!' cried Ben. He tried to think of an argument that might sway his father. 'We need a servant to replace Mr McStewart,' he said quickly. 'Have you ever been a servant?' he asked the convict.

Was that a smile? A crafty, smug smile that said, *I've got you now.*

'Just so happens I have,' the man said. And added, 'Master.'

CHAPTER 3

Mr Huntsmore returned to the quarterdeck, leaving Ben, the convict and the sailor by the hatch, now closed again. The convict was too weak to wash himself, and Ben didn't have enough strength to haul up the seawater required. But they managed it, with bucket after bucket of cold water grudgingly hauled up by the sailor.

'What's your name?' asked Ben at last, when the bundle of skin and rags next to him was almost clean. The man's body was emaciated, and his eyes watered, still growing accustomed to daylight after the months below.

''iggins,' said the man, spitting out a tooth and then another, and wiping his bloody mouth on his sleeve.

Ben looked in horror at the yellow objects lying on the deck. He had not known teeth could get as long as that.

'Higgins?' he repeated.

'That's what I said. What's yours?'

'My name is Ebenezer Huntsmore. Can you walk, Mr Higgins?'

A shake of the head, more lice than straggly hair. 'Better lend us yer shoulder, Sneezer.'

'My name is Ebenezer.'

Higgins smiled innocently. 'Weren't that what I said?'

Was that another sly grin? Ben remembered how the convict had found the strength to haul himself up the rope to the deck. How many reaching arms had he pushed past to make his way up to the light? How many desperate hands had he pushed away to get what he needed from the water and food buckets? For the first time Ben realised that sending a rope down into a hold full of convicts was the way to bring up the most ruthless, not the most deserving.

'What was your crime?' he asked. Please, not murder. Don't let Higgins stab us in our beds. But murderers were hanged, weren't they, not sent to the colony?

'Bein' poor,' said Higgins flatly.

Ben felt a spurt of anger. He had *saved* this man. He should be given gratitude, respect.

'Apart from that,' he snapped.

'I were a fence, weren't I.'

'I don't understand.'

The look was unmistakeably one of contempt now. 'I had a fencin' ken. Coves brought me stuff they nicked and I sold it on. Had a cross crib too, and a tribe of kinchin coves I was trainin' to be thimblers.'

The words were meaningless, but Ben suspected they meant nothing good.

'I'll take you to the servant's quarters,' he said coldly. It was just a hammock next to the owner's cabin, roughly partitioned off with a blanket. But it would be a palace compared to where Higgins had been.

Higgins shaded his eyes with his skeletal hands and tried to peer around. 'Where are we?'

'Waiting off Sydney Heads. The pinnace has gone to fetch a pilot. We should be ashore soon.'

'And I'm goin' to be your servant. Fancy that.'

'Unless Father objects again.'

'He the captain?'

'No. Father owns the ship.'

'Does he now. Well, ain't that good. Come on now, Sneezer, give us a hand. Me shamblers ain't too steady.'

'I told you what my name is!' Ben said, but reluctantly put his arm around the convict. The man's bones seemed as thin as a rat's.

'You got spare clobber?' Higgins asked as they limped their way across the deck. 'Clothes,' he added when he saw Ben didn't understand. 'Can't be a gentleman's servant in rags.'

The man was scarcely as tall as Ben was, and far thinner. McStewart's clothes would be too big, but he could cuff the trousers, tie the belt tight.

The skeletal arm tightened a little around Ben's shoulders and Higgins gave a faint triumphant cackle. 'Well, look at me now, with the gentry as me crutch.

Come on then, Sneezer, let's get me some decent grub. I'm fair gut-foundered.'

Ben knew Higgins wouldn't talk like that to his father. But even so, he said, 'I'll find you some food.'

Dressed in proper clothes that hid his skeletal frame, with what was left of his hair combed back, Higgins looked human again. He stared at the ham Ben had set out on the cabin table, the wheel of cheese, the plum pudding and squares of jellied soup, then snatched a slice of pudding.

'This is gentry grub,' he muttered through the crumbs. 'This what the crew eat on this ship, Sneezer?'

'No,' said Ben shortly. He had felt ashamed at eating so well while the men who worked had to eat salt beef blackened with age and so tough they had to cut off bits that couldn't be chewed, and ship's biscuit that was sour with weevils.

His father had laughed when Mama had protested. 'You want to feed sailors ham and pudding?' he'd said. 'No wonder the estate never made a shilling.'

Mama had said no more.

Higgins ate ravenously for a quarter of an hour, tearing chunks off with his fingers, washing them down with ale. He'd never make a servant, Ben thought. But at least he'd get a meal or two and some respite from the hell below.

Higgins stopped eating at last, looking regretfully at the unfinished wheel of cheese. 'Rum grub that,' he said hoarsely, and pulled a shred of ham from the ruins of his teeth. He looked at it, then began to chew it again. 'How's about a kip, Sneezer?'

'I beg your pardon?'

'A sleep, matey. Rest me shamblers. Don't think I've slept proper since Plymouth, not three to a bunk. Though we all got a bunk to ourselves now mostly, what with so many dead.' He met Ben's eyes. 'But somehow you don't feel like sleepin' sound when you might not wake up at all.'

'I'll show you your bunk,' said Ben. He hesitated, then helped the convict to his feet again.

Higgins made his way uncertainly out the door and collapsed on the hammock. Once more he was a pile of bones. A snoring pile of bones.

Mr Huntsmore didn't mention Higgins when he came back to their cabin late that night. He must have dined with Captain Danvers. He put a candlestick on the table, undressed, pulled on his nightgown and cap, and slid into bed. The sheets hadn't been changed since McStewart died. Ben soon heard the faint whistle that meant his father was asleep.

Ben gazed at the ceiling in the flickering light of the candle his father hadn't bothered to snuff out. Its wood had been polished before they sailed from Plymouth, but now soot stained the area around the lamp hooks. And even in here, the cleanest, most private place on board the ship, the stench of convicts and the filthy bilges filled the room.

This is my home now, thought Ben. For though he and his father would go ashore while the ship was unloaded, careened and restocked, they'd soon be aboard again, hunting their fortune.

And what of Higgins? He did not know.

Ben woke to footsteps across the cabin floor. The ship still creaked idly around them. The pinnace hadn't returned.

'Your tea, Mr Huntsmore, sir. And Master Ebenezer.'

Ben sat up on the trundle bed and stared. Higgins loomed above them, a tray in his hands that held Mama's teapot, two of her china cups and a plate with some of the oaten biscuits she had carefully baked three times so they'd survive the voyage. No one had served them tea in the morning since McStewart had died.

Ben reached out automatically for the cup and a biscuit, then recoiled at the sight of Higgins's skull-like face. The convict's thin hands trembled slightly, and his red eyes squinted at the light in the cabin, but despite all that he looked ... like a servant, thought Ben. It wasn't just that he'd dressed himself in McStewart's clothes. He was polite. No, more than that — he was deferential, which Ben knew Higgins was not. And how did he know the correct way to serve a gentleman tea in the morning?

'I have taken the liberty of sponging your suit, sir,' said Higgins. Even his accent had changed. Not quite that of an upper servant but not close off it either. 'I h'endeavoured to h'iron h'it in the galley, but h'it is not what I might h'achieve on shore.'

Ben's father took the cup of tea thoughtfully and sipped. 'What is your name again?'

'Higgins, sir.'

'Have you seen domestic service before?'

'Third footman to a merchant, Mr Bigges, sir.'

'And you left because ...?'

'I could see better h'opportunity h'elsewhere, sir.'

'And yet you ended up in His Majesty's prison.'

'H'unfortunately yes, sir. And now I h'am serving your tea.'

The two men looked at each other, evaluating.

Finally Mr Huntsmore nodded. 'Very well, Higgins. Do you wish to continue in my employ when we land?'

'H'it would be an honour, sir,' oozed Higgins.

'And more comfortable than breaking stones to build new roads,' said Mr Huntsmore dryly. 'Very well. If you continue to give satisfaction, I will arrange to have you assigned to me for the months we are in New South Wales. Thank you, I do not need help dressing. By the way, if my watch, necktie or any article is misplaced, you will hang for it.'

'I would h'expect nothing less, sir.'

Higgins backed out almost politely, but Ben saw a gleam in his red crusted eyes.

CHAPTER 4

The ship's pinnace returned with a pilot mid-morning. The *Golden Girl*'s main sails were hoisted and filled with wind, and she slipped through the narrow passage between the headlands into the harbour.

Ben leaned over the rail. The harbour was so vast! It was so different too, strange yet beautiful. The excitement he'd failed to feel for the last few months began to flicker.

His first impressions were of dazzling blue and olive green, fingers of drab-coloured trees and black rocks enclosing the most gigantic harbour he had seen. Its waters were calm after the restless seas outside, and ruffled by a breeze that smelled of a strange smoke and unfamiliar trees. The sky seemed too high, too deep a blue for winter ... and the trees didn't know the rules: none seemed to have had the decency to lose their leaves. They were thin-topped, as if the fierce sun had sucked away their branches and foliage.

A dark-skinned woman in a canoe that was floating

low in the water looked up at him and laughed. She wore only a string belt, with objects hanging from it. Ben tried not to stare at her. The canoe had a tiny fire at one end, where a naked black child grilled a fish on a stick. It was the first fresh food Ben had smelled since leaving Rio and the first time he had felt true hunger.

More canoes appeared as they sailed further into the harbour. A fire flickered on one of the golden coves, and he saw black women sitting on the sand and young people diving in the lapping water, laughing, splashing, swimming. He had never seen people swim before.

Those boys might be Young Lon or Tugger, he thought, and wondered where they were now. Had Mr Nattisville let their families stay at Badger's Hill? Mama had left her pearls with the rector so they might be sold to help those most in need. There had been no time to sell them herself, nor could she risk her husband finding out. The rector had promised to write with news, but Ben knew they would probably sail again before any ship brought a letter. He thrust away the memory of his friends. He had been unable to reassure them when he'd said goodbye and was just as helpless now. His only hope of returning to Badger's Hill, of buying back the land, was this wild venture at the end of the world.

A flock of birds flashed overhead, their reds and greens too bright. Seagulls hovered around the ship, their cries different from the gulls' calls back home.

Creaking and flapping, the *Golden Girl* veered past a tiny island. The distant shore had proper houses now, each sitting within distinct squares of garden, pasture and orchard. Some looked neat; others substantial.

The ship swerved into another branch of the harbour. That must be the port, Ben realised. At first glance it was like the other ports he'd seen on the voyage: rough wooden buildings on the western side of one of the two wharves, and a four-storey sandstone building that must be the Commissariat store, with workshops, sawpits, boatsheds and what looked like a watchhouse within a paling fence. A Navy ship was already docked there.

Dirt lanes ran higgledy-piggledy up the slope behind the wharves, crammed with the kind of taverns Ben had seen by the docks in London. They sold cheap gin to sailors and bowls of stew the owners swore contained neither cat nor rat. Huts straggled above them on one side of the port, with sagging roofs or collapsing mud walls, but the other side showed cobbled roads leading up to more substantial streets and buildings.

'Puny little place,' said Mr Huntsmore behind him.

Ben straightened and turned to his father. He wore the newly sponged and ironed clothes, and a ruby pin in his cravat matched the ruby on his finger.

'What happens now, sir?' Ben asked.

'You can go ashore if you like. I've an agent here who'll

take you and the luggage to the house I've hired. I'll stay aboard to see to the unloading of the cargo.'

'You mean the convicts, sir?'

'No, the real cargo. We've ten cases of porter, twelve barrels of tar, five rolls of cloth, four cases of saddlery, a hundred jugs of turpentine, five cases of hats, ten cases of shoes, two boxes of pins, eight boxes of nails, one case of umbrellas, twelve cases of pickles, three chests of tea and two of coffee.'

Ben blinked. It was an impressive list to remember. But then this was his father's trade, even if he called himself a gentleman.

Mr Huntsmore gazed at the town before them. 'This place has to import most of the necessities of life. The goods should fetch a good price.'

Ben tried again. 'The convicts —'

Mr Huntsmore misunderstood. 'Yes, Captain Danvers informs me we still have a good amount of the stores provided for the convicts left too. Four cases of cheese, six of biscuit, one of salt butter, eight of flour, though they are not the same quality as the rest of course. No doubt we will still find a buyer. I'm told the custom is to auction the goods on board as soon as a ship arrives.'

'But, sir, when will the convicts be taken ashore?'

His father looked at him impatiently. 'The convicts can wait. They have been down there for more than five months, boy. Another few days will make no difference.'

Except to those who die, thought Ben. Or who go mad in the filth and darkness. Was Higgins mad?

'About that Higgins chap,' said his father. 'Do you wish to keep him?'

Ben stared at him. 'You told him you'd have him assigned to you.'

His father shrugged. 'And have him spit in my coffee if I said no? But Captain Danvers tells me it is almost impossible to get trained servants in the colony. That ruffian may be the best we can manage for a while.' He smiled. 'He may also be … enterprising enough to stay in our employ when we leave.'

Ben didn't like Higgins and didn't trust him. But he was the only person he knew in the colony now, besides his father. And what would happen to Higgins if he said no? Would he be sent back down into the stench and death and darkness with the others?

'I would like him to stay, sir,' he said, trying not to let his reluctance show.

'Very well. Will you go straight to the house with him, or stay to watch the bidding?'

It was a test, Ben knew. *Are you worthy to be my son?* It was also a chance to learn something of his father's business. Latin and Greek were of no use to him now.

'I will stay, sir.'

'Good lad. We've been invited to dine with Governor Macquarie tonight — he's the man to impress. The

Governor's word can secure us land grants and convicts to work them, as well as government contracts to supply the colony. That's how fortunes are made here.'

'But you said we'd go back to England, sir.'

'Oh, we will. No life for a gentleman here. But it would be rash to pass up the chance for investment while we are here. Tell Higgins to make sure your best suit is pressed for this evening.'

Mr Huntsmore gave Ben a smile and a pat on the shoulder, and strode off towards Captain Danvers.

Ben turned back to the rail. Men yelled from the wharf, most dressed alike in dun-coloured ragged cloth. Convicts, but not in chains. This colony was a prison in itself.

Sailors hauled at the capstan, dragging the *Golden Girl* the final yards alongside the wharf so she could be tied up.

They had arrived.

Ben and his father left Higgins giving orders to the convict maid and gardener in the rough wooden house Mr Huntsmore had arranged for them. Higgins seemed good at ordering others around, though Ben still doubted he had seen much domestic service.

When they arrived at Government House, Ben found it had spacious stone rooms and polished furniture, though back home it would have been deemed sufficient for an agent rather than a person Mama would dine with. Wood fires flickered in the reception room and in the dining room, but though they blazed high and hot, they smelled wrong. Still, Ben was glad of their heat after the cold of the ship's cabin with just its tiny coke brazier.

Dinner was only two courses. Ben sat in the middle of the long table, while his father sat next to Mrs Macquarie, a comfortable-looking woman well-dressed in puce silk who kept him engaged in conversation. Ben felt more than tired, as if most of his body still floated on the ocean, leaving a shell of a boy behind. The ground felt odd too, as if he were still going up and down while it stayed still. He helped himself to slices of roast mutton, which didn't taste like the mutton of home — tougher and stronger-flavoured. The stuffed fish was the wrong shape too, but there was familiar mint sauce to accompany the mutton, and buttered parsnips, roasted potatoes and carrots, as well as the first real bread he had eaten since leaving Rio de Janeiro.

Scraps of talk floated down the table.

'In a few years I have no doubt Sydney will be as fine and opulent a town as any,' declared Mrs Macquarie. 'My husband already has the plans drawn up for the buildings a true city needs. Once the roads are surveyed straight and cobbled, and a proper road is built to Parramatta and then on to the Hawkesbury, we shall really see the colony forge ahead. An ordered, civil society.'

'And one ripe for investment, Mrs Macquarie?' asked Mr Huntsmore.

She laughed. 'I cannot see where your profits might be better spent, sir.'

'Indeed, madam. Mr Moore and I are meeting tomorrow.' Ben's father nodded towards a solid-looking man sitting on the other side of Mrs Macquarie. 'He is looking for capital for his ship-building business.'

'Mr Moore is an excellent and most Christian man,' said Mrs Macquarie. 'And his wife does much good among the poor.'

Ben's father gave a dutiful smile.

Mrs Moore, who was sitting next to Ben, looked up as her name was mentioned. She had been quiet so far.

'I am so sorry for the loss of your mother, Master Huntsmore,' she said to Ben. 'The death of a mother is most grievous.'

Ben looked at her, startled. She was dressed as a gentlewoman, but her accent was that of a servant. And yet she was dining at the Governor's table.

'Thank you, Mrs Moore,' he managed.

'Will you be staying in Sydney long?'

He realised he didn't really know. He had been too numb to ask questions at the beginning of the voyage, and too ill later.

'Just long enough for repairs and to stock the ship again, I think, and find more crew to replace those lost at sea.' He thought it better not to mention the typhoid.

'That's a pity. This is a beautiful country, Master Huntsmore.'

'Indeed,' he said politely.

More conversation floated down from the top of the table. The Governor was speaking to the woman on his right, an officer's wife, though Ben hadn't caught her name.

'The French remain a great concern indeed,' Governor Macquarie said. 'We are at their mercy if they choose to attack us here. The colony has few defences even about the harbour.'

The woman looked slightly affronted. 'But you have your troops, sir.'

Governor Macquarie patted her hand. 'I warrant they are good men and experienced, but how can a colony as small as ours defend an entire country? What if Napoleon establishes a military base to resupply his ships in the west or the north? It might be years before we even knew of it.'

Ben met his father's eyes and for the first time he felt a spark of pride. Surely the French would be less inclined to try to settle on this land if the merchant ships of their Dutch allies vanished along its coast? We are acting on the orders of the Prince of Wales himself, he thought.

Maybe … maybe even Napoleon himself might be on the ship the *Golden Girl* took. Napoleon might come south, looking to extend his empire among the fabulous wealth of the Spice Islands, and the Huntsmores would stop the war and free Europe from the tyrant. Being a privateer had seemed slightly shameful back at Badger's Hill. Here, at the table of the Governor, a man who had fought so honourably for his country, in a colony that might be attacked any day by the French, Ben felt for the first time that their enterprise was also a duty to King and country. He found that he was smiling.

'You are enjoying the roast mutton, Master Huntsmore,' remarked Mrs Moore. 'It must be a welcome change from ship's fare.'

Ben nodded. 'You soon grow sick of ham and plum puddings and portable soup.'

Mrs Moore laughed. 'I wouldn't know. I travelled down in the hold, not in a cabin.'

Ben tried not to show his shock. This woman in a silk dress had been a convict! He saw Mrs Moore's expression and realised she knew exactly what he was thinking.

'This is a place of new beginnings, Master Huntsmore,' she said quietly. 'It has been for me and for my husband. He was a ship's carpenter, and now he is the most prosperous businessman in the colony.' She smiled at Mr Moore across the table, a smile of love, gratitude and pride.

The second course was brought in: roast ducks garnished with oranges, a dish of fresh peas with butter, an apple pie, a blancmange and a currant jelly. The fresh food was good, but Mama would not have served such simple fare to a curate after church. But things were different here at the end of the world, where ex-convicts sat with gentlefolk at the dinner table, and even the seasons did not behave as they should.

I won't be here long, Ben consoled himself. Soon the *Golden Girl* would sail to meet the enemy. He glanced at his father, who was smiling at something Mrs Macquarie had said. This was not just an adventure, a way to quick riches. They were going to fight the enemy. And win.

'How long do we stay in the colony, sir?' Ben asked his father in a low voice as they walked back down the hill to the house where they were staying, two convict servants with flaming torches lighting the way before them, as well as for protection against thieves.

It was strange to think that almost everyone in this small town was or had been a criminal back home, with only those who offended again in chains. But the streets were empty, apart from a wandering goat. All convicts had to be in their quarters by the last bell.

'A month at least to repair and restock the ship and find the crew to man it. Captain Danvers will see to that. And after,' his father shrugged, 'that will depend on the winds. It will take us seventy days perhaps to ride the westerlies around the south to get back to the west of the continent.'

Ben stared at him. 'Around the world, sir? You can't be serious. Why not just sail back the way we came?'

Mr Huntsmore laughed. 'You landlubber. The Roaring Forties blow westerly winds, which only get stronger as you go further south into the Fifties and Sixties. It is nigh on impossible to sail to the west around the bottom of this continent from here, at least in a ship as large as ours. We will be sailing far south, into iceberg country. But if we get the right winds, we shall do well enough.'

What if we don't? thought Ben. But he had learned that his father did not like the possibility of good luck to be questioned. Instead he asked, 'Sir, how does one ship capture another?' He knew ships fired cannons at each other in war, but that was to sink the enemy vessel, not to board them and take their cargo.

His father glanced around, then lowered his voice. 'We wait behind an island Danvers knows where passing ships can't see us. It's not much of a harbour, but there's fresh water and it will do. We will have lookouts along the coast who will light signal fires as soon as they sight a ship. Captain Danvers is Navy trained. He's taken four ships before in war. He wasn't a captain then, but this time he'll get a third of what we take, with another third divided between the crew. Danvers has the charts we need too — Dutch ones, found on a French ship — that show him the rocks, the winds and the currents. When the lookout alerts us to a ship, we will sail at night so we can get close without being seen. And then we fire.'

'But won't the Dutch merchantmen fire back?'

Mr Huntsmore nodded as if he approved of the question. 'English cannons have a longer reach than the Dutch and French ones. We aim for the sails, the decks, the captain's and the crew's quarters — enough to cripple the ship, but not sink her. And then we board,' he grinned, 'and take her.'

'But what use is a crippled ship?' Ben asked.

'That's why we're carrying spare spars, sails and masts, lad. If we can, we'll patch her up and take her back to England, or to Sydney Town to refit. If not, she and her crew are bound for Davy Jones's locker.' He shrugged again. 'But by then we'll have her riches aboard the *Golden Girl*.' He stopped walking suddenly and put his hands on Ben's shoulders. 'I'm glad you're with me, lad. I left you in your mother's care too long. A man needs a son. And we'll be fighting for your future. A grand one.'

'Yes, sir.'

Adventure, Ben's mind whispered. You will sail the oceans, see whales and mermaids, fight for treasure. He might even make his own fortune ...

His father was still looking at him. 'Perhaps you should stay here till we return,' he said. 'It's going to be dangerous, not just the fighting but facing the Southern Ocean against the wind. Much worse than the journey here, though not so long.'

Stay here with Higgins, in this colony of mud? Miss the chance to be a hero?

'No, thank you, sir.'

His father clapped him on the back. 'Good lad. You truly are my son.'

Perhaps I am, thought Ben as they continued their walk down the muddy hill.

CHAPTER 5

Ben slept for the next two days, his body needing to adjust to a world that no longer swayed and wandered under his feet, and to regain the strength he'd lost to the fever. He woke only to eat from the trays Higgins brought him in bed, and then slept again.

On the third day Ben awoke and suddenly found himself eager for life beyond his room. There was no bell pull to call a servant, but he found clothes that had been washed and pressed in a roughly made cupboard. He put them on and made his way down the narrow stairs.

'You're up, lovey!' The maid of all work, Maggie Three-Tooth, looked like an old woman, though she was probably no more than thirty. Only young women were sent to the colony. 'You go into the parlour and I'll bring your breakfast.'

'Thank you,' said Ben. 'Is my father there?'

'Oh, no, lovey, he's gone down to the docks already. Now you sit down and I'll bring a couple of nice boiled cackleberries for you — the hens are laying even in this chill. I've soda bread fresh-made too.'

Maggie Three-Tooth smelled of sweat and rum and her apron wasn't clean, but her gap-toothed smile was friendly. She cooked plain stews and soda bread on the hearth, for the house had no oven, as well as spit roasts and boiled vegetables, Welsh rarebit and potato cakes. Higgins had carried all of them up on Ben's trays over the past few days.

The parlour was small, with rough wooden walls, a planked floor and a table that wobbled. Each chair wobbled too. Ben sat on the least wobbly one as Maggie carried in a tray.

'Here you are, lovey, and look! Mr Higgins got some butter for us. Ain't seen butter for an age. He's a true wonder that man.'

'Where is Higgins now?' Ben asked.

'Out marketing. The master gave him money.'

Ben noticed Maggie's brief displeasure that the money hadn't been entrusted to her. He wondered how much of it would stay in Higgins's pocket. Still, according to Mr Huntsmore, who had visited Ben briefly each evening, Higgins seemed to be managing the house surprisingly well. And Ben had seen for himself that the convict stood straighter now, his body quickly filling out. He'd also seen that Higgins hadn't bothered to hide his amusement at the pampered boy who could stay abed so long.

Ben had just finished the eggs and two slices of bread and butter — Maggie didn't seem to know that breakfast required toast — when the door opened and Higgins grinned in at him, showing gaps amid his yellow teeth.

'Mornin', Master Sneezer,' he said, his mocking tone not quite an insult.

'Good morning, Higgins. Maggie said you've been marketing.'

'That I have. And not just for the mutton you'll be eatin' for dinner.' He tapped his nose.

Ben thought of Maggie's scent of rum. Higgins's breath smelled of it too. 'You've been drinking rum, haven't you?'

'And what if I have?' Higgins's grin grew wider. 'Rum's used like money here — your pa will've found out that already.'

The servant's accent Higgins had put on for Ben's father was gone. Now the convict spoke in the same tone he'd used when Ben had first pulled him from the hold.

'Who are you?' demanded Ben.

Higgins laughed. He grabbed a chair and sat on it, leaning back, all servitude vanished. 'I told you, Sneezer lad. Me name's 'iggins.'

'You weren't ever a footman.'

'Well, no, but ain't no need to tell your father that, eh? I were sent from the workhouse to be a boot boy, but I kept me eyes open. I know enough to play the lackey if I have to.'

‘Why don’t you pretend with me too?’ Ben asked.

Higgins reached over and took an uneaten slice of soda bread and butter from Ben’s plate. He bit into it and chewed. ‘’Cause I like you, Sneezer. You remind me of the whippersnappers I was trainin’ back in Lunnon Town.’ He smiled, but there was iron behind it. ‘I know boys,’ he added softly. ‘I know you, lad.’

‘I’m not afraid of you!’

‘You are, you know. So scared you might widdle in that nice suit of yours. But you needn’t worry, Sneezer lad. I ain’t ever goin’ to toby you.’ Higgins lost his smile. ‘I look out for my boys.’

‘I am not one of your boys!’

‘You are now. Not much you can do about it.’

‘I can tell my father!’

Higgins sat back, grinning again. ‘Tell him what? Oh, dearie me, that I’m a criminal — a shuffler or a dimble-dambler? A thatch-gallows here in New South Wales who came in the hold of a convict ship? Your pa knows full well what I am. That’s why he lets me stay, see.’ He tapped his nose once more and looked at Ben shrewdly. ‘Your pa’s hirin’ crew, and a certain sort of crew, I heard. He’s lookin’ for soldiers gone bad, those who can use a cannon or a musket and wield a sword as well. Now what would a nice gentry cove want with cannons, eh, Sneezer lad?’

Ben was silent.

Higgins took another slice of Ben's bread and spread it thickly with butter. 'I want to make me fortune,' he said softly. 'Workin' for your pa is goin' to make it for me. And actin' the servant on his ship will get me back to Lunnon Town as well. I got a nice nest egg waitin' for me there, even if some varlet's moved onto my territory. So I warn you, little paddle-pate, you keep your bone box shut. Play me wrong and one day, when you're close to the rail, you'll feel a shove, and you'll be in the water and shark meat. And I'll be on the other side of the ship, all innocent.' He gazed at Ben, all pretence gone. 'I'll look out for you, Sneezer lad. That's what pals do. But you got to look out for me too.'

Ben pretended to concentrate on scraping out the last of his boiled egg. Higgins was right. He'd done nothing to make Mr Huntsmore dismiss him. He might even claim that the rum he'd bought had been used to trade for cheese or butter. But nor would Ben let himself be intimidated. He was the master here, not one of the sorry street urchins Higgins had terrified. And soon he was going to face the King's enemies.

He pushed his plate away and stood. 'I'm going down to the harbour to help my father. And if you — or Maggie — are drunk tonight, you'll be dismissed.'

Higgins smiled up at him. 'Yes, master.'

It was easy to find the harbour, stretched blue below him. It was even easier to find the wharf as every road seemed to head that way. Most of the dwellings Ben passed were huts with sagging walls and rotting roofs, but here and there were substantial cottages of logs, plaster or even stone, with long neat orchards and tethered goats gazing hopefully at vegetable gardens. And untethered goats too. Ben stepped aside to let a mean-eyed animal trot past him on the muddy road, confident that its horns would let it go wherever it wanted.

'Warder! Clean fresh warder!'

It took Ben a moment to realise the cry was 'water' and that the boy was selling the presumably fresh water from the buckets that dangled from a yoke over his shoulders.

The huts gave way to taverns, some solid, others as squalid as the huts further up the hill. Men and a few women sprawled drunk against the walls. Most wore the dull garb of the convict: dun-coloured trousers or a shabby dress, colourless except for the stains.

A gap-toothed woman leered at Ben from a doorway. 'Fresh pies,' she offered. 'Genuine sheep.'

One of the drunks said, 'Genuine rat, more like.'

The woman strode over and kicked him. Ben saw that her bare feet were caked with dirt. 'The only rat near my place is you, Long Bill.'

The man warded her off with a laugh. 'Opossum then. Opossum pie, anyone?'

Ben felt a hand sliding into his pocket and turned sharply. An urchin stared up at him, skinny, ragged and so filthy it was impossible to see the colour of his skin.

'Spare a penny, mister?'

'I don't give to pickpockets.'

The wheedling tone turned threatening. 'Gimme your jacket then. Nice one, ain't it?'

Ben had learned fisticuffs as well as Greek and Latin from the rector. He could fight off one thin boy, but not the drunks around him. He glanced at the men, but they seemed intent on their tankards again.

'You will not take my jacket,' said Ben steadily, and he forced himself to continue towards the dock, alert for any footfall behind him.

None came.

The wharf was crowded, men circling a cart where an auctioneer called out prices.

'One case workboots, best quality! What am I bid? Two pounds for boots like these? You won't get a single pair for that. Ten pounds? Do I hear twenty? Forty? Eight barrels of rum? Now that's more like it. Do I have nine barrels of rum? You'd rather pay in coin, sir? Sixty-five pounds? Sixty-four? Do I have a rise on sixty-four? Sold for sixty-four pounds to the gentleman in the hat. The next lot is another case of boots, men's riding. Any of you officers want a true smart pair of boots? Here's yer chance ...'

They were auctioning the goods that had not yet sold from the *Golden Girl*, Ben realised. He watched, the colony's sun surprisingly hot and heavy on his neck, as lot after lot was sold. At last he moved into the shade.

Then it was over. The crowd moved in a single tide away from the wharf. Ben spied his father, deep in conversation with the auctioneer and Captain Danvers. Mr Huntsmore broke off and strode towards him.

'Ben! I hoped you'd be well enough to come down today.' He grinned. 'Excellent prices at this auction too — I estimate we'll make more than five hundred pounds after commission. I'm about to negotiate with the chandler for the ship's supplies — food, rope, sails and nails and such like that we might need. It's time you learned about those things.'

Ben nodded, and his father smiled and put an arm about his shoulders. 'Good lad. We'll have to make do, of course — salt mutton instead of salt beef. The ship's biscuit here is mostly weevils, but Captain Danvers says that dried corn can be boiled up instead, and the mush is easier to eat than biscuit.' Mr Huntsmore's eyes were bright and excited. 'She'll be ready to sail within a month,' he added softly. 'And soon she'll be a golden girl indeed.'

The chandler's shed smelled of rancid butter, stale biscuit and the omnipresent stink of rum. Mr Huntsmore had told Ben that the chandler, Mr Porter, boasted he'd been a ship's quartermaster, fighting against the French. Now he sold whatever the convict transports and whaling ships that called into Sydney Town needed.

'Best salt mutton,' said Mr Porter.

Mr Huntsmore poked at the lumps in the barrel of brine. 'More fat than meat.'

'Fat gives the men more energy.'

'Goes off faster too. I'll give you a quart of rum per barrel.'

So Higgins was telling the truth, thought Ben. Rum really was money here. He hadn't realised that the *Golden Girl* had carried so much of the liquor. His father must have known its value.

Mr Porter shook his head. 'A quart for this good meat? Four quarts, and that's a bargain.'

'Two. And I won't ask questions like how much goat or hopper meat is mixed up with the mutton.'

Mr Porter laughed. 'Two it is then. Now, the corn comes dried, parched or ground into meal. Parched corn has been cooked then dried — all it needs is soaking. Dried is cheaper, but you need more charcoal or wood to cook it.'

Ben listened to them dicker about the price.

'And for you and your lad, I've got the best hams in the colony,' Mr Porter added, 'as well as preserved fruits in honey. Better than lime juice against the scurvy.'

'Four hams, thirty flasks of fruit,' Mr Huntsmore said. 'And you can deliver the rope and sailcloth by the end of the week?'

'I can. And the stores will be ready for you by the end of the fortnight.'

'Excellent. Ten per cent of the price when the rope and sails are delivered, full price on delivery. Feel free to inspect the rum before then.'

Mr Porter grinned. 'I will, sir. And on delivery too. No watered rum gets past me.'

'I didn't think it would. Come, Ben, it's time we —'

'Excuse me, sir,' interrupted Ben, 'but the sailors will get scurvy living on salt mutton and corn mush.' Especially as they were now facing a longer journey than even the voyage here, with no ports to stop at.

His father shrugged. 'Sailors always get scurvy.'

'But they'd be stronger if they didn't,' said Ben quietly.

Mr Huntsmore looked at him thoughtfully. 'What do you suggest? If you're going to say plum puddings, you can think again.'

'Sauerkraut, sir. It's what Captain Cook fed his men and not one of them died of scurvy. It's cheap and lasts well.'

'Well, Mr Porter?'

'I can do you sauerkraut, sir. A pint of rum a barrel.'

Ben looked at Mr Porter steadily. 'There are cabbages in just about every garden in the colony. I saw them on my way down here. We could make our own before we sail.' Or Maggie could, he thought. He'd seen sauerkraut made back home: the cabbage just needed salt and pressing. 'One pint of rum for six barrels.'

'The barrels alone cost that!' protested Mr Porter.

'One pint, and we give you six empty barrels in exchange,' Ben said, glancing at his father.

His father nodded. 'Better for our cooper to be repairing barrels than sitting on his backside in a tavern.'

'You drive a hard bargain, sir.' Mr Porter spat on his hand, then held it out to shake and seal the deal.

Ben felt a true smile stretch across his face for the first time since he had lost Badger's Hill. The *Golden Girl* had made honest money, bringing goods to a colony that needed them. And he'd made a better bargain for the stores than his father could. If this was going to be his life till he could buy back Badger's Hill, he would be good at it.

CHAPTER 6

The air blew clean and salty as they came out of the chandler's, and Ben could smell a faint tang from the thin-topped trees that clothed the promontories across the harbour. Sunlight flashed silver on the bright blue water. The *Golden Girl* swayed alongside the wharf; she was the only ship in the harbour now. The Navy ship must have sailed during the days he'd spent sleeping.

'Good thinking back there,' said Mr Huntsmore. 'Good bargaining too. We're going to need strong men. Our crew will be fresh while the Dutch will be weak from the voyage.'

Ben hadn't even thought of that, just of the crew he'd seen on the voyage: their legs so swollen the skin became tight and shiny, their black toothless gums. Some had been too weak to move from their hammocks and had been among the first to die of the fever.

A straggle of convict workmen in dun-coloured smocks shuffled past, two men with whips guiding their progress down the wharf. Soon after, a gust of wind carrying the smell of rotting flesh made Ben look around. The convict gang was still on the *Golden Girl*, and the hatch had been pulled open. Someone let down a ladder, and hands reached down to help the first filthy skeletal frames into the sunlight.

Bodies were laid upon the decks. Those who could rolled over to cover their faces. Others stared at the sky, too weak to move. Ben remembered what Higgins had looked like, all bone and rags, but at least he'd had the strength to move. These men's only sign of life was the movement of their hands as they tried to shield their eyes from the unrelenting harbour light.

Three days, thought Ben in horror. We have been docked three days and all that time the convicts were left down there in the stinking dark.

The stench filled the cove now, and his father grimaced. 'Back to the house, I think. Don't worry — Danvers will make sure the ship is well-scrubbed before we sail.'

It was as if Ben had been suddenly drenched with a bucket of cold seawater. He'd let himself be seduced by his father's dream of riches and his own imagined opportunities for heroism against the enemy. He had wanted to see his father as a hero and an adventurer, but Branwell Huntsmore was a man who saw other people as mere cargo. A man who saw Badger's Hill as just profit or loss. He *was* a pirate, even if he called himself a privateer.

Ben had to get away from him. He had to get away from *here*.

He fumbled for an excuse. 'Excuse me, sir, I ... I promised Maggie I would buy some eggs for her.'

His father frowned. 'Higgins is supposed to do the marketing.'

But Ben was already running — down the wharf, past the chandler's and the grog shops with their stench of rum and privies. Away. Away. Away.

A year ago he could run for hours. Now, twenty minutes left his legs weak and his lungs hunting for breath.

He stopped and looked around. The shanties by the cove and the neat houses with their gardens, orchards and tethered goats lay behind him. Up on the hill, a convict gang hammered at rocks, breaking them into smaller cobbles, perhaps for one of the roads Mrs Macquarie had talked about at dinner. They were grim-faced men of dust and sweat, their bodies bowed with work. Mrs Macquarie had seemed a kind woman, and the Governor's vision for the colony sounded good, yet suddenly Ben realised that their grand ambition would be built with slave labour, just as his father's profit from this voyage had come from convicts too. And the fortune Ben dreamed of would be the stolen loot of other merchants. Did that make him as criminal as any convict?

Ben tore his gaze away from the labouring men and looked around. He had come to an open area that was obviously a market. People were packing up trestle tables and loading them onto carts as most of their produce would have been sold by mid-morning. Should he try to buy the eggs he'd offered as an excuse to his father? He had coins in his pocket, but no basket to carry the eggs in, and Maggie had said the hens belonging to the house they'd hired were laying well.

He stepped back as a cart trundled past carrying two well-dressed women seated on cushions. Two men in convict drab were yoked to the cart instead of horses. Most of the stall holders seemed to be men too, not the women he was used to in the market at home. Ben realised he had seen only a handful of women since he came here.

He was hungry now, and desperately thirsty. But the only stream he had passed was thick with stinking algae, and he didn't want the ale or rum that seemed to be the only drinks for sale here. He doubted a colony like this would have a teashop. He moved past the market area, then sat with his back to a tree, feeling as empty as the barrels he had promised the chandler. Everyone he'd loved was dead or across the ocean. Everyone he trusted too. He no longer even trusted himself. The boy he had been a year ago would never have dreamed of stealing someone else's treasure. But the boy he'd been a year ago had been part of Badger's Hill.

He closed his eyes. Maybe, when he opened them, he would be back at Badger's Hill. Mama would be in the library, and Cookie would be singing as she made jam. Young Lon would call for Ben at the back door and they'd go rabbiting.

There weren't any rabbits in this land. No beauty, and no honour either. It was a place where criminals dined at Government House. He covered his face with his hands to hide his tears.

'Are you all right?' A girl looked at him with concern. She was about the same age as he was and dressed in a blue dress rather than convict drab.

Ben scrambled to his feet.

'Sally? What's wrong?' A man approached in the rough garb of a farmer, but the two horses whose reins he held looked good, both carrying bulging saddlebags.

The girl gestured to Ben. He flushed, rubbing at his eyes, embarrassed to be found crying.

'Here.' The man offered him a stoppered flask.

Ben hesitated, then lifted it to his mouth, expecting just to wet his lips with rum for politeness's sake. But the liquid was a bit like tea and sweet with honey. He drank more deeply, then stoppered the flask and handed it back.

'Thank you, sir. What is it?'

'Sarsaparilla tea. Or a native flower that we call sarsaparilla.' The man held out a calloused hand. 'I'm Tom Appleby. This is my oldest daughter, Sally.'

Ben shook it. 'How do you do, sir, Miss Appleby. I'm Ebenezer Huntsmore.'

'New chum?' Mr Appleby laughed when he saw Ben didn't understand. 'You a new settler?'

Ben shook his head. 'My father owns a ship, the *Golden Girl*. We'll be sailing again soon.'

'I saw it in the harbour,' said Sally. 'Papa bought some of the cloth it carried. Are you going to be a ship's captain one day?'

'I prefer farming. You have a farm, sir?'

'I do indeed. Up on the Hawkesbury. Though one day,' Mr Appleby nodded towards the high, blue, distant mountains, 'I'm hoping to cross those.'

'No one knows what's beyond them,' said the girl excitedly. 'Lakes or rivers or maybe an inland sea.'

'I didn't know there were free settlers here, sir,' said Ben. 'I thought everyone was a soldier or a convict, with a few merchants to supply the ships.'

Mr Appleby glanced at his daughter. At last he said, 'I was a convict. Chimney sweep and thief, sent here when I was ten years old. Now I'm a farmer and a good one. Lad, are you in trouble?'

Ben hesitated again. His entire life was wrong. Did that count as trouble? He cast a quick look at Sally. She smiled encouragingly.

'Yes,' he admitted.

Mr Appleby fastened the horses' lead ropes to a

branch. He rummaged in his saddlebags for a large tin, then sat down by the tree. He gestured for Ben to sit again too. Sally spread her skirts beside them.

'Here,' said Mr Appleby, passing Ben the tin. 'The world looks better on a full belly.'

Ben reached inside. It was full of hearth cakes. 'Thank you.' He bit one. It was sweet with dried currants. 'They're good.'

'I made them,' said Sally proudly. 'And I made the butter and dried the currants too.'

Mr Appleby smiled. 'Every bit home-grown, our own flour and eggs too. Have another.'

'Thank you. Is the Hawkesbury very far away, sir? Mrs Macquarie said there was no road there yet.'

'No road, but a good track. Sally here is a grand rider. At least she is when she's not trying to jump fallen trees.' Mr Appleby looked at his daughter mock sternly, then returned his gaze to Ben. 'You thinking of running away, lad?'

Ben hadn't been. He hadn't even thought that this land might have farms like the ones he knew. All at once he longed to be among crops again, away from the sea, away from the smells of sickness, greed and death.

'Do you know someone who'd employ me?' he asked impulsively. 'I know a lot about farming, sir.'

Mr Appleby shook his head. 'You won't find a job as a farm labourer, nor as an overseer, lad. Not in the colony where any man with land can have convicts assigned to him, and get rations to feed them for nothing too.'

Ben stared at him. 'You run your farm with convict labour?' Once more his gaze swept up to the men breaking rocks.

Mr Appleby followed his glance, then looked back at him. 'I do,' he said frankly. 'Convict labour creates this colony, lad. How else can we afford to clear the land, or build the roads? But a convict's life depends on who he's assigned to. I was sent to one of the best men I've known, who's now godfather to my Sally here. The men on our farm live and eat as well as my family do.'

'But many don't,' said Ben flatly.

'No,' admitted Mr Appleby. 'Many live condemned to rations that were stale when they left England, and with the fear of the lash. Convict labour is this land's greatest curse as well as its salvation. But a convict isn't a slave, lad. No matter how badly he's treated, every man here knows that within a few years he'll have served his sentence, or get a ticket of leave.'

'Are there no jobs for a free man?'

'Many, if you have a skill or experience. Almost none for a lad your age. You're a mite too young to be a farm manager.' Mr Appleby looked at him carefully. 'Does your father beat you? Starve you?'

Ben shook his head. 'I had typhoid on the voyage here,

that's why I'm thin. My mother died of it. My father treats me well.'

It was true. Ben was well-dressed, well-fed. All his father had done was lose Ben's home, his mother and all he loved. None of that, nor even what he planned to do next, was illegal.

'You're scared of going to sea again?' Mr Appleby's voice was sympathetic.

'Not … not really.'

'Then what's wrong?'

Ben met the kind eyes. 'My father treats people like cattle. Worse than cattle, because cattle are worth money. He doesn't care if they live or die.'

'I've known men like that,' said Mr Appleby quietly. 'Officers of the Rum Corps, captains of convict transports. I was lucky to arrive here under Captain Phillip. He forced us convicts to eat fruit in every port and nearly all of us survived — more than would have if we'd stayed back in England. But most of the ships since …' He shook his head. 'More convicts die than live. They always will while men are greedy and are paid for those they take on board, not those who live to walk ashore.'

'Sir, I don't need a wage,' said Ben desperately.

'Can't he come and live with us?' asked Sally eagerly. 'He could share Frederick's room. He's my brother,' she added to Ben. 'Have you ever worked with sheep?'

'Yes. I can —'

Mr Appleby held up his hand. 'Hush, Sally, you don't know what you're saying. I'm sorry, lad. I can't break the law and take a son from his father. I could be charged with kidnapping.'

'But it wouldn't be kidnapping if he wants to come,' argued Sally.

'In the eyes of the law it would. And I'm just a farmer with no influence, not a shipowner who can bribe a magistrate to do his bidding. I've got one conviction behind me. If I were charged with a second offence, I'd lose my farm, be sent to Van Diemen's Land, or worse. What would happen to my family then, eh?'

Sally was silent.

'I ... I see,' said Ben. 'I'm sorry. I shouldn't have asked.'

He had been stupid. The *Golden Girl* was still the only way he had of getting home to England, away from this land of criminals, thin soil and colours too drab or too bright. He would be a fool to trade that hope for life on a farm in the colony. Capturing the Dutch treasure was still the only way he might buy back Badger's Hill.

'We need to be on the road soon,' said Mr Appleby. 'Or we won't reach home by nightfall. Can I give you some advice, lad?'

Ben nodded.

'How old are you?'

'Fourteen next month.'

'Seven years then till you reach your majority. Same amount of time I had to serve as a thief. But I managed it, and so can you. Just survive, lad. That's what I told myself when my master forced me up those chimneys. That's what I whispered day after day on the ship that brought me here. Just survive, then one day you can make the life you choose, just as I've done. Can you do that?'

Ben looked at him. A former chimney sweep. A prisoner. One of the wretched trapped in the hold of a ship for half a year, or even more, if he had been held a prisoner in the hulks on the river instead of a jail on land. If this man could survive, and thrive and now be happy, then he could too.

Ben met Mr Appleby's eyes. 'I'll survive, sir.'

'Good lad. Learn what you can, find out what you truly want in life — and learn what kind of man you don't want to be too. And if you need me, really need me — if something happens to your father, or you really need to vanish ... Well, I was younger than you and desperate, and someone helped me then. I wouldn't have my life and farm without them.' Mr Appleby smiled at his daughter, then looked back at Ben. 'There's an inn called the Sergeant's Arms. Ask for the sergeant, tell him your story and he'll send a message to me. No promises, but if I can help you without risking my family, I will.'

'Thank you, sir.' Ben met the green eyes that belonged to an ex-thief, yet Tom Appleby seemed to be the most honest man Ben had ever met.

'It can be a good life here in New South Wales,' added Mr Appleby softly. 'A grand life. There's land here for whoever can farm it. And if that's what you choose when you're old enough, I'll do whatever I can to help you get it.'

'Me too,' said Sally. 'And maybe, if your father's ship comes back to Sydney Town, you could come and visit.'

Now his panic had receded, Ben wasn't sure he wanted to visit a New South Wales farm — a few paddocks carved out of this land's ugly thin-topped trees. But these people had shown him the first true kindness since his mother had died.

'Thank you,' he said. 'I would like that very much.'

CHAPTER 7

Four weeks more of Maggie's stews, spit roasts and soda bread, while the ship's hold was cleaned, her decks scrubbed, her sails mended, the holes in her hull the rats had gnawed filled. The coopers and the carpenters hammered, and the stores were loaded.

Four weeks of Higgins's obsequiousness when Mr Huntsmore was near, and his knowing comments when he was not.

Four weeks while Captain Danvers gathered more crew members to replace those lost to typhoid and scurvy. There'd be almost three times the usual number of crew; men who would slink on board the *Golden Girl* at night, and stay down in the hold till the ship was at sea.

'Best we know nothing about it, son,' advised Mr Huntsmore. 'I'll warrant some of the crew haven't served their sentences yet. But Danvers knows the kind of man we need.'

Criminals, thought Ben. Convicts. Ex-soldiers turned highwaymen who knew how to fire a musket and wield a sword. And others who knew how to manoeuvre sails even in the lash of the southern winds.

Mr Huntsmore spent much of the four weeks consulting merchants in the colony. Prices here were high for everything from tea to cloth, all of which must be imported, he told Ben. Rum was the most valuable import, especially now Governor Macquarie had stopped the notorious and corrupt NSW Corps monopoly. The Sydney Town to Calcutta run was proving lucrative, carrying barrels of whale oil and whalebone that was used for all sorts of items that needed stiffening, from umbrellas to corsets, then bringing back tea, cloth, spices, rice and other items the colony needed. The Dutch ship would give Mr Huntsmore back his fortune, and the trade route between India and Sydney Town might be a way to invest that fortune profitably, with less risk than sending ships around the Horn back to England.

Twice Ben and his father went on picnics organised by the wives of the 73rd Regiment who had come out with Governor Macquarie. The picnickers travelled in small open boats to beaches across the harbour, where convict servants cooked damper in the ashes, and flies settled promptly on the pies and spiced beef. The cooked damper was as solid as a rock, and it was difficult to tell where the ash finished and the bread began.

None of the officers seemed to have sons or daughters Ben's age; or if they had, they'd been left at school in England. Even Mrs Moore's son, Andrew, had been sent to England for his education. Ben spent the picnics watching the Indian women (for that was what the officers called the native race here) fishing in their tiny bark canoes. Once he saw a young black-skinned man standing motionless in the water for an hour, about fifty yards away from the picnickers and yet ignored by them, his spear poised. Suddenly it flashed and he hauled up a giant fish, the spear in its side, its scales glinting as it twisted in its death throes. Ben clapped. The young man turned and grinned at him, holding up the fish triumphantly. Ben laughed, and clapped again.

Mr Huntsmore broke off his conversation. 'What's so funny?'

'Not funny, sir. The Indian man over there just caught a fish.'

'Remarkable achievement,' said one of the officers dryly, 'to catch a fish.'

Laughter rippled around the gathering.

And yet it had been remarkable, thought Ben as the young man and his fish vanished into the trees' shadows. To stand still for so long so the fish didn't suspect your presence; to spear it so fast and accurately before it could speed away. But there was no point trying to defend the young man's skill to people who hadn't even seemed to realise he was there.

The first urchin arrived at the Huntsmores' rented house during their second week in Sydney Town. Ben opened the door when he heard the knock. It still felt odd to act as butler. But the house had no doorbell, and neither Maggie nor Higgins could hear a knock from out in the kitchen.

Ben stared at the thin, ragged boy on the doorstep. 'Yes?'

'You Mr 'iggins's son?' the boy demanded.

'No, I'm —'

'Does 'e live 'ere then?'

'Yes.'

The boy held out six buttons in a grimy hand. ''E wanted buttons. Said I'd get six baked potatoes for 'em.'

'I don't know,' began Ben as Higgins appeared behind him.

The convict took the buttons, then gave the boy a brief tap on the ear. 'Deliveries at the back door only. You'll get your potatoes there too. No, not through the house, boy. Nobs only through the front door.'

He gave the urchin another cuff, and the boy grinned and ran around the house towards the kitchen door.

'You're getting beggar boys to do the marketing?' demanded Ben.

Higgins looked innocent. 'Marketing? No. Just gettin' together a few of the necessities.'

'Those buttons were stolen?'

Higgins shrugged. 'Your pa needs new buttons on his coat. No buttons for sale in the markets or at the chandler's, except for wooden ones, which wouldn't suit your pa.'

'You asked that boy to steal for you?'

Higgins looked at Ben levelly. 'That boy's been a thief since he was old enough to slip his hand into a pocket. Half the young'uns here don't know their pa nor ma. You goin' to tell him to take them buttons back? Snatch his potatoes from him?'

The boy reappeared munching a baked potato with the speed of someone who knew the only safe place to store food was in his belly. Ben was silent.

More urchins arrived with various items and left with baked potatoes. Higgins began to sport a red velvet waistcoat for his jaunts beyond the house. The scissors that had been lost on the voyage were replaced. A set of kitchen knives arrived for Maggie. The household had tubs of fresh butter, which almost never appeared in the market, and were used to make the boiled puddings they'd need on the voyage — far superior to those made from the rancid salt butter shipped from England. There was even a pocket-knife for Ben, which looked surprisingly like the one he had lost on the voyage. He wondered now if one of the crew had stolen it while he was sick and it had now been stolen back. Or was this a similar knife taken from its lawful owner?

Ben looked at Higgins's smile as he held out the knife, hesitated, then took it.

'Thank you, Higgins,' he said.

Higgins winked at him. 'Told you I looks after me own,' he said.

'Letter for you, young master,' said Higgins when he brought in the tea tray late one afternoon. As Ben's father wasn't there, his tone was insolent even if the words were respectful.

'For me?' Ben asked. 'Has a ship come in?' Maybe it was a letter from the rector back home.

'Not from a ship,' said Higgins. 'One of the stall holders in the market were askin' about an Ebenezer Huntsmore. He give it to me.'

Ben took the letter. No envelope, no stamp, and no money to be paid to receive it or Higgins would have asked for it. It was just a sheet of paper — rough paper that might once have been wrapping paper — kept closed with a lump of melted beeswax, but no seal pressed into it. He opened it and saw the name at the bottom — Sally. He smiled, then noticed Higgins was still waiting.

'Who's it from?' Higgins asked.

'I thought you'd have opened it,' said Ben shortly.

Higgins grinned, showing the gaps in his teeth. 'Would have if I could've read it. Didn't get no learnin', or not the kind that taught me me letters.'

'It's from a friend,' said Ben.

'What kind of friend? Government House has its own seal, and I reckon the officers do too. And men like your pa.'

'She's a farmer's daughter, and the rest is none of your business.'

Higgins laughed. 'You're my business, sonny lad. Young'uns have been my business for the last ten years.'

'Well, I'm not going to pickpocket for you,' said Ben. 'Go away.'

He had never been rude to a servant before. But Higgins was … Higgins.

'Yes, master. Certainly, young master,' said Higgins, and he pulled the warped door shut behind him with exaggerated care.

Ben looked at the letter again. Sally's writing was neat — neater than his — and tiny, to fit in as many words as possible, though she hadn't written across the page as well as down it, as so many did to save paper.

Dear Master Huntsmore,

I hope this finds you in good health, as it does me. It was good to meet you in Sydney Town. I have been worried about how you are, so Papa said I could write to you and say that if your father agrees, we would be very glad for you to visit us here if there is time before your ship sails.

I think you would like this farm. Papa says it is not like farms in England, where the houses are made of stone and the fences too, and it is green and wet all the time, and the sheep get footrot and sometimes the wheat rots too and even the potatoes. I do not think I would like an English farm even if the houses are larger.

Our house gets bigger every year as Papa and the men build new rooms after every harvest. They built new convict quarters this year too as we now have fifteen men working here. The men are clearing more land, ringbarking the trees then burning them, then grubbing up the roots. Some farmers don't bother with the roots, which Papa says is short-sighted as you cannot plough properly with roots still in the ground.

I have a pet cow called Betty and my horse is called High Lady. You met her at the market. If you don't have a horse, I would be happy for you to ride her, but Papa says you could ride his horse too. Frederick said you can't ride his horse, but I think he will say yes because if he won't let you ride his horse, I won't make him any pancakes. He is two years younger than me and should do what I say, but he doesn't think so!

There isn't any other news, except eight of the sheep had twins and we have to bottle-feed two of them, and the young hens have begun to lay and Frederick shot a native cat trying to eat the chickens. The dingoes can be a problem, but now we have enough men to guard the sheep. I also found a wild beehive last week and got lots of honey. Papa says that in England the bees sting. England does not sound a hospitable country, with stinging bees everywhere and footrot as well.

If you deliver an answer to the Sergeant's Arms, they will see it reaches me.

Your respectful friend,

Sally Appleby

PS This is the first letter I have ever written, so I hope I have done it correctly.

PPS I hope you can visit.

The house had no study, much less a library. Ben crossed to his father's room, took a sheet of writing paper from the waterproof compendium and sat at the narrow table, dipping the pen into the inkwell.

Dear Miss Appleby,

Thank you for your letter. I wish I could come and visit you, but we are going to sail this week, as soon as Captain Danvers says the winds are right.

I wish I could show you a farm in England. It is colder and wetter than this colony but beautiful, and the land is neat with lanes and fields. We never got blight on our wheat at Badger's Hill as we were careful to grow it in the sloping paddocks, not by the river, and we grew a short-stemmed variety that matures even when it is a short summer. It does not crop as well as the long-stemmed varieties, and you cannot use the stems for thatch, but it is more reliable.

He blotted the words, then hesitated. It hurt too much to write more about Badger's Hill.

I am going to send this to the Sergeant's Arms. I hope they can send it to you as I don't know the address of your farm.

I hope this reaches you before our ship has sailed.

He blotted the paper, dipped his pen in the inkwell again, then added:

Would you perhaps be coming to the market again soon? I will be there every day till we sail, just in case.

Please present my best wishes to your family.

I remain yours respectfully,

Ebenezer (Ben) Huntsmore

He folded the letter, wrote *Miss Appleby, Hawkesbury River, care of the Sergeant's Arms* on it, automatically looked for the bell pull to call a servant, then took a candle along to the kitchen to light it so he could seal the letter with wax.

The kitchen was a separate room behind the main house so that stray coals from the kitchen fire couldn't burn down the entire house. Higgins sat at his ease on a chair near the window, its wooden shutters open to catch the breeze from the harbour, while Maggie chopped cabbage at the table. The kitchen fire was banked, with only a few coals glowing.

Ben waited for Higgins to stand when he entered the room and ask what was wanted. He didn't. Ben flushed, then crossed to the fire and lit the candle himself. He held it out so the wax could drip onto the folds of the letter.

'Writin' a reply, are you? Want me to deliver it?' Higgins still didn't get up. Instead he stretched out a hand for the paper.

Ben hesitated. But he had no wish to face a public house by himself, nor the pickpockets and beggars around it. He pressed the candle wax firmly with his thumb, then passed it to Higgins. 'You need to take it to an inn called the Sergeant's Arms.'

'I know that one,' said Maggie. 'It's by the market, not the docks.' She winked at Higgins. 'You're out of luck, matey. Sells more ale than rum, and more steak and kidney pies than either.'

'What do I want with a steak and kidney pie with a good mutton stew waitin' for me here?' Higgins replied.

He rose lazily, stretched and ambled out the door.

An hour later he scratched on Ben's door, then opened it. 'The sergeant cove says your young lady will be at the market day after tomorrer. Meet her at the stall sellin' apples two down from the water tank. Best be there early, if we ain't sailed already.'

'So soon!' Ben hadn't thought Mr Appleby would have anything more to sell at the market after their last visit to Sydney Town.

Higgins stared at him. 'You ain't figured it out yet?'

'What do you mean?'

Higgins sighed. 'I ain't as green as I'm cabbage-lookin', Sneezer. Here's you, the son of a shipowner, all rich and respectable like, and there's her, daughter of two ex-cons. Course you're a bit young, but no pa is goin' to turn down the chance of a match with a cove like you.'

Ben flushed. 'You read my letter!'

'Can't read, matey. Remember?'

'You gave it to someone else to read then.'

'Course I did. I told you — I keeps an eye on me lads.'

'I am not your lad!'

'But I says you are,' said Higgins softly. He looked at

Ben for a long moment, then added suddenly, 'Stay here when the ship sails. His Nibs'll let you, if you ask nice. You could gammon him, tell him you got the fever again. I can smudge a bit of soot about your eyes, make you look as if you're sweatin'.'

'No!' said Ben.

'Why not?'

'Because it would be cowardly. And cheating.'

'And stealin' Dutch treasure by sneakin' up on 'em ain't cheatin'? It ain't cowardly to stay safe, boy. Only a bottlehead risks his life when he don't have to. Let your pa bring home the bacon while you stays safe.'

'The Dutch are our enemies. It's our duty to fight them.' Ben tried to convince himself too.

'Good thing they're rich then, ain't it?'

Higgins shut the door. Ben heard his footsteps retreat down the hall. Both the threat and the insight whirled for attention in his mind. How dare Higgins! But what if he was right? Should Ben stay here? No. His honour demanded that he sail with his father. If he was going to share in the treasure, he must share the risk. How could a convict like Higgins understand honour?

Nor did he think Sally's letter was part of a plot to have him marry her. Mr Appleby seemed too honest to be involved in trickery despite being an ex-convict. And Sally had wanted to help him before she knew who his father was.

It would be seven years before Ben could marry anyone without his father's permission, which Mr Huntsmore certainly wouldn't give for the daughter of an ex-convict. Ben wouldn't even be in New South Wales when he was old enough to marry or even have thoughts of marriage.

But he liked Sally. She obviously liked him too. He hoped the *Golden Girl* didn't sail till after he'd met her again.

CHAPTER 8

Two days later the hoped for winds still hadn't arrived, though Captain Danvers was optimistic there'd be a wind change the next morning. They were to sleep on board that night, to sail beyond the heads with the tide.

Ben left Higgins to carry his portmanteaux to the ship after he'd dressed carefully in his best breeches and coat. He'd be conspicuous in this land of drabs and rags, but he wouldn't feel comfortable meeting a young lady — even if she was the daughter of an ex-convict farmer — in more casual clothes.

Sally hadn't said what time she would meet him. He suspected that the Applebys might not even own a timepiece. The convict work bell had just sounded as he walked down the lane from their rented house. Men in convict-issue clothes strolled casually to their workplaces, except for the chained work gangs, who limped between their overseers and their whips.

Dogs scratched, and men milked goats in the nearby gardens, but there were no women to be seen. It seemed that the few women in this colony were soon taken as servants and lived in their masters' houses rather than the convict barracks.

Ben wondered what Higgins's lot would have been if he hadn't hauled him up from the hold. A work gang? No, Higgins was too sly for that. He'd have ingratiated himself into an easier role somehow.

The market stalls were already in place, the stall holders folding the tents they'd slept in or unloading the wagons they'd slept beneath. Here at least there were some women: a cheese-seller as fat as her cheeses; and two younger women on a stall selling baskets of eggs, bunches of red radishes and sacks of maize still on the cob.

Ben tried to work out which apple stall was the second from the water tank. There were many apple stalls. Apples were as plentiful as cabbages and rhubarb at this time of year.

Nearby, a convict in a sacking apron hauled up a dead sheep slung on a hook. The man slit the skin and began to punch the hide away from the flesh. A pair of yellow-eyed dogs lay watchful, waiting for scraps.

Cries began to rise around Ben, familiar from his weeks in London: 'Pies! Fresh pies!'; 'Fisho! Fisho!'; 'Cockles and mussels! All alive-o!'; 'Lavender! A penny a bunch!'

Ben wondered who in this colony would buy lavender. Officers' wives, he supposed. Impulsively he held out a penny. 'A bunch, please.'

The wizened convict grinned at him, showing black gums. 'Make it threepence and I'll tie it with a ribbon. Pretty ribbon for your pretty lady.'

Ben had only seen women selling lavender back home, but here he supposed it was a job for any man unable to do heavy work. 'Yes, please. A ribbon.'

He took the bunch, and its scent suddenly reminded him of his mother, of the linen chests at Badger's Hill. Mama had the maids put fresh lavender bags in every linen chest each summer ...

'Master Huntsmore?'

He turned. Sally wore a brighter dress today, a new yellow one not faded by the colony's too-strong sun. Her hair was loose, tied back from her forehead with a matching ribbon.

She smiled at him tentatively, curtseying as he bowed. 'I'm so glad to see you. I thought you might have sailed.'

'Please call me Ben. We sail tomorrow with the tide, I think. You ... you look pretty.' He held the lavender out to her.

She blushed. 'Thank you. You can call me Sally. Mama and Papa are just beyond the market.'

They must have camped overnight, Ben realised. He followed Sally through the growing market crowd and over a slight rise. The land here was almost park-like, with scattered trees — attractive if you ignored the drab colours — and shaggy tussocks that weren't grass, the quartz-bright soil gleaming between the clumps. A few tents were still standing, and hobbled horses picked at nosebags or the tussocks. A pen of sheep complained. Ben wondered if they were destined for the butcher's knife.

The Applebys were camped under a thin-leafed tree by a water butt made from a half-barrel, evidently put there for the stall holders to water their stock. The three of them stood as he approached: Mr Appleby, in what might be his best coat, and the woman who must be Sally's mother, as slim and blonde as Sally, with a much younger boy by their side.

The boy grinned. 'Sally's got a follower!'

Sally glared at him.

'Hush, Frederick,' said Mrs Appleby. 'Mr Huntsmore will think you have no manners at all.' She gave Ben a slight curtsey. 'I'm pleased to make your acquaintance, Mr Huntsmore.'

He bowed politely. 'A pleasure, Mrs Appleby, Mr Appleby, Master Appleby.'

'We've got pies for breakfast!' said Frederick, failing to bow entirely. 'They ain't got maggots in them either, because Ma made me sew them in oilcloth soon as they were cooked to keep the flies off.'

'Won't you sit down?' asked Mrs Appleby, gesturing to a patchwork rug.

Ben sat as Mr Appleby stirred the coals of the fire nearby. Mrs Appleby opened a basket and began to place food on the blanket. Small meat pies and a larger one Ben thought must contain fruit; a fresh cheese in a tin container; real bread, made with yeast, the first true bread he had seen since dinner at Government House; butter, slightly melted, in another tin can. There was a single knife to cut the bread and spread the butter, and a pannikin for each of them, which Mrs Appleby filled with sarsaparilla tea from a tin on the fire.

Ben sipped the hot sweet tea, then bit into a pie. Mutton, seasoned with herbs, and possibly the best he had ever eaten. 'This is delicious, Mrs Appleby.'

She flushed with pleasure. 'Sally helped with the baking.'

'We have an oven now,' said Sally. 'Papa made it from an ants' nest.'

Ben didn't see how an ants' nest could be an oven, but nor did he want to seem ignorant, so he said nothing. He bit into the pie again.

'Did you know that if you leave a sheep's head on a meat-ants' nest, it's bare in three days?' asked Frederick.

His sister gave him a look and changed the subject. 'Mama used to cook at Government House.'

Ben glanced at Mrs Appleby. He wondered what crime she'd been sentenced for. Was she free even now? Maggie had told him that convict women were usually permitted to marry even before they had served their full sentence, and then assigned to their husbands. But there was no polite way to ask.

Mr Appleby smiled at his wife. 'She could have married any officer in the colony. Instead she chose a would-be farmer with a dozen sheep and two shirts to his name.'

'And a land grant on his marriage,' said Mrs Appleby.

'Well, yes, there was that.' He took her hand.

'I knew just what I was doing,' said Mrs Appleby firmly.

Suddenly Ben realised Higgins had been completely wrong. Undoubtedly the Applebys were glad for Sally to have the friendship of a free man's son, and a shipowner at that. But Sally was no village girl with few opportunities for a good marriage. She was one of the few free women in a colony where men outnumbered women ten to one. She could cook, tend a farm, and she was beautiful. Sally would marry where she chose.

He smiled, suddenly more relaxed than he had been since the day of the Harvest Home feast back in Badger's Hill. Indeed, when he shut his eyes, he felt he could have been there: the taste of good food, the bees humming in the tree above, the scent of horses and blossom.

He opened his eyes to find Sally smiling at him. 'Will you try the apple pie, Master Huntsmore? I mean Ben.'

'Thank you.' He bit into it. It was as good as the mutton pies, a real taste of home.

'When does your ship sail?' asked Frederick. 'Can I look on board? Where are you sailing to? What cargo are you carrying?'

'Hold!' Mrs Appleby laughed. 'Let the young man eat his pie first.'

'We sail for Calcutta with tomorrow morning's tide,' said Ben, flushing at the need to lie. But that was the story his father had told him to tell. 'We carry wool and seal oil to trade. We'll pick up a cargo of spices there, for England.'

'Can I see your ship?' demanded Frederick again.

'I … I would have to ask my father.'

Who would almost certainly refuse, partly because he would see no profit in an acquaintanceship with a colonial farmer, but also in case sharp eyes saw that the ship carried only enough cargo to avert suspicion from the chandler, who assumed Mr Huntsmore had bought the rest of his cargo directly from the Marsdens or the Macarthurs or other wealthy landowners who had no need of an intermediary. The *Golden Girl* needed to travel light and swift.

Frederick seemed undeterred. 'Have you ever seen a mermaid?'

Ben shook his head.

'Been wrecked then?'

'No.'

Frederick looked disappointed. 'I heard of a ship that was becalmed for almost a year and the sailors ate each other, and then —'

'Fred, we need more firewood,' said Mr Appleby calmly. 'Would you mind gathering some?'

'But, Pa, all the sticks around here have been picked up already.'

His father gazed at him.

'Yes, sir.' Frederick sighed and stood. 'I would like to see your ship, Mr Huntsmore, if your father says yes. And if you need a cabin boy —'

Frederick caught his father's expression, bowed swiftly and headed off towards the distant trees.

'He's a good lad,' said Mr Appleby. 'Please pay him no mind. We would not presume to trouble your father.'

'Nor is Frederick going to be a cabin boy,' said his mother firmly.

Ben wondered what they would say if they knew where the *Golden Girl* was truly headed. Both Mr and Mrs Appleby had been thieves when they were very young, but it was obvious they were not now. Mama would have liked them, he thought. They were a little like Badger's Hill's tenant farmers, the kind you joined for Sunday dinner sometimes after church, or drank parsnip or rhubarb wine with in their parlours.

Mr Appleby cleared his throat. 'I have a farewell

present for you, lad.' He reached into his coat and pulled out a sheet of cheap brown paper.

'Thank you, sir,' said Ben politely, taking it. It was a map, drawn simply and by an amateur's hand, for it bore none of the neat calligraphy or embellishments of a professional mapmaker. But the outline was clear and looked exact, and the lines of longitude and latitude had been marked with a straight edge where they were supposed to be, for parts of it were familiar to Ben.

'It's a copy of Mr Flinders's new map of New Holland,' said Mr Appleby. 'The whole of it, made when he sailed around the entire land a few years ago. It's more accurate than the maps most sea captains still use, for theirs are made up of the chart markings of different explorations all pieced together. This is the continent entire.'

'Thank you, sir!' Ben said again. 'It's a most precious gift. Did you make it?'

'No, Frederick drew it.'

'Frederick!' Then Ben added quickly, 'I'm sorry, sir, I didn't mean to imply —'

Mr Appleby laughed. 'That Fred is a ruffian? Well, he is, but he writes and draws a neat hand too.'

Which means that Fred must have some schooling, thought Ben, though he didn't like to ask what quality of school was available here.

'You might like to follow the course of your ship till you leave the coastline. And if you ever come back, maybe the map will show you your progress towards us,' Mr Appleby said as he helped Mrs Appleby to her feet.

'I need to buy a frying pan, if there's one to be found today,' she told Ben. 'Sally, will you entertain Master Huntsmore till we return?'

Sally blushed. 'Yes, Mother.'

She and Ben sat silent till her parents had disappeared over the hill.

'I like your family,' said Ben.

'Thank you. May … may I ask you something, Master Huntsmore? I mean Ben.'

'Of course.'

'May I write to you? I don't mean to be forward,' she added quickly. 'I know you may never return to New South Wales. We will probably never meet again, but I would be so interested in what you'd write of other lands and your time at sea.'

She didn't know what she was asking. Nor, if the *Golden Girl*'s expedition was a success, could Ben write of it. Not just because his father would wish their hunting ground to be kept secret, but because war and privateering weren't topics that a young lady should hear about.

Yet he found himself saying, 'I'd like to write to you. Very much. My father's agent in London will know where to forward a letter to. Please do write to me.'

To his surprise, he found he meant it.

CHAPTER 9

Five hours later Ben sat in his and his father's cabin aboard the *Golden Girl*. The scent of lavender polish on the wood reminded him of the lavender he'd given Sally. But the ship still stank of death. He hadn't had the courage to ask his father how many of the hundred and twenty convicts taken on board at Plymouth had survived. He was too afraid that his father might neither know nor care.

The ship creaked about him and he heard the furled sails flap like giant imprisoned bats. His father's voice gave orders to Captain Danvers, and there were calls from the crew above and the sudden thudding of feet. The ship lurched as the sails were hoisted.

A scratch on the door. Higgins grinned at him. He'd filled out even more in Sydney Town, but nothing could change his weasel-like features. 'We're off. Want to catch a last glimpse of your sweetheart?'

But Sally was gone, riding in the farm cart with her family back to the Hawkesbury, carrying the frying pan and the bunch of lavender, as well as the memory of a few hours with a boy from home. No, not home, Ben realised. Neither Mr nor Mrs Appleby seemed to have any longing for the land of their birth, and Frederick would probably rather sail to a cannibals' island than to England. And Sally?

'One day I'm going to cross the Blue Mountains,' she'd told him during those magic hours together. 'Papa and Mama crossed half the world to come here, a place no one from England had seen for nearly twenty years, and then only just for a few days. I want to see new lands too. Drove sheep across the mountains. Find an inland sea maybe, or a new river.'

'The River Sally?' Ben had teased.

She'd laughed. 'I don't need a river named after me. I just want to be there. Do things. Look over my acres when I'm old and see my great-grandchildren and think, *All this is a farm because of me.*'

Suddenly, reclaiming Badger's Hill seemed tame. And yet to do it they'd need to face the enemies of the King and seize enemy treasure. That wasn't tame at all.

'You don't want to visit England?' he'd asked her.

She looked surprised. 'Why should I?' She laughed again. 'England has already been discovered. But I'd like to hear about it,' she added quickly, 'if you'll write.'

It cost sixpence to send a letter to England — Ben had sent one to the rector, telling him about his mother's death and their arrival here, and asking how the servants and tenants were faring under their new landlord. The Applebys must be doing well if they could afford sixpences to write back and forth to England. Five months to get a letter, five months for your reply to travel back to England, assuming the ship didn't sink or the mail chests get sodden in a storm. Once Ben arrived back in England, he and Sally might exchange one letter each a year perhaps ...

'Ain't you comin' up on deck?' Higgins asked, still waiting for Ben's answer.

Ben shrugged.

'Scared, boy?'

'No!'

'Well, if you ain't, you should be,' said Higgins flatly. 'We're headed down to iceberg country, and then into battle. You know why your pa's carryin' so many crew? It's not just to outnumber the Dutchies. It's 'cause half of 'em will be dead afore this voyage is ended, cut down or taken by the scurvy or shot or drowned.'

'Then why did they join the ship?' Ben replied.

'You really don't understand, do you? Oh, I've heard your pa moan about havin' to make his fortune back again, but what he made on the voyage here is enough to keep him and you in comfort all your lives. This is about making himself, and you, rich is all. But for them like me ...' Higgins shook his head. 'Every man on this ship — yes, even the captain too — knows what it's like to have the hunger eat at you, till you try to drown it in the gin 'cause you can get enough gin to make you drunk for a penny, but bread costs threepence.'

Ben stared at him. Higgins met his eyes.

'We knows most of us won't see the end of this voyage alive. But the crew shares a third of the gold taken, not to mention what we can grab for ourselves. The fewer of us left, the more treasure there'll be to share — and it'll be enough to keep each man fed and to build a new life.'

'What kind of life do you want?' Ben asked, curious.

Higgins grinned. 'Like what I had before, but better. A tavern of me own, a mob of boys to work for me.' The grin vanished. 'Back in Lunnon Town, 'cause that's where my woman's waitin' for me, but she won't wait seven years. Two maybe, if I can get back in two. That's where this ship is goin' to take me.'

'I didn't know you were married.'

The grin again. 'I'm not.'

'Mr Higgins ...' Somehow the 'mister' had slipped into Ben's speech. 'Is it going to be very bad?'

'Yes,' Higgins said flatly. 'Worse'n your pa will admit to himself. Men like him only see what they want in their future. It's goin' to be hard sailin', or worse, and hard fightin' too. We got a good chance, but that's all. A chance. Why d'you think I told you to stay in Sydney Town?'

'Because you thought I was a coward,' Ben said.

'Bein' scared don't make you a coward. Well, unless you can swim, it's too late now. Come and say goodbye to Sydney Town, boy.'

Ben followed him up to the deck. The ship was approaching the first small headland out from Sydney Cove, and he saw blue water, blue skies and white caps where the breeze ruffled the waves.

He looked back at Sydney Town. The stop-work bell must have sounded on shore for the streets looked empty, except around the rum shanties by the wharf. Decent men would be tending their gardens, the women their cooking pots, the thieves and cut-throats practising the crafts they'd brought from England, the Governor perhaps dreaming of yet another grand building to be constructed at the end of the world. Perhaps Governor Macquarie might even make this place of mud and rags somewhere people wished to live, Ben thought, not just those forced to come here by law or poverty.

Seagulls soared above them and, even higher, a vast bird like an eagle circled. No Indian women fished this afternoon, but an Indian man in a far larger canoe hauled in a bulging fishing net out by a small island. To Ben's shock, one of the *Golden Girl*'s crew stopped scrubbing the deck, ran to the rail and called out to the fisherman in an incomprehensible gabble.

Ben stared. The sailor had black skin! And not the blackness of the ex-slaves from America or Jamaica he had seen in London, but the colour of one of the Indians of New South Wales, even though he was dressed like the other crew in ragged sailcloth, his feet bare.

'Danvers! What's this?' Ben's father had appeared from the forward deck. He pointed angrily to the Indian sailor. 'I said I wanted men who could sail and fight.'

'That's Billy-Boy, Mr Huntsmore. He's crewed on half a dozen ships before. Some of the Indians really take to it. Billy-Boy knows this coast, sir. I'll show you. Hey, Billy-Boy! Come here.'

The young man stopped his exchange with his friend and ran over to the captain. 'Yes, sir?'

'Tell Mr Huntsmore here what the wind will do in the next two days. Big wind blow from where, eh?'

'Big wind blow from that way, boss.' Billy-Boy pointed to the north. 'One day, two days. Wind stay strong.'

'Back to work, Billy-Boy,' said Captain Danvers.

'Yes, boss.' The young Indian made some sort of signal to his friend in the canoe, then walked back to his bucket and holystone.

'Let me run my ship, sir,' the captain added to Mr Huntsmore in a low tone.

'Very well, Danvers.' Mr Huntsmore headed below towards his and Ben's cabin.

Ben stayed up on deck. Partly because he wanted to see the country he would probably never glimpse again; and partly because he didn't want his father to guess his fear.

He was afraid of the voyage, the vast waves again, the violence to come. But he was also curious. He had only seen Indians in their canoes or wandering the streets. He hadn't thought they would be able to crew a boat.

He crouched by Billy-Boy, who was again scrubbing the deck with the holystone to keep its surface from getting smooth and slippery.

'Billy-Boy, can you understand me?'

The young man looked up. 'Yes, boss.'

Ben tried to think of the simplest way to ask where the Indian sailor came from and why he chose the danger of the sea. 'You like being on big canoe?'

Billy-Boy stared at him, expressionless.

Ben pointed to the canoe behind them, then to the deck of the ship. 'That small canoe. This big canoe. You like big canoe?'

'Yes, boss.'

'Why? We go to big storms. Big waves.' Ben pantomimed cold, then pointed south. Suddenly he didn't want this simple savage to die because he hadn't understood the danger they were sailing towards. Perhaps he might even be able to swim to shore from here. 'Bad!' He shook his head. 'Lots of danger! You go home.' He pointed to the shore. 'Safe, eh?'

Billy-Boy looked around. No one was close enough to hear their conversation above the competing noises of sails and seagulls.

'I can speak English properly,' he said calmly. 'And I know the winds, the tides, the song of the whales and the tracks the fish take through the seasons.'

Ben stared. His accent was that of an educated wealthy man, not even that of a servant. 'How?' he asked.

'My friend taught me. He's a sailor too — Nanberry White. He was adopted by Surgeon White as a boy.' Billy-Boy shrugged. 'My people usually speak several languages. Maybe it's easier for us to learn a new one than it is for Englishmen.'

'Then why don't you speak proper English?'

Billy-Boy laughed. 'I am speaking it. But not to Captain Danvers.'

'Why not?'

'White men like to feel superior. So I speak like they expect me to.'

'But not to me?'

'You're the first person to tell me we're heading into danger.' Billy-Boy glanced over at Captain Danvers, who was yelling something to one of the sailors leaning on a yard above the deck. 'The captain just asked me about the winds. He didn't tell me why he wanted to know. But why wait for a wind from the north unless the ship is heading into the stormy south, not to Calcutta?'

'Do you know why?'

'Yes, but only because I overheard the other sailors talking. We're going to raid another ship. Steal its gold.'

'Not steal,' Ben said. 'Win. We have permission from the Prince of Wales.'

Billy-Boy looked unimpressed. 'I like battles,' he said. He looked back at the land again, then at Ben. 'And my name is Guwara.'

CHAPTER 10

Guwara had been right — the northerly rose early the next morning. For four days the *Golden Girl* sped south, timbers creaking, sails taut, the men yelling from yards as she did exactly what she was meant to do: ride the waves speedily and safely despite the rolling. They sailed far off the coast, in case ships heading to the colony wondered why they were heading south when the usual route away from Sydney Town was to the north. The land became a dim blue line again, against the richer blue of the sky.

Ben spent the first days at the rail, watching the distant land change: mountain ranges rose and fell; jagged islands rose from the sea, then vanished as the ship sailed past. A pod of whales passed far to starboard, leaping black and white against the rich blue of the sea.

He felt uncomfortable to be dressed like a gentleman in coat, breeches and boots, while the crew wore shabby sailcloth and worked barefoot. Back home, except for church or social occasions with other gentry, he had worn the same kind of clothes as his friends, even if his were newer. Nor was he comfortable standing idle while others worked, sanding the deck, furling and unfurling the sails as the wind strength changed, each watch busy until the ship's bell called them off duty to gulp down a pannikin of salt-mutton stew in the galley, then sleep in the hammocks vacated only minutes before by the shift taking over from them. With more crew on board, the hammocks were in even more demand now than on the voyage to New South Wales. Ben tried to think of a job he might do on board. But the owner's son could not scrub the deck, or pick maggots out of the mutton, nor did he know how to trim the sails or even navigate.

On the voyage from England, Captain Danvers had chosen his crew carefully: men he had sailed with several times before, who knew to show deference to the ship's owner and his son. The new crew were surly towards Ben, most pretending they hadn't seen him instead of greeting him politely. Even Guwara, so friendly that first day, ignored Ben now.

The sailors looked resentfully at this boy idly matching the coastline against his brown-paper map, a boy who'd go below to a proper bed in a cabin warmed by a charcoal stove, with a servant to serve his meals of colonial ham, cheese, preserved fruit, raised pies, oat biscuits and plum puddings made by Maggie on shore, all kept in oilcloth in the trunks in the cabin. Higgins brewed the

Huntsmores' tea or coffee on the small galley fire, and Mr Huntsmore drank port and claret from his private store, while the crew only had their daily ration of rum and water, with shards of the ice that rimmed the water barrels. The Huntsmores' limited diet on the ship was more than most of these men had ever eaten, or could dream of eating — unless this voyage was successful and they shared the gold.

Slowly the sea lost its colour, greying as they passed Van Diemen's Land, then turned west on that strange route across the bottom of the world that would eventually bring them around to the western coast of New Holland.

Ben spent most of his time in the cabin now. The winds were strong and unrelenting, and while this gave them speed, it also meant the *Golden Girl* rolled and lurched in the swell. A misstep on deck could lead to death. If a man slipped over the rail into the cold water, he wouldn't survive more than a minute or two. And the ship would sail relentlessly on, unable to turn back into the wind. The waves spat icy froth, and some rogue waves rose so high they could even sweep away men up on the mast.

Weeks passed, and then months. Wind and water ruled here. Each day was a battle to survive them, a fight that Ben had no part of. But slowly, being in a small ship on a vast and dangerous sea faded into normality, and then to boredom. Even on calmer days there was little to see but sea and sky and the occasional flight of sea birds.

Ben re-read the dozen books he and his father had brought from England, including *The Aeneid* in Latin, added by Mama so he might not lose his proficiency. The voyage of Aeneas from Troy to Italy seemed irrelevant now, as did studying both Latin and the ancient Greek language necessary to enter university in England. Ben would almost certainly never go to Oxford as Mama had planned. If he were able to buy back Badger's Hill — *when* he bought it back — he would never leave the place again. But what else was there to do except write in his journal? And there was little to note in that, beyond the distance the ship had travelled, the strength of the wind, or the storms that rolled him out of bed or crashed the china.

Mr Huntsmore spent most of his time in the cabin as well, leaving Captain Danvers to the lash of spray and bite of wind on the quarterdeck. For the first time he spoke to Ben about his life, long rambles about the deals he'd made, the wealth he'd won gambling with the Prince Regent. Ben lay quietly on his trundle bed and half-listened, preferring to remember Badger's Hill instead, taking each detail out from his memory to treasure again. His father never mentioned Ben's mother nor Badger's Hill. Perhaps both had just been business speculations to him, unsuccessful ones. His father never talked of the deals or ships he'd lost.

Today's story involved cargoes of slaves to Bermuda, and the profit to be made in cargoes of rum, port or sugar.

Ben muttered, 'Yes, sir, indeed,' in the pauses. At last he could stand it no more. 'Excuse me, sir, I need to go on deck.'

'Use the chamberpot,' said Mr Huntsmore impatiently.

'The wind has dropped and I could do with the fresh air,' Ben lied.

He went up the companionway onto the deck. The sky and sea were grey again, and the world seemed leached of colour. The crew looked grey too, bundled in whatever clothes or rags of sail they could find, their feet wrapped in rags too. The wind blew harsh and strong, but at least today it was no longer a struggle to stay upright.

Ben had used the head — the lavatory seat at the bow of the ship — and was heading back when he saw it: a gleam of white like a giant tooth shining with blue shadows, perhaps two hundred yards away. He hesitated, not sure what he'd seen. But there it was again, the only colour in this world.

Iceberg.

His feet knew it before his mind did. He was already scrambling back along the deck to the quarterdeck, where the captain was pacing and talking to the helmsman.

'Iceberg! Ahead of us, Captain.'

'What?' Captain Danvers wheeled around and peered ahead. 'I can't see. Are you sure, boy?'

'There, sir!' It was closer now. But still the captain didn't seem to see the small white berg among the grey.

Then suddenly he did.

'Iceberg full ahead!' he yelled at the helmsman. 'Hard to port, man, if you don't want to face Davy Jones's locker!'

The helmsman hauled on the ship's wheel in an effort to pull the ship to the left of the berg.

'Move to the rigging, ye sons of harpies!' shouted Captain Danvers. 'Run!'

Men ran, slipping and sliding. Hands hauled the sails to gain even more momentum so the ship could change direction. Too much and they would hit the iceberg before the ship could turn. Too little and the ship couldn't change course. Men clambered along to trim other sails and keep them taut.

The ship began to turn.

The iceberg loomed closer.

Ben could make out the mass of it below the water now, a small island of ice with only the tip pointing up into the air.

'If we hit it, run to the ship's pinnace,' Mr Huntsmore muttered grimly as he appeared at Ben's side. 'It's stocked ready for use. We take Danvers and two others, to sail for us and navigate.' He handed Ben a pistol. 'Shoot any other man who tries to board it.'

The pistol was cold in Ben's hand. He shoved it under his belt, then covered it with his coat. He could shoot, as any country boy could shoot. But could he shoot a man who was desperate to save himself from ice and drowning?

He found Higgins standing close to him. 'Just checkin' you don't slip, Sneezer,' the convict muttered.

'Or you plan to follow me to the ship's boat if we hit the iceberg,' said Ben.

Higgins grinned sourly. 'That too.'

Could he shoot Higgins? He didn't know. But he knew his father could. Higgins would be no use in the pinnace as crew or navigator.

The ship shuddered. For one flash of terror Ben thought they had hit the iceberg, but it was the wind gusting into the sails as they turned.

The iceberg loomed closer, almost at the ship's prow. Close up it looked more blue than white. Ben stared at it, smooth, silent, deadly, almost luminescent, as if it held strange beasts locked in its heart, its tip so innocently small, with such vast danger below the water line.

And then, suddenly, it was gliding past them, or they had sailed past it. It was only yards away, but that was enough. The ship plunged onwards, further and further, till the berg was left safely behind.

Someone gave a hoarse cheer. Other voices joined in.

'Where there's one, there may be others. We need to change course, Mr Huntsmore, head north,' said Captain Danvers.

Ben's father stared at him. 'That will lose us time. I'm not going to wait on the shores of New Holland if we miss the trading season this year.'

'We may lose more than time if we try to sail through a sea of icebergs,' said Danvers.

'We saw one iceberg, Captain, and a small one at that. There is no need to panic.'

Danvers's expression seemed to carefully not change. 'It's my decision, sir, as captain of this ship. I am merely informing you that I am making it.'

Mr Huntsmore frowned. 'Wait. My son saw the iceberg before any on the ship.'

'Indeed, sir. The boy has sharp eyes, even for a lad.'

Ben knew that scurvy and long exposure to the sunlight at sea meant sailors gradually lost their sight. Those few who managed to reach old age were mostly blind.

'Then let him keep watch,' his father said. 'He'll be able to tell if there are more icebergs.'

Captain Danvers hesitated, then shook his head. 'In seas like this, the waves can hide a berg till we are nearly on it. We were lucky to be able to turn in time.'

'Then send him aloft! He can see to the horizon from there.'

'What? You don't know what you're suggesting, sir. I doubt the boy could even climb up the rigging to the top platform. Even experienced men fall in seas like these.'

'Men weakened by scurvy,' said Mr Huntsmore. 'I'll warrant my son is as strong as any man on this ship.'

Ben knew he wasn't. He had been well-muscled from farmwork before they left England, but the fever and inactivity had taken their toll. He was suddenly aware of Higgins close by, silent, watchful, listening.

'I want to go,' said Ben.

He had watched the men clambering up the shrouds, suspended out from the mast as they headed up around the futtocks, no rope or net to protect them if they fell or a wave swept them away. The thought of climbing those ropes terrified him. Yet in a strange way, it was that very fear that made him determined to conquer it. If he was to share the *Golden Girl*'s fortune, then he should share the danger.

'Well?' demanded Mr Huntsmore. 'If my son sees no more icebergs, will you continue on this course? There can be a stray iceberg even to the north, can there not?'

'That's true, sir. But sending an inexperienced lad aloft ... With all due respect, sir, I captain this ship, not you.'

'And with all due respect, Captain Danvers, as owner I can relieve you of your command whenever I wish. My son has volunteered for this. You can do it, can't you, Ebenezer?'

Fear made Ben's breath shallow. 'I have watched how it's done, sir.'

'Sir, I do not think —' began Higgins in his most servantly voice.

'You are not paid to think, Higgins! Nor to give orders to my son or me. Ebenezer, here, take my coat.'

It was sealskin: waterproof and warm. It was also too long for Ben and would make it impossible to climb. He shook his head.

Higgins bent close to him. 'You're bein' crazy brave. Don't even try it, lad.'

Ben gazed up at the rigging again. Even the thought of letting go of the ropes for long enough to tie himself onto the top platform — if he managed to get up there — was terrifying and probably impossible.

But if he didn't, they might miss the Dutch ships for another year — the spice trade depended on the annual monsoon winds. Another year before he could get Badger's Hill back. A year in which his father might even be declared bankrupt. Ben suspected that if that happened, his father would not face disgrace by going back to London. He would take his gold to the Americas, or some other land where his name wasn't known.

And what if there were icebergs already to the north of them? The *Golden Girl* might be wrecked even as she sought safety.

Captain Danvers gazed at him, evaluating. Ben could guess his thoughts. Ben was not crew, nor any loss if he vanished. If Mr Huntsmore wished to risk his son, then let him.

'Very well,' Danvers said abruptly. 'If the lad can do it, and if he sees no more bergs to the horizon, we will keep course.'

'Thank you, sir,' said Ben quietly.

'Sneezer —' began Higgins.

Ben shook his head at him, suddenly unable to speak. He did not even look at his father.

He slipped off his shoes and stockings. The cold air directly on his skin made him gasp as he walked across the rolling deck to the gunwales. He would have to climb up onto the gunwales and swing one leg out to reach the shrouds before he could start the long climb aloft to the top platform. For a brief period he would be outside the comparative safety of the ship and suspended, clinging onto the rigging, above the churning waves. Higgins was right. Ben had been crazy to agree to this. But if he didn't, and if there were icebergs to the north of them, he might be doomed to death in the grey ice water anyway.

Higgins was still at his side. 'Don't look down, Sneezer,' he whispered. 'And keep breathin'. Terror makes you hold your breath.' He lowered his voice still further. 'When you feel like your hands and legs are givin' way, just remember it's goin' to be easier to get up there than tryin' to turn round to go back.'

Ben wondered how many young thieves Higgins had coached to climb up to high windows back in London.

He wondered how many had survived.

CHAPTER 11

Two-thirds of the way up Ben knew he had agreed to the impossible. The rope under his hands and feet was wet and half-frozen, needles of ice digging into his skin. The ship seemed to roll in every possible direction, shifting with each wave or gust of wind.

He had managed to get this far only by calling on every reserve of strength. But now he had to go around the futtock shrouds, hanging on almost upside down till he could edge his way up and onto the top platform attached to the mast.

Don't look down, Higgins had said. And yet he did.

The world lurched. White spray, grey sea, the tiny figures down on the deck. Almost all the crew seemed to be watching him, even the cook. Guwara's dark beard was fringed with ice as he gazed upwards.

Ben realised he was holding his breath, just as Higgins had warned. He breathed, then breathed again. Higgins was right. He didn't have the strength to get back down. He had two choices: to let go and die, or keep going.

He stretched out his hand again, trying to push his feet against the rope to support his body as best he could. One hand up, another, then another ... He was nearly there.

And now the last push up onto the platform.

His hand grabbed wood, then slipped on the thin layer of ice coating the top. He felt his body fall. But one hand still gripped the rope and one foot was still wedged against a ratlin. He tried again, digging in with his fingernails now, pushing with his feet, a mighty lurch that took him up and over.

A length of rope like a rat's tail curved across the platform. His numbed hands managed to tie it around his waist. He leaned back against the mast, crying in pain, terror and relief.

Somehow the tears gave him strength. He had not been able to cry before, not where someone could hear him. But only the wind and clouds saw his tears now, and even then they froze on his cheeks almost instantly.

At last he realised someone was yelling below. It was Captain Danvers, demanding to know what he could see. Ben suddenly remembered why he was up there. He cleared the tears from his eyes and peered at the sea ahead of them.

Captain Danvers had been correct. Down on the ship, the view was obscured by waves. Here, the grey horizon stretched all around, broken only by froth and the deeper grey of currents. And there was the first iceberg he had seen. Its gleam gave him confidence that he could recognise others.

But no matter how carefully he searched the horizon, there were no more to be seen.

'All clear!' he yelled, wondering if the captain could hear above the groans of the hull, the wind whistling through the rigging and the slap of waves. He made a chopping gesture, hoping Danvers would understand that. Evidently he did, for the ship did not change course.

Ben watched. Grey and grey, and more grey still. Grey that surged and so was the grey sea. Grey that floated and shifted and was cloud. Grey that raged and buffeted. He hadn't known that you could see wind too. He could almost hear its words ...

He forced himself to watch for what was there, not to try to grasp what wasn't. Grey sea. Grey sea. No white at all. Grey sea ...

A bell sounded below. He ignored it, gazing at the grey sea, hunting for a glimpse of white.

A voice below. The captain's, a practised bellow above the wind. 'Come down now, lad. Climb down.'

Leave the security of his perch, to climb down that vast distance to the deck with numbed fingers and cramped legs? He could not do it.

He had to do it.

He fumbled with the rope, gripping, holding. He no longer thought, but let his body take over to survive. Down and under, and then down again …

This was the most dangerous moment of all: level with the gunwales but outside the hull of the ship. Ben could feel his legs shaking. His feet had lost all sensation. His fingers were blue and bleeding from the ice crystals in the ropes. All his strength and determination ebbed …

'Just survive,' the wind muttered. They were the words Sally's father had said. All Ben had to do was survive, and he would have a life beyond this pain, beyond the waves and wind. If he survived, he would live in a world of green again. He would return to Badger's Hill.

Slowly he crabbed sideways along the shrouds, forcing his hands to grasp the ice-daggered, frozen ropes. Even more slowly he transferred one leg and then the other around the shrouds. Now he was outside the edge of the ship's hull. He glanced down at the white and turquoise of the waves crashing below. A few seconds in that water and he'd be dead. He focused on gripping the rope again, though his body had lost almost all feeling except pain. At last he was on top of the slippery wooden gunwales.

The world swam about him. For a moment he thought he had fallen, that the sea had claimed him at last. Then hands grabbed him. Black hands. He caught a glimpse of Guwara's face and felt him stagger as he caught Ben before he hit the deck, then supported him. More hands helped him to stand. His legs trembled uncontrollably. His feet and hands shrieked in agony now they were moving again. He tried to walk, staggered, felt arms on either side of him.

'Good work, boy.' That was Harry One-Eye, the cook.

Mutters of 'well done' came from either side, and hands helped him to the companionway and carried him down.

'See! I said the boy could do it.' His father was triumphant, up on the quarterdeck with Captain Danvers, as if there had never been any doubt or risk.

The cabin. Warmth. Ben held his hands above the coke brazier, almost screaming with the pain.

'Drink this, Sneezer.' Higgins held out something warm.

Ben tasted the bite of spirits. He drank more deeply and felt the world shudder. For a moment he thought the ship had struck an iceberg, one that he had missed seeing. But it was his own body that lurched. I am drunk, he thought. And my body will go no further.

Hands undressed him. He fell into a deep black hole. And slept.

He woke suddenly, thrown against the wall, then falling back onto the bed. The cabin lurched about him. Iceberg!

The ship righted again. No, a storm. His hands and feet burned. So did the skin on his face. But he was alive.

'You're awake then.'

Ben looked up at Higgins's face. The ship lurched again, sloping up, up, up. Higgins braced himself against the wall as the cabin suddenly crashed down the other way.

'No sign of more of them icebergs,' he said. 'You were a fool, boy. Brave, but a fool. Here.' He handed Ben a stoppered flask.

Ben took it carefully, his hands hurting even more as he bent his fingers. It was coffee, cold but sweet. He sipped it cautiously so it didn't spill.

'Captain's ordered the fire put out in the galley,' Higgins said. 'Too dangerous in a sea like this. But there's plum puddin' or cheese.'

Suddenly Ben felt ravenous. 'Both, please.'

'Yes, master.' The tone was sarcastic, but nonetheless Higgins crossed to the chest where the Huntsmores' personal food supplies were kept. He returned with both pudding and cheese neatly on a plate, marred only by the imprint of his thumbs on them to stop them sliding off.

'Is all well up top?' Ben asked.

'One man overboard. Boney Figgs. Slinker Harris has a broken leg. Bone's pokin' through, so he'll probably die of it. Apart from that it's bruises and a bit of frostbite is all so far. You did a good job on the lookout yesterday, Sneezer. We'd have been goners without you seein' that iceberg, and the crew know it. Good thing too.'

'Because the ship might have sunk?'

'That too.' Higgins looked at Ben thoughtfully. 'We're headin' for fightin', Sneezer. The crew are in it for the gold. A week ago not one of 'em cared a ha'penny what happened to you. They wouldn't have put a knife into you, but they wouldn't have stirred 'emselves to stop one either.'

Ben felt the last mouthful of cheese go hard in his throat. 'And now they would?'

'Mebbe. Mebbe not. Do another turn up on the lookout and they'll think more kindly of you yet.'

It made sense. Ben's father commanded loyalty because he promised them wealth. The crew had no reason to care what happened to Ben. He didn't want to go back up to the lookout. He was even more frightened than he had been the first time, especially as the ship surged up and crashed down and rolled with the following wind.

But still he said, 'I'll go up on deck and offer to take another turn.'

Higgins shook his head. 'Not yet, you won't.'

Anger flared. 'You can't give me orders.'

'I just have. And if you've got sense, you'll follow 'em too. Go up on deck now and they'll expect you to do another watch today. Chances are it'll kill you. You ain't got the experience or strength in a sea like this. The deck is rollin' and pitchin' now, but up top the movement's much wilder. More than yesterday, and that was wild enough. Wait here till it calms and your body's stopped achin', then go up. They'll think you're still asleep, recoverin'. Or, more likely, won't think of you at all.'

'But I need to —'

'Use the chamberpot,' said Higgins impatiently, then grinned. 'I been usin' it meself while you were sleepin'. Less chance of goin' overboard throwin' mess into the sea than tryin' to sit astern. Give it a few days more afore you goes back on deck. But that was grand work, Sneezer. A fool's choice, an' a brave one.'

Higgins reached over and helped himself to a slice of plum pudding. 'Grand puddin'. Never had me a puddin' like this in Lunnon Town. Real toff's food, this is.'

Toff's food, Ben thought. He had taken his birth as a gentleman for granted. One did one's duty, as the lower orders did theirs. But yesterday he had done the work of a common sailor, and it was possibly the proudest moment of his life.

CHAPTER 12

Ben felt the change in the ship's movement a week later. They seemed to be meeting the waves side-on, as if riding in a carriage on a potholed track. His hands had recovered, and his feet too, but he still hadn't been up on deck.

'We're tackin' north,' said Higgins, bringing back the chamberpot.

Ben saw that deadly tooth of ice again in his mind. 'Icebergs?'

'Nah. If the captain's right, we're nearly back where we was when we sailed to New Holland the first time, way down south of the western coast, but headin' north this time, not east. We'll be seein' land soon, Sneezer.'

'And if he's wrong?'

'Then we're lost,' said Higgins cheerfully. 'Ain't much we can do about it, except enjoy them plum puddins while we can.'

Ben swung his legs off the bed. 'I'm going up on deck.'

Higgins nodded thoughtfully. 'Probably a good time to.'

'I wasn't asking your permission,' said Ben shortly.

He pulled on his oldest, warmest trousers, his jacket and one of his father's coats, then climbed up the companionway. His legs and arms still felt stiff. One of the crew nodded to him as he passed. It was a small gesture, but the first acknowledgement he'd had from any of them.

The swells ran strong and deep, but they were regular and the ship rode them easily. Ben's father stood with Captain Danvers on the quarterdeck. Ben hesitated to go up to them. No one, not even the owner's son, went onto the quarterdeck without permission. But to his relief, Captain Danvers hailed him.

'Good morning, Master Huntsmore. Come to have a lesson in the use of a sextant?'

Ben wasn't sure if the offer was a joke or not. 'I'd like to be the lookout up on top again, sir.'

'No need,' said Danvers. He smiled. 'Save your eyes for the scenery. We should approach the coast by afternoon.'

'But I would like to, sir.'

'Bored below? That's my lad,' said Mr Huntsmore.

Captain Danvers regarded Ben, his expression hard to read. 'Very well,' he said at last. 'Be ready for the change of watch at the next bell. You know what to look for up there?'

'Anything except sea and sky, sir?'

'Not quite. This route has been well-mapped, but not quite well enough. Look for white water where there should be none — there may be a reef. Keep an eye on the horizon, and if it shrinks, yell a warning and get down from there fast. There are rogue waves in these waters that can splinter a ship in seconds if you don't meet them right. Call out whales too — a surfacing whale can capsize a ship. And dolphins — the men like to bet on them. Land too, of course, though I doubt we'll be within sight of it during your watch. Oh, and other ships.'

'Dutch ones, sir?' Would the battle happen so soon?

'In this latitude any ships we see are more likely to be American sealers or Englishmen.' The bell that told all the time of the ship sounded below. 'Up you go, lad.'

'Thank you, sir.'

Fear prickled, almost terror, but excitement too. Ben felt his father watching him thoughtfully as he walked over to the ropes.

To his surprise, Ben enjoyed being a lookout the second time, once he'd made the still-terrifying journey up the shrouds and tied himself onto the top platform securely.

There was no true privacy on a ship, nor silence. Not that it was silent up there either, but the wind blew away all but the loudest sounds. He would never make a sailor, never make another voyage once he returned to England, but for the first time he understood why men like Guwara chose to go to sea. For the feeling of being one with the waves and sky; the adventure of waiting for the line on the horizon that might resolve to be cloud or land.

The wind increased, lashing and buffeting. Ben was used to it now, even when spray was thrown up so high that it splattered ice drops against his face and coated his hair with froth. This was as close as a man could come to flying. It was exhilarating, almost as if he were an eagle riding the sky.

When he climbed back down, he was smiling still, despite the pain in his feet and hands.

They saw the coast of west New Holland just as the dusk drew purple curtains across the sky: a darker line that could have been cloud or waves if it had not been exactly where the captain's sextant said it should be.

The crew reefed the sails, keeping just enough up to hold the ship steady overnight so they could navigate any reefs or islands in daylight.

Ben woke with the dawn, pulled on his trousers and scrambled up the companionway, his feet as bare as any sailor's. There was the western coast, flatter-looking than the east and on their starboard now, but too far off to make out details.

'Come on up, lad,' called Captain Danvers from the quarterdeck.

To Ben's surprise, Guwara stood next to the captain.

'No storms ahead then? No wind changes?' Danvers was asking him.

Guwara shook his head. 'Not sure, boss — birds strange here. Don't think so, boss.' He gave Ben a half-grin.

'Off you go then, Billy-Boy. Food time, eh? You go get food. He's not as useful here as he is on the east coast,' Captain Danvers added to Ben as Guwara ran back towards the companionway. 'But he's been right so far about the winds.'

'Where do we head to now, sir?'

The captain looked surprised. 'Your father hasn't told you? We'll anchor behind Shark Island, just off the Swarte Swaene-Revier. That's the Black Swan River. A Dutchman found it more than a hundred years past, and a Frenchman mapped it a few years ago. I haven't seen his map, but I met a man who's copied it. There's fresh water on the island and game. The island curves, making a harbour of sorts.' He shrugged. 'Sailing up the river would be better, but there's a sandbar across its mouth.'

'So we hide behind Shark Island till a Dutch ship comes by, then we chase them?'

Captain Danvers shook his head. 'They'll be bigger than us, and most likely faster.'

'So how do we catch them, sir?'

'We lure them in towards us. They'll be thinking the *Golden Girl* has been abandoned, the crew dead of fever or thirst maybe.'

As we nearly were, thought Ben, thinking of how the ship had been almost helpless when so many crew had died of fever on the voyage out.

'But won't they get suspicious when they see the English flag, sir?'

'That's why we'll be flying the flag of Holland. It's a dangerous coast and many a ship's been wrecked here. Every ship knows to look out for fellow countrymen who might be stranded.'

'But … but isn't flying another country's flag against the law?'

'Yes,' said Captain Danvers briefly.

'But …' Ben stopped at the look on the captain's face.

'I can't say I like it,' said Danvers harshly. 'But those are your father's orders. And we're doing the Prince of Wales's bidding, and these ships are those of our enemy. And,' he added grimly, 'there'll be none left to tell the tale when we're done. Go below, Master Huntsmore, and have your breakfast. We need more experienced sailors than you up on the top today.'

Ben's father sat in the single chair in their cabin while Higgins set the table with a linen cloth, silver cutlery and the china plates that were packed away with the cloth after each meal. Then came the food from the chest — oatmeal biscuits baked in Sydney Town to eat with their cheese and ham today, raisins, dried apples, sugarplums, and claret too.

Mr Huntsmore nodded to the convict. 'You may go.'

'Yes, sir. If that will be all, sir.' Higgins backed from the room, bowing.

'Where have you been?' Mr Huntsmore asked Ben.

'I was talking to Captain Danvers, sir.'

'I don't want you consorting with the crew.'

'But he is the captain —'

'Don't you "but" me, young man. Once you let underlings become too familiar, you lose authority. We are on a ship of thieves. Even Danvers wouldn't be on the *Golden Girl* if he could get a better berth. I expect my son to act like a gentleman.'

'But you sent me up to watch, sir!'

'That was necessary. Idle chatter isn't. Understand?'

'Yes, sir,' said Ben. What else could he say? But his thoughts were his own.

CHAPTER 13

The *Golden Girl* hummed. There was no change in routine Ben could point to exactly, just the heightened sense that all aboard were waiting to get closer to this western land, waiting for battle, for gold ... or for death.

Ben had never seen a battle, but almost every ancient Greek or Latin textbook the rector back home had made him study had been about long-ago wars. Ben had no reason to think battle would be any less bloody now. The *Golden Girl* might be able to cripple a Dutch ship with her cannons, but there would still be hand-to-hand combat to gain its treasure.

He waited till evening to speak to his father, spending his time studying the map Mr Appleby had given him. The Black Swan River was marked on it, as well as many small islands, including the curved one that must be Shark Island. He'd wondered if he should risk his father's anger by showing the map to Captain Danvers, in case it had islands or reefs the captain didn't know of. But this western coast had been well-mapped by many hands and had been an established trade route long before the English came to New Holland. He doubted there was anything new along this part of the coast that Captain Danvers needed to know.

At last Higgins brought their dinner: boiled potatoes with salt butter, ham, biscuits and plum pudding.

Ben cleared his throat nervously. 'Father?'

His father looked up from the account book he was scribbling in. His annoyance seemed to have subsided. 'Yes, son?'

He hardly ever calls me by name, Ben realised. It's as if I exist only in relation to him, as his son.

'When we meet the Dutch ship, how ... how should I fight?' he asked. 'I am a fair shot, but I have never studied sword play.'

'Sword play?' His father looked amused. He put down his pen, wiped its nib, then corked the ink bottle. 'You and I won't board the ship ourselves. That's the crew's job.'

'They ... they will die for us?'

Mr Huntsmore looked impatient. 'Men do die. Ships' crews and men in battle. Generals stay behind the line to direct the battle, and that is what you and I will do. We will be in this cabin with the door well-bolted until the fighting is over. You still have the pistol?' he asked sharply.

'Yes, sir.'

'Keep it hidden. You know how to reload it?'

'Yes, sir.' Young Lon's father, the gamekeeper, had shown him that, as well as how to hunt with a musket. Badger's Hill seemed very far away now.

'This cabin is reinforced,' Mr Huntsmore went on. 'It won't withstand cannon shot, of course, but I've ordered Captain Danvers to keep this part of the ship on the far side of the attack.'

So it would be Captain Danvers who marshalled the attack, Ben realised, for all his father's talk of generals in the rear. The men would fight and die, and his father would take the profits. Just as he had from so many other ventures in which men had died from shipwreck or disease.

Ben wondered suddenly how much of his comfortable life had been won through the deaths of others. Even heroic Sir Roderick Montclaire, the founder of Badger's Hill, had won his land by conquest. Had Sir Roderick ordered his men to take the hill while he stayed in the rear?

'Sir, why have we come if we aren't going to fight?' Or lead the fight either, he thought.

His father gave a bark of laughter. 'And let Danvers have my ship, treasure and all? Give him half a chance and he'd sail off with her, paint another name on her at the next port, and I'd never see her again. But Danvers won't risk mutiny. News like that gets around. Men won't sail with a mutineer.' He changed the subject quickly. 'What's that on your bed?'

'A map of New Holland, sir. Someone I met in the colony gave it to me.'

'Let me see it.'

Ben handed it over reluctantly.

But his father gave it only a cursory glance. 'A copy of Flinders's map. The Governor has one too. I had a copy of it made for Danvers.'

Of course the Governor would provide ships that called into Sydney Town with the latest map to copy. Ben took his back and folded it carefully in his jacket. He returned to sit on his bed and wondered what he would say if he could write to Sally now.

Dear Sally,

Tomorrow, or the day after, we will reach Shark Island to await a Dutch ship. We will fire on it and cripple it, and our crew will take its treasure while my father and I hide. I had thought I would be fighting the King's enemies to win a fortune, but instead ...

He could not say the words.

He sat silently as Higgins arrived to remove their dishes and the leftovers he would undoubtedly eat himself. He always cut more slices of ham or pudding than Ben and his father would eat.

At last his father blew out the candle. Ben listened to the creaks of the ship, the slap of waves, the flap of sails above, the scratch as rats gnawed the hull, as the long hours passed as he tried to sleep.

They reached Shark Island the next afternoon, manoeuvring carefully around its rocky edges to the smoother water facing the mainland. The *Golden Girl* had already dropped off four men at two positions further south to stand lookout for Dutch ships. They were in pinnaces, fore-and-aft gaff-rigged, single-masted cutters that could be rowed as well as sailed.

Each pair of men had a barrel of water, stores and a hatchet so they could cut and erect a pole, guyed with ropes to keep it steady, with a crosspiece from which they would take turns looking for sails on the horizon. The first pair would light a signal fire as soon as they glimpsed a ship. The second would light another fire to alert those on the *Golden Girl*.

Ben watched from the rail as men lowered the longboat to go ashore on the island to look for the fresh water the mapmaker had indicated. Shark Island was low and sandy, except for a vast dune covered in scrub and scraggy trees. Thin lips of waves rose up the sandy beach and flopped back.

Birds rose in angry complaint at the disturbance of the ship's boat's arrival, strange birds with strange cries. Seals and sea lions flapped across the sand and slid into the waves, as if they knew they'd need a safer resting place now men had come. The air stung with the smell of bird dung, sharper than the tang of sea and sand.

The mainland looked dry and sandy too, with clumps of dull-leafed shrubs, barren compared even to the tall, thin-topped trees of the forests of the east. But the river glimmered blue and inviting. Then suddenly Ben saw them — a tiny fleet of black swans, as dark as their name, gliding out from the reeds at the edge of the river.

'Good eatin' on a swan.' It was Higgins, at his elbow.

'How do you know?'

''Cause only the King is allowed to eat 'em.' Higgins gave his gap-toothed grin. 'I reckon we'll all be eatin' swan soon, eatin' like kings.'

Ben watched the swans paddling over the shallow water where it rippled across the sandbank, unaware of the threat on board the *Golden Girl*. They weren't just meat, he thought, like the convicts weren't just cargo. But Ben ate meat. And the comfort of his life was based on human cargo ...

'Are you going to fight too, Higgins?' he asked impulsively.

'Course. Only them what fights gets a share of the takings.'

‘And my father.’

Higgins gave a secret smile. ‘And your pa of course.’

‘But you haven’t been in the Navy, have you?’ Ben asked. ‘Or the Army? How do you know how to fight?’

‘I been fightin’ since I were a sparrow. Don’t you worry about me. The streets I come from are better trainin’ than any battlefield.’

Ben stared at him, taking in the wizened features, the claw-like hands. Higgins laughed and cuffed him lightly about the ear. Ben flushed at the indignity.

‘I can take care of meself, Sneezer.’

The longboat returned with its two barrels of fresh water, all it could carry. Men hauled them aboard and sent down empty ones. This time Guwara clambered down the ladder to the boat as well, carrying two long spears and a short one, each with sharp-barbed tips. Ben wondered what there was to hunt on the island now the seals and sea lions had taken to the water. Surely no spear could catch birds on the wing. The men would have to use their muskets.

He stayed on deck, sitting on a coil of rope while sailors scrubbed the deck around him or mended sails ripped in the southern gales, and the carpenter mended a cracked spar. He waited for the sound of muskets to show the men had found game. But the only sounds were the lapping of the water and the high raucous cries of a mob of black-feathered birds overhead, too small for swans. There wasn't even any sign of the Indians that Mr Flinders had said lived on this side of New Holland too, though far inland he thought he saw a smudge that might be smoke.

'Ahoy there!' someone called.

Ben ran to the side of the ship and looked down. The longboat had returned and was sitting low in the waves. The water barrels must be full again. The two sailors clambered up the rope ladder, carrying bloody sacks on their backs. Guwara followed them, carrying only his spears.

Ben glanced around quickly, in case his father saw him consorting with the men. But there was no sign of him. 'I didn't hear any shots,' he said.

'Didn't need to waste powder,' one of the sailors said, gesturing at Guwara. 'Billy-Boy here reckons hoppers are good eatin' — better than that salt mutton. And guess what else he got?' The man grinned, showing a gold tooth that he must have got in Sydney Town if he was an ex-convict, Ben thought, for anything so valuable would surely have been stolen from him in a convict hold.

'What?' he asked.

The man leaned close. 'Billy-Boy speared us a shark, though he says he ain't gunna eat it. Them Indians got strange ideas sometimes. It's a good omen, lad. We'll be eatin' shark tonight instead of sharks eatin' us!'

The two men took their haul down to the galley, while other sailors hauled up the longboat. The *Golden Girl* needed to be ready to move quickly if any sails were seen. Guwara lingered, gazing across the scrubland.

'You're a good hunter,' said Ben tentatively.

'Yes,' said Guwara.

'Could you teach me how to use a spear?'

It was an impulse, something to lessen the boredom of waiting. His father would be furious, but Ben didn't regret asking.

Guwara assessed him for so long that Ben flushed.

'I'll teach you,' he said at last. 'But not on the ship.'

'Why not?'

'No man touches my spears but me. If the others see you do it, they'll want to try too. They'll break them. You and I take the boat out at first light tomorrow.' And he strode over to the hatch.

CHAPTER 14

The ship stank of boiled hopper that night. It was so tough that Mr Huntsmore pushed his serving away and demanded ham instead, though he accepted a cut of the shark, which Harry One-Eye had dressed with lime juice and butter.

The wind rose again in the night. It was still so strong in the early morning greyness when Ben went to meet Guwara that he had to lean forward to stay upright on deck. Mr Huntsmore was still asleep in the cabin. Ben wondered what he would say when he heard his son had spent the day with an Indian. But his anger would be worth it to learn to use a spear.

He nodded to a sailor who was already scrubbing the deck and to two men with fishing lines dangling over the rail.

Guwara was already waiting for him, spears in hand, a pile of sacks at his feet.

'Captain says we can take the boat,' he told Ben. 'I said I'd get more meat without the men making so much noise.'

He nodded at Ben to pick up the sacks.

I'm the owner's son, thought Ben. I don't carry sacks.

Guwara laughed, seeing his thoughts. 'A warrior only carries his spears.' He waited.

Ben picked up the sacks, then followed Guwara down the rope ladder to the waiting ship's boat.

Warriors, it seemed, did not row either. Ben pulled at the oars, and soon felt blisters forming. It had been more than a year since he'd rowed on the lake at Badger's Hill. Thankfully, it only took ten minutes to row across the bay to the sandy beach that curved towards the mainland. Birds yelled at them and at each other and at the rising sun.

Ben pushed off his shoes, pulled up his trousers, then leaped into the shallows to heave the boat up the sand. It didn't move. He tried again, embarrassed.

Guwara grinned. He jumped out too, his bare feet landing in the water, and grabbed the edge of the boat as well. Together they eased it up onto the beach. Then Guwara leaned into it and picked up his spears.

The sun rose higher. The wind grew hotter, but didn't lessen.

By midday, Ben had learned that Guwara's spears were made from the flower stalks of a special tree that didn't grow on this side of New Holland, bound together with the tree's sap and with hopper sinews. But another kind of spear could be made from a branch soaked in hot water, then buried in hot wet sand to straighten it, because only a truly straight spear would fly straight.

But Guwara wouldn't let Ben bury the stick he'd chosen. 'Only a warrior may make a spear.'

'How do I become a warrior?' Ben thought of the battle to come.

Guwara gazed at the white beaches on the mainland, as if remembering. 'You learn,' he said at last. 'You study the country, the law, the skies. And then you enter the circle and …' He stopped, smiling.

'And what?'

'And then you find out what makes a warrior. But a boy can learn to cast a spear. First you need to learn to stand, like this. Now keep your hand steady. Level the spear to your eye so the point is on the place you want it to land.'

By the time the sun rode down the sky, Ben had hit the bush he was aiming at five times, and tussocks he hadn't been aiming at more times than he could count. But he was just beginning to understand the movement and balance needed to cast a spear, and also the amount of strength he would need to cast one hard enough to kill even one of the small hopping animals in the scrub about them.

At last Guwara took the spears himself. 'Stand like I do,' he said quietly. He straightened and lifted one leg, one elbow, hiding the spears close to his body.

Ben tried to copy him. Within minutes his leg ached, his shoulders too. The wind snickered, buffeting them.

A hopping creature peered from behind a bush. It bounded out slowly, followed by another. Guwara didn't seem to move. Only his spears flickered, cutting the air. The animals lay twitching on the sand, then were still.

Guwara nodded to Ben. 'Put them in the sack.'

'Should I skin them? Gut them?'

'The crew can use the insides as bait to fish with. The hides will keep us warm when we travel south again.'

Ben bent to the still-warm bodies and thrust them into the sack. 'I've never seen anyone move so fast.'

'You'll do better tomorrow,' Guwara told him.

'Thank you, Mr Guwara.'

A laugh. 'No mister, just Guwara. Though I have other names too.'

'Why do you use Billy-Boy?'

'I don't. The white men do. But not a boy who uses my spears.' He grinned. 'One day I may tell you all my names.'

'Thank you,' said Ben, humbled.

Suddenly Guwara held up a hand for silence. He pointed into the waves by the beach. A school of bright fish flickered through the water, each no larger than a man's hand, and then a hook-shaped fin. The water was so clear Ben could see the outline of the massive twisting body underneath it, the jaws that looked set in a savage grin. Shark.

Guwara passed the spear to Ben.

He couldn't do it. He would lose the spear in the water. Guwara would need to swim after it, even though he was a warrior, because the stupid white boy couldn't even swim ... But if Guwara swam after the spear, the shark might kill him.

Ben cast the spear.

It struck, lurched. The giant shape surged out of the water, rolled, taking the spear with it. Ben splashed towards it as the vast mouth opened further, lunged ...

The shark jerked back as another shorter spear flashed into its belly, Guwara still gripping it. The giant fish shuddered, twisted, trying to wrestle away, but Guwara held firm.

Ben managed to grab the first spear again. The shark struggled, its tail flashing, lashing. Then suddenly it lay limp below them in the water, its life gone.

Ben leaned on the spear, half-triumphant, half-terrified, wholly exhausted and exultant.

Guwara laughed, not even out of breath. 'Tomorrow you will do it better,' he said again, then stopped and pointed south.

Smoke rose from the mainland, a thin spire in the sky.

'Signal fire,' breathed Ben.

'Yes. Too much smoke to be from people who live here.'

Ben stared at him. 'I didn't know there was a colony in the west. There are no houses.'

Guwara looked at him impassively.

'You mean Indians,' said Ben. 'I'd forgotten that Mr Flinders said some Indians lived here too.'

A pause. Then Guwara said, 'I am a Cadigal man, just like you are English. The people here are Noongar.'

'How do you know? From Mr Flinders?'

'We know,' said Guwara shortly. 'We trade. I ask the ... the people who talk, who trade and know many languages ... to ask what nations live here in the west when I knew we were coming.'

'But how did they find out? We're so far away from ... from your people?' It was as if a new world was opening up. An impossible world, where Indians knew more than Englishmen.

But all Guwara said was, 'We must hurry. The ship must leave.'

Mr Huntsmore was already up on the quarterdeck with Captain Danvers when Ben and Guwara clambered up the ladder. Sailors immediately hauled up the ship's boat and fastened it securely to the side. Others hauled on the massive chain that held the anchor, while others swarmed up the shrouds to set the sails. Ben hoped he and Guwara hadn't delayed the sailing.

The ship surged northwest as her sails filled. Mr Huntsmore gestured for Ben to join him and Captain Danvers. It seemed Ben had escaped his father's anger, possibly even a beating.

'High tide too,' Ben's father was saying to the captain as Ben climbed the steps. 'And the wind in the right direction.'

Ben peered out to sea, but even his young eyes could see no sails. The ship must still be far south.

'How long till the ship gets here, Danvers?' demanded Mr Huntsmore.

Captain Danvers glanced up at the sails, then the cloudless sky. 'In this wind? Three hours if they are carrying full sail, but I doubt they'll risk that at night, not with the rocks around here.' He grinned. 'The timing couldn't be better.'

'So what do we do now?' Ben's father asked sharply.

Captain Danvers smiled. 'We wait for morning, when they will come to us.'

Two hours later Shark Island was behind them, and other islands too. The mainland was a blue haze over to the right, almost lost between the smudge of sea and sky. At last Captain Danvers ordered the billowing sails furled.

The wind came in hard, cold breaths. The *Golden Girl* rocked as the waves crashed against her sides, white froth coating the roughened wood of the deck. As the sky and sea faded into greens then grey, men ran to check powder and shot, and to move cannons and cannon balls so the ship still balanced straight upon the sea.

Ben sat on the coil of rope and watched the activity till Higgins came to fetch him.

'His Nibs wants you. Time for some gruntin' peck and murphies. Ham and potatoes,' he added when he saw Ben didn't understand the thieves' cant.

Ben stood up stiffly.

'You scared?' Higgins asked.

'No.'

'You'd be bird-witted if you ain't. It's goin' to be bad, Sneezer. Keep mum and do what yer pa tells you.'

'I thought you didn't like him,' Ben said.

Higgins shrugged. 'He's a flash cove and a mongrel, but he knows how to save himself while others die for him. Stick with him tomorrow and you should be right. Now move yer pins. I want me grub, and I can't eat till His Nibs is finished.'

Supper was cold: cold potatoes and cold shark meat for the men; cold ham, potatoes and pudding for Ben and his father. The hopper and shark meat that Guwara and Ben had caught would not be cooked tonight. It sat preserved in salt in a barrel. The ship dared not show a gleam of cooking fire in the darkness, or a hint of smoke tomorrow, lest the Dutch ship see it. The

Golden Girl must seem to be lying abandoned in the morning.

It was hard to sleep, the rolling and yawing of the waves too unpredictable. Nor was Ben able to imagine what tomorrow might be like. Maybe nothing would happen at all. The Dutch ship might slip past them in the night. Some captains did forge ahead despite the darkness, especially if bad weather was coming. Or perhaps the Dutch ship had sailed further west so as not to risk shipwreck near the coast.

And what were the ship's crew and passengers dreaming of now? Their own fortunes, once they had sold the cargo they were carrying and bought a cargo at Batavia to take home?

At last he dozed, but it was a strange sleep. He saw snakes coiling around tree limbs, apple pies in the Sydney Town market, Sally's face, and Mama's too. And a rolling hill of golden wheat, not the gold they hunted now ...

CHAPTER 15

Ben woke to a knock on the cabin door. Captain Danvers stood there, holding a candlestick.

'Mr Huntsmore, sir, I'm sorry to disturb you, but it's almost dawn. Would you give permission for Master Huntsmore to climb to the top again? His sharp eyes may see a ship before any of the men.'

Ben's father yawned and nodded. His eyes met Ben's. *Do what is necessary*, his look said, *but do not be familiar. Remember what I said.*

Ben dressed quickly, envying the sailors who did not have to dress each morning or button up boots. He clambered up the companionway, following the candlelight. The last faint stars still shone above, with a faint haze beyond the shore where the sun would rise. The wind blew strong and cold, though in gusts now instead of the ceaseless roar.

He bent to unbutton his boots again. Stupid to have put them on for a one-minute scramble up to the deck, but he could imagine his father's face if he'd seen his son go through the door barefoot. Ben's heart beat faster than a horse could gallop. At least he was playing a part in this adventure, not simply hiding below.

He pushed off his socks and clambered up the shrouds, felt the wind tug at his shirt and tickle his ears with cold. Finally his fingers found the cross-edge of the top platform above the futtocks. He hoisted himself up and clung there, monkey-like. It was easier this morning than it had been perched above the vast seas of the Southern Ocean, but he still needed to cling tight, for the waves that dashed against the ship's hull were sharp and unpredictable.

Grey washed across the dark horizon. The stars vanished. Colour seeped back into the world. Blue sky. Blue sea and wind-curled white caps. But no sails marred the thin line of the horizon.

He watched.

Men vanished down the hatch, emerging with pannikins of cold meat and potatoes. Of course, he thought, it might be hours before they had a chance to eat again. One of the sailors doled out mugs of lime juice laced with rum.

Ben could hear a strange grinding noise, almost kitchen-like, then recognised it. The sharpening of swords and knives on a grindstone.

He watched.

The wind blew.

A shark circled the *Golden Girl* in the clear blue water, and then another. Did the sharks sense there'd be blood in the water this afternoon, bodies to feast on? Or did they always prey here in such numbers, growing fat on the fish that bred near the river's mouth?

He watched.

Surely the Dutch ship should have reached this far north by now. It must have gone further out to sea, as he'd thought last night, running with the wind swiftly, safely, to Batavia.

And yet ...

He saw a cloud down south, and then the smallest speck of white.

'Ship ahoy!' he yelled.

The wind carried his words into the emptiness, but the men below had seen his gesture. Captain Danvers signalled to him to come down.

He moved carefully, aware of how stiff his hands and feet had grown, retracing his progress across the futtocks and down the shrouds. He staggered as his cold feet found the deck, then straightened.

'Position?' demanded Captain Danvers.

For a moment Ben didn't understand. The Dutch ship was on the sea and heading north. And then he did. 'Further out from the shore than us, sir, but not by much, I think. She'll see us.'

‘She may already have seen us if there’s anyone aboard with eyes as good as yours. Right, lads, get below. And you too, Master Huntsmore, if you please.’

‘Sir, is there nothing else I can do?’ asked Ben.

The captain considered him. ‘I doubt Mr Huntsmore would allow it,’ he said at last.

‘Could I help the wounded? My mother tended to the tenants back home.’

‘Can you stitch a wound, or cauterise one?’

‘No, sir. But I can tie up a wound, if it is not too bad, and straighten a broken leg.’

‘And what would your father say about that, eh?’

‘I would like to help, Captain Danvers, if I may be of use.’ He did not answer the question about his father.

He glimpsed Higgins behind him. Had he come with a message from Ben’s father, demanding to know what was happening? But Higgins seemed to be listening, not waiting.

Finally Captain Danvers nodded. ‘Harry One-Eye will do the cauterising. You can help him with the wounded once the day is won. Till then, stay out of the way.’

‘Yes, Captain.’ Ben ran to the hatch and scrambled below.

Mr Huntsmore sat at the table, already dressed and breakfasting on ham and pudding and a dish of nuts.

‘Well?’ he demanded of Ben.

'I saw the ship, sir, right on the horizon. She'll be here in a couple of hours, I think. Captain Danvers has ordered everyone below.'

'He should have reported to me.'

'I think he is busy, sir.'

'I should hope he is. But he should also be reporting regularly.'

Ben sat on the bed, and forced himself to eat and drink. Neither he nor his father spoke. Ben wondered if his father's anger masked apprehension. He had risked everything, even his life and his son's, on what would happen today. By tonight they would be rich, or dead.

Ben moved over to the porthole in their cabin. There was still no sign of the ship behind them. Perhaps she had circled around to be sure the *Golden Girl* really was abandoned before coming closer.

At last Mr Huntsmore sat back, his meal finished, a glass of claret in his hand.

Ben shifted on the bed. 'Will I take the dishes out, Father?'

'Higgins will see to it,' said his father shortly.

'Captain Danvers may have given him orders for the battle, sir. And I … I'd like some water.'

Mr Huntsmore nodded. 'We may well be in here for some hours. Take the jug. Hurry.'

'Yes, sir.'

Ben ran for the door, unbolted it, then halted. Men crouched by the companionway, swords in hand or armed with muskets. They turned almost as one to stare at Ben. He stepped back at the sight of their expressions. Hatred.

He had never been hated before, or had not known it if he had been, but he understood it. Today these men might die, while Ben and his father hid in the safety of their cabin.

'I ... I'm looking for Higgins,' he stammered.

The men moved apart to reveal Higgins sitting on the lowest step, a pair of daggers in his belt. Were they his, Ben wondered, or from the *Golden Girl*'s store of weapons?

He tried to make his voice authoritative. 'Higgins, we need some water in the cabin.'

Higgins stared at him. For a moment Ben thought he was going to refuse, tell him he could fill the jug from the water barrel himself.

'As you wish,' he said at last. At least he hadn't called him Sneezer.

Higgins moved to the barrel in the corner and took the jug from Ben, then bent to turn the bung to fill it.

Ben stood beside him, his back to the waiting men. 'I have something for you,' Ben whispered. 'Here.' He slipped the pistol from his belt. 'There's only one shot. You aim it by lifting it to your eyes and —'

'I know how to use a pistol,' said Higgins quietly.

He slipped the weapon under his belt so his servant's coat covered it, then handed Ben the jug.

'Thank you,' said Ben.

Higgins said nothing, just walked back to the others at the companionway.

Mr Huntsmore was at his desk writing in his logbook when Ben returned. Ben put the jug in the small rack that kept it from toppling in rough seas, just as a bell rang. And the world exploded.

Ben put his hands to his ears automatically. The floor rocked.

Shot after shot followed, the *Golden Girl* shuddering each time. Had the Dutch ship realised they were enemies and attacked them? But then Ben realised the vibrations were from the retort of their own cannons. Charge after charge. He ran to the porthole again, but all he could see were white-frothed waves and the shadows of waiting sharks. The Dutch ship must be on the other side.

He had to see what was happening! Surely it didn't matter if anyone on the Dutch ship saw movement now — they knew they faced an enemy. He crossed to the door.

'Where are you going?' his father asked. 'Come back at once!'

Ben pretended he hadn't heard.

He ran up the companionway, empty of men now, and through the hatch. And there was the Dutch ship. It was twice as high as the *Golden Girl* and half as long again, and close enough to see the faces of the men on deck. Ben saw it was high-masted, or rather had one high mast. The other two masts were already crumpled on its deck, sails trailing in the sea; and waves washed into a jagged hole just above its waterline.

The Dutch ship shuddered as a cannonball shot from its amidships towards the *Golden Girl*. Ben ducked instinctively, but the cannonball fell into the waves, at least twenty yards from the *Golden Girl*. Just as Ben's father had said: the *Golden Girl* was smaller, but her cannon reach was further than the Dutch ship's. And with two masts down, the Dutch ship couldn't manoeuvre close enough to cause any damage.

Another shot. The Dutch ship's final mast collapsed.

A ragged cheer spread through the *Golden Girl*. The enemy ship was stranded now, at the mercy of the waves. It couldn't be long before it sank.

But if it sinks too soon, we'll lose the treasure, Ben thought — just as Captain Danvers yelled, 'Forward! Full sail, you sluggards! Get moving, you dog-faced sons of monkeys! Move!'

The *Golden Girl* surged forward. Another cannonball flew from the Dutch ship, closer this time. The *Golden Girl* changed course.

‘Each man to his station!’ Danvers shouted. ‘Grappling hooks at the ready!’

‘Ready, Captain!’

‘Charge! A gold ducat goes to the first man to draw blood!’

The coil of rope Ben had sat on so often had become a snake topped with hooks. As he watched, a burly sailor swung it round and round above his head and let it fly. It landed on the deck of the other ship, skidded across it, then hooked on fast near the rail. Another hooked rope whirled out, and it too held the Dutch ship fast.

Hands reached up the ropes, the men sweating and straining as they pulled. The two ships clashed together in a shock of wood on wood and creaking ropes.

Suddenly both decks were crowded with men holding muskets, swords and daggers. But the *Golden Girl* had twice the crew and so far they were unhurt. The crew upon the other deck looked already blood-stained. One man’s arm showed bone, Ben saw, and yet he held his sword steady.

A cheer, and the *Golden Girl*’s crew leaped across to the neighbouring gunwales, leaving her decks empty, except for a boy.

Men died, their necks slashed open, their insides toppling out. Men died slowly, crying in pain upon the deck. All around, men died.

Ben watched from the *Golden Girl*, unable to move or look away. He had not realised how men died in battle, not when he was back at Badger's Hill, dreaming of ancient Greek adventures, or at Government House, proud to be facing the enemies of the King.

Some men did not die, and that was almost worse. They screamed for help, for water, for bandages to staunch their blood.

Ben had not known that blood smelled like cold iron, that the insides of men smelled like slaughtered pheasants hanging in the larder, that even the cold wind could not blow the smell away.

He had not known that so much musket shot left a haze of smoke that smelled of sulphur, the stench of hell. Nor could he help the *Golden Girl*'s wounded men. There was no safe place upon the Dutch ship's deck to take them. A wounded man was still an enemy.

The battle filled the world — the clash of swords, the musket shots, the stink of blood and sulphur — yet at the same time it was so very small. Two dots on the vastness of the sea, the giant, mostly empty continent beyond them.

Suddenly boots landed on the *Golden Girl*'s deck. Ben stepped back, hoping he was hidden in the companionway. Dutch sailors, bearded, bloodied, swords in hands, slashed at their enemy. Others followed, Dutch and English. The fighting became even fiercer on the *Golden Girl* than on the doomed Dutch ship.

Because it was doomed, Ben realised. It would have only one ship's boat, or two at most, possibly already holed by the *Golden Girl*'s crew to stop any Dutchmen escaping with the story of what had happened on this day. Only one ship and its crew would sail away from this battle. The Dutch sailors' only hope was to capture the ship that had attacked them.

Ben had to get back to the comparative safety of the cabin. His father was right: he shouldn't be out here. He hadn't even thought to bring another pistol.

Even as he thought it, a hand grabbed him, held him up, a dagger swung ...

And dropped, the body that held it dropping too as a pistol shot rang across the deck. Ben looked up to see Higgins by the ship's boat, a sack at his feet and the pistol in his hand. Higgins had saved his life. Or given him seconds to escape.

Ben half-tumbled down the steps and grabbed at the cabin door. It did not move.

He beat on it. 'Father! It's me!'

For long seconds he thought his father could not hear, or would not. At last he heard the bolt pulled back and the door opened a crack just large enough for him to squeeze through.

His father shot the bolt again. 'Well?' he demanded.

'The Dutchmen are trying to take over the *Golden Girl*. But I think our crew are winning.'

And dying, he thought, while we wait here.

'How is the Dutch ship? Sinking yet?' Mr Huntsmore paced across the cabin and back again. 'If she sinks before we can unload her, we will have to begin all over again — repairs, new crew ...'

'The ship doesn't look like it'll sink soon, sir, but it's taking on water fast.' Ben hesitated. He could not stay in this room while others died for him. Even if the men hadn't been fighting for his fortune, he realised, he couldn't stay here and do nothing while they suffered. 'I'm going out again to help, sir.'

'You will do no such thing.' Mr Huntsmore strode over to the door as Ben pulled back the bolt. 'Ebenezer!' he yelled as Ben slipped through the doorway, but made no further move to stop him. Ben heard the bolt snicker shut behind him again.

He paused, but this area below deck was still free of fighting. He made his way up the companionway cautiously. The noises had changed in the time he'd been in the cabin. Men still yelled, screamed, sobbed, but the clash of swords, the bark of cannon, even the blast of musket fire had vanished. Only the stinking sulphurous yellow smoke remained. And the blood.

But there were no bodies lying on the deck, except for a few sailors slumped in exhaustion. As Ben watched, he saw why. Two men carried a bleeding crew member down the hatch towards the galley and Harry One-Eye, while another two threw a screaming Dutch sailor over the rail. And over on the Dutch ship, a line of men in strange leather trousers stood by the furthest rail. Ben stared as a single sword thrust cut their necks, toppling them over into the sea.

For the sharks, he thought. We ate the sharks, now they eat us.

Somehow, despite the Governor's words, despite his love of England, Ben could not think of the Dutchmen simply as enemies. They too had crossed the seas, survived the waves, the doldrums, scurvy, cliffs, reefs and icebergs. What was the word of kings and governors compared to that? But they were dead. And men still alive on the *Golden Girl* needed tending.

He ran over to the hatch that led to the galley, his boots sliding in blood that seemed to become more slippery as it congealed.

He grabbed the top of the companionway and climbed down into the galley. There was no sign of his father.

CHAPTER 16

Time seemed to stop. The world became a series of flickering moments as sailor after sailor limped down or was carried to the galley, bleeding, limbless, screaming or too quiet as they slowly died from loss of blood.

Ben helped hold men down as Harry One-Eye used a red-hot iron to cauterise bleeding stumps of wrists, or wounds on arms or legs. In one case, a foot that dangled was quickly cut off and the stump seared, the man collapsing into unconsciousness that Ben hoped was respite, however brief, from pain.

Footsteps thudded above. Ben heard his father giving orders for the disposal of the riches from the Dutch ship: the chests of gold and ducats to his cabin; the bolts of rich cloth and the stores to be taken to the hold. Even the ship's fresh-water kegs would be brought on board.

Ben held water to the lips of a man with blood still seeping from the edges of a cauterised wound across his forehead. Somehow he was still conscious, even giving

Ben an almost grin. 'We got 'em,' he whispered. 'We got 'em good.'

'Yes,' said Ben.

He wondered if Higgins had survived, or Guwara. Or were their bodies lying on the Dutch ship? There had been only one shot in that pistol, and Higgins had used it to save Ben's life. Had that moment of kindness led to his own death?

Captain Danvers appeared. His left arm was tied with a rough bandage. Red seeped below it.

'There you are,' he said to Ben. 'Your father wants you.' And he vanished up on deck again.

He didn't call me Master Huntsmore, thought Ben. He glanced at Harry One-Eye.

'Off you go, lad.' Harry looked and sounded strangely sympathetic. 'All of us must do the captain's bidding.' He hesitated, then added, 'You did good here, lad.' And then, 'I'm sorry.'

What did he mean? Sorry about the wounded men, the dead? But none of that was Harry's fault.

As Ben climbed the companionway, his body felt as if it were wading through jelly, his mind filled with so many bloody scenes that the ship and sea seemed unreal. He looked around. A team of weary-faced sailors scrubbed at the deck, while others hauled up buckets of seawater to sluice away the slippery gore. Others carried tankards of rum among the working men, giving each a few gulps before passing on to the next. One of them hesitated next to Ben, as if to offer him a drink, then passed on.

Ben looked over at the Dutch ship. The grappling hooks must have been released while he was below decks. The ship floated half a mile away perhaps, one end underwater. Bodies floated in the water too. Some, perhaps, were still alive. But they wouldn't be for long. No one else on the *Golden Girl* looked over the rail. No one was launching the ship's boat to save those in the water. Death by sword, or death by drowning — what was the difference, Ben thought, even to the sharks?

Then he saw Higgins. The convict was leaning against the ship's boat. He didn't rise when he met Ben's eyes, but nodded in acknowledgement, his expression impossible to read. There was no sign of Guwara.

'Son! Over here! You'll want to see this,' called Mr Huntsmore. He was up on the quarterdeck with Captain Danvers.

Ben walked slowly across the deck and up the steps. 'What, sir?' he asked. His head ached. His tongue felt too thick for his mouth.

'Fire!' yelled Captain Danvers.

Two cannons blasted below and the hull of the Dutch ship exploded in a haze of splinters. The rest of it shuddered then slowly rolled, down into the ocean. A vast wave, perhaps two yards high, spread out from where the ship had been. Ben felt the *Golden Girl* bounce as the wave passed underneath them.

A few of the *Golden Girl*'s crew cheered. But most kept to their scrubbing, barely looking up.

'Excellent,' said Mr Huntsmore, turning away from the whirling debris where the Dutch ship had gone down. He clapped Captain Danvers on the back. 'We've done it. Good job, man.'

'A good job indeed,' said Captain Danvers quietly.

That grand ship is gone, thought Ben, leaning on the rail, trying to breathe in the freshness of the wind instead of the sour stench of blood and men. Vanished as if it had never existed. He realised he hadn't even seen the ship's name. Perhaps no one would ever know where it had been lost or why.

How long would it be before the families of the men who'd died here realised their fathers, brothers, husbands would not return?

The wind filled the *Golden Girl*'s sails again, sending them southwest, away from the wreckage-strewn water. Ben wondered where they were headed now. To Shark Island, to let the crew rest and recover before facing the southern gales again? Or would they resume sailing north?

Down on the deck, sailors still scrubbed. Others hauled at ropes; and the ship's carpenter hammered at damage to the deck and the gunwales.

Higgins still leaned against the ship's boat. He might have taken part in the fight, but he looked as if he felt it beneath him to do any other work beyond serving the Huntsmores.

Captain Danvers began to walk, a little unsteadily, down to the main deck. Ben and his father followed. Suddenly the captain stopped.

'What is it?' demanded Mr Huntsmore.

Captain Danvers smiled grimly.

Suddenly Ben realised that the sailors scrubbing the deck had shoved their holystones under their belts and were rising to their feet. Other men emerged from the hatches, slowly converging around the captain, Ben and his father. Wounded men, men who limped, men who supported others, exhausted men — but excited too, as if the battle had just been the beginning of their adventure. Every one of them was bloody, though from their own wounds or those they'd killed or helped, Ben couldn't tell.

And there was Guwara at last — unhurt. The dark-skinned man moved slowly to the outside of the crowd of sailors, his expression impossible to read.

Only Higgins remained apart, still leaning against the ship's boat.

Ben looked at the faces around him. What was happening?

'Seize them,' Captain Danvers said.

Ben felt two strong hands pull his arms behind him. A rope bound his wrists tight.

'What in the name of Hades is going on here?' Mr Huntsmore struggled as his hands were bound too. 'How dare you! Danvers, I demand you let me go.'

'Demand all you like,' the captain said, and nodded to Six-Toed Sam. 'Get his pistols from his belt.'

'This is an outrage! I will see you hanged, man!'

'I doubt it.' Danvers smiled wearily at Mr Huntsmore. 'You see, it's like this. You have two choices. You and your son can die by the sword; or we throw you overboard and see if you can swim.'

'Don't be ridiculous, man! The sea is alive with sharks. This is mutiny!'

Ben realised he had never seen the captain look amused before. 'Ah, you've noticed, have you, Huntsmore? Always did think you were a bit slow on the uptake.'

The men laughed.

'You'll never get away with this!' Ben's father yelled.

'Why not? Dead men tell no tales. Those were your very words, Huntsmore. Give us a few weeks and the *Golden Girl* will have a new name, a new history, and never appear in any port she's been to before. And every man on board will be free of New South Wales forever. So what shall it be? Shooting, or man overboard?'

'I demand,' blustered Ben's father, then stopped,

obviously trying to come up with a demand that might be met.

'Or we could take it nice and slow,' suggested Danvers. 'Would you like that, *sir*?' He spat out the last word. 'Maybe chop off your fingers first, so you can feel what it's like for all those you expected to give their limbs for you today. And then your arms, your legs ...'

'Stop it!' yelled Ben.

'Sorry, little master,' said Danvers, a small flash of sympathy in his eyes. 'You're not like your father, but we can't risk having you tell anyone what happened here. It's fish food for you too.'

'Excuse me, Captain.' The crowd turned to look at Higgins, still leaning against the boat. 'You promised each of us who fought today a share for our work.'

'I did.'

'Well, the lad helped, even if his father is a pox-ridden mongrel. That boy saved us down among the icebergs. And he helped with the wounded today. I reckon the whippersnapper deserves a share too. Let his life be his share. That's what I say.'

Silence. Ben could hear his heart beating. He didn't look at his father. A dutiful son would say, 'I will die with my father, an Englishman to the last.' But he didn't want to die. Nor had he ever really felt this man was his father. He had just filled the space, now and then, where a father might be.

Captain Danvers looked around the men.

'He did his part up on that mast,' said someone. 'No complainin' either.'

'Can't trust 'im. Curs breed true,' said another voice. 'The pup'll be as bad as 'is father.'

Harry One-Eye stumped forward. Blood crusted his arms, his shirt, his trousers. Other men's blood. 'Let the boy live,' he said quietly.

'You're forgetting something,' said Danvers slowly. 'If we let him live, he can tell the authorities. We'll all be known as mutineers. And that means the rope in any port in the Empire. Even the Frenchies and the Americans hang mutineers.'

'Only if we take him with us, Captain,' said Higgins quietly. 'Put him ashore. Even if he's rescued, we'll be long gone. The *Golden Girl* vanishes, and us too.'

'He won't survive ashore,' said Harry One-Eye. 'Not a boy alone, on a coast like this.'

'A slow death, not a fast one,' Captain Danvers said. He looked at Ben. 'Which do you want, lad?'

'Put me ashore,' said Ben, and added, 'Please.' I could have said 'us', he thought. I should be pleading for my father too.

Even as he thought it, Mr Huntsmore said, 'But what about me?'

An arm moved from behind Ben. A sword slashed, and a red stain grew across Mr Huntsmore's neck, severing his head from his body. He fell to the deck, his feet twitching, then lay still.

Ben gave a cry. He kneeled by his father's body, gazing at his face. I should be grieving, he thought. But he had been grieving for the past year, for Mama and Badger's Hill; and today for the men lost in the battle. There was little left for this cold-eyed man who had killed not for survival, like so many here had been forced to do, but for wealth.

'More scrubbin',' muttered someone as blood pooled on the deck.

Hands grabbed Mr Huntsmore's limp body, lifted and heaved. Someone else grabbed the head.

Ben struggled to stand, and forced himself to watch as they carried his father's body to the rail and threw it over. I should pray for him, he thought. I should feel ... something. Perhaps I am dead too, and haven't noticed.

'You've earned a chance, lad,' Captain Danvers said. He nodded towards a blue smudge to the east. 'See that? It's an island, bigger than Shark Island. Rottnest, the Dutchies call it. They say it's full of giant rats a man can catch with his bare hands — and maybe a lad can catch them too, if he's fast. The maps say the island's got fresh water. Keep those young eyes of yours peeled and light a signal fire if you see a ship. If you're lucky, another Dutch ship might find you and take you to Batavia.'

'But we are at war with the French and Dutch!' Ben said. And there was no chance an English ship would sail this far north. Why bother when the Dutch controlled the shipping route, and the fastest way to Sydney Town was with the winds down south?

Captain Danvers gave a tired smile. 'I wouldn't worry about that, lad. Chances are you'll never reach the island anyway. But we'll give you iron and flint to make a fire. We'll even give you a knife.' His gaze hardened. 'It's more of a chance than most men get. More than your father gave my son.'

'I don't understand.'

'My boy Nate was first mate on the *Silver Queen* eight years ago, one of your father's ships. Word in London was there was plague in Bombay that year. But profit was everything to your father. And profit he got, because few other ships ventured to Bombay to carry back tea that year. But my son lost his life.'

'I'm sorry,' said Ben.

He wondered if he should tell this man how Mama had been lost on one of his father's voyages too. But the captain already knew that. And this was all the mercy he would show Ben.

CHAPTER 17

The *Golden Girl* moved with purpose now, the waves lifting her rather than tossing her from side to side. The blue smudge that must be Rottnest grew, till it became green and rocks and sand. Ben sat with his back to the mast. No one met his eyes, not even Higgins. Guwara had vanished, presumably below.

At last Captain Danvers ordered the mainsail furled. 'Volunteers to take the boy ashore?' he yelled.

Silence. Bare feet shuffled on the deck that had been scrubbed again, though the stains of blood remained.

Captain Danvers turned to Ben. 'Sorry, lad. I'm not going to order any man to take you. There are rocks around the island that aren't on my map. It's not safe for a ship like ours to sail closer. If no one volunteers ...' He shrugged. 'Don't suppose you can swim?'

'No, sir.'

Someone sniggered. 'Might be time you learned then.'

Ben looked around the men on deck. 'Please,' he said.

More silence.

He sensed that most were not antagonistic to him, but nor would they risk their lives for him, taking the ship's boat to an unknown beach. Each man here had a chance of life now with his share of the treasure, a far better share than under an owner who would have taken a third for himself. Why should they risk that life for Ben? None of them even knew him.

Except, he thought, for Higgins. He looked for him, and found him still leaning against the boat.

'I saved you once,' Ben said to him.

Higgins shrugged. 'You saved me another week down in the hold is all. I'd survived down there for months, I could've managed.' He met Ben's eyes. 'And then you had me as your servant in exchange.'

Ben said nothing. Higgins was right. He probably would have survived, and might even have ended up on this very ship once he'd recovered on shore, though without the food and care he'd enjoyed in Mr Huntsmore's service it would have taken him longer to regain his strength. And Higgins had already saved Ben's life once — which was possibly something he didn't care to mention in front of his fellow mutineers.

Why *did* Higgins save me? Ben wondered. He must have known the mutiny was planned. Captain Danvers had obviously filled the ship with men who were loyal to himself. If Higgins hadn't been part of the plot, it would have been easy for the others to shove him overboard in the southern storms.

He gazed around for Guwara. Surely he would help him? But there was still no sign of him.

Higgins heaved himself slowly to his feet. 'I'll take the pup to the island,' he said expressionlessly.

'You're no sailor,' said Danvers. 'We can't risk losing the boat for the sake of one boy.'

'I used to be a ferryman back and forth across the Thames. I know enough to get to that island and back.'

Had Higgins really been a ferryman? Or was this yet another lie? But at least it gave Ben a chance.

Captain Danvers looked around at his men, as if assessing their temper. But once again there was no active antagonism towards Ben, even if they would not help. All of them had seen him climb the mast amid the storm and help Harry One-Eye with the battle-wounded while his father sat comfortably in his cabin.

At last the captain nodded.

Higgins clambered down the ladder first. The pinnace rocked as he settled himself on the seat. Ben followed him, the flint and knife tucked under his belt. He should have asked if he could take a bag of clothes too, and the food chest from the cabin, even some money so that if a miracle occurred and a ship picked him up, he would not be penniless in Batavia, an enemy who did not speak the language.

'Hoist the sails, Sneezer,' said Higgins.

Ben fumbled with the ropes, but then his fingers remembered how he had done it before on the lake at Badger's Hill, even though that didn't have waves that pushed and bounced. Higgins stood stiffly and trimmed the sails, expertly enough for his claim to have sailed on the Thames to possibly be true. The small craft began to bob unsteadily away from the ship.

Ben looked up at the rail. Most of the men had moved away, though Captain Danvers still stood there, gazing down at them.

Suddenly something moved. A figure clambered up on the gunwale, then dived, graceful as a sea eagle. A dark head emerged above the waves, swimming towards them using a strange sideways stroke, the other hand holding his spears.

Guwara.

A few heartbeats, and Guwara's hand grabbed the side of the pinnace. He threw his spears into it, then hauled himself, dripping, in too.

'Come to join us, Billy-Boy?' asked Higgins softly.

Guwara didn't reply. He gathered his spears, checked their points, then sat at the other end of the boat. Watching for sharks? Watching for rocks? Watching in case one of the crew decided on a final revenge and sent a shot at Ben?

At least his presence meant the *Golden Girl* would get her boat back safely, thought Ben bitterly. And the spears would stop him attempting to overpower Higgins and escape with the boat. But escape to where? Even if he were to push Higgins overboard, which he would not do, the *Golden Girl* would easily overtake him.

Ben looked back at the ship. His father's, until just a few hours ago. Now Ben had lost everything: his parents, his home, his future. He had only his life left, and months or even years of solitude and struggle. He should be weeping. But in truth he felt he had lost his life more than a year ago, when the carriage had left Badger's Hill for the last time. Nothing since had seemed truly real, except perhaps those hours with Sally, who had reminded him of the friends he had left behind.

He looked at the island in front of them. Seagulls yelled and soared and balanced on the ever-present wind. Grey shapes moved on the rocks. Seals. He could spear one for food if he had a spear. He doubted that Guwara planned to leave him any of those he held so carefully. At least he had shown Ben how to make a spear. Then Ben realised Guwara had never shown him how to finish the spear, how to make the bone barbs or attach them to the wood.

The boat changed course, and now the island hid it from the *Golden Girl*. Ben could see more rocks and then a beach, the sand as bright as sunlight. Perhaps he could fish from there. If he unravelled his stockings, the wool might become a fishing line. He might be able to grind the buttons of his jacket to make hooks ...

'Well?' Higgins asked Guwara softly. 'What happens now? Your choice, friend. You got the spears.'

Guwara laughed.

Ben stared at him. What was so funny? They were leaving him here to die, or at best to live scavenging among enemies.

Guwara stood and trimmed the sails, swiftly and expertly. They billowed, taut as canvas eggshells. The boat surged through the waves. Suddenly Ben realised the beach was getting further away. The boat was heading due east, towards the mainland, the *Golden Girl* still hidden from view.

He looked at Higgins, then at Guwara, and tried to keep his voice steady. 'What's happening?'

Did they plan to kill him out of sight? But Higgins had saved his life. And he'd thought Guwara was almost a friend.

'What are you doing?' he asked again.

'I'm savin' your poxy life,' said Higgins shortly. 'An' I think Billy-Boy here has the same idea. Now hush up.'

The freshening wind pushed the boat hard east. They were nearly at the mouth of the Black Swan River. Guwara steered expertly towards what looked like a shallow channel at one side of the sandbar.

Ben looked back. There was still no sign of the *Golden Girl*. Did Higgins and Guwara plan to leave him on the mainland instead of on Rottnest Island? But that made no sense. Ships stayed as far as they could from the rocky coast; and it would be impossible for Ben to cross this mostly unknown continent on foot. His only chance of rescue was on the island.

The boat sped past the first bar of bright white sand, then lurched and stuck. Deceptive waves rippled around them.

Higgins swore. 'Curse it, man, they'll be after us soon.'

Guwara leaped from the boat, sinking to his knees in sand, then gestured to Ben to do the same. Ben took off his boots and stockings, then carefully jumped out too. He felt the sand creep up almost to his thighs. They pushed, but the boat didn't move. Nor, Ben realised, could he.

Higgins swore again. He held out a hand to Ben, heaving him back into the boat. Guwara had already freed himself. Ben watched him swim to the other side of the boat.

'Get out! Both of you!' he yelled, in the excellent English he had used only with Ben before.

'I'm not …' Higgins began, then evidently realised he had no choice but to obey.

Ben leaped further from the boat this time. The sand below him was firmer and ankle deep only. A splash and a glug, and Higgins landed next to him, giving a muffled exclamation and pressing his thigh with his hand.

Guwara pushed at the pinnace with one hand, keeping himself afloat with the other. The boat began to move. Ben ran forward and grabbed the prow. His legs sank into the sand again, but the boat's momentum helped him now. A few more minutes and it floated clear.

He grabbed its edge and hauled himself in. Higgins followed, still cursing under his breath. Guwara clambered in beside them and adjusted the sails again. Once more they billowed above and the boat sped down the river, then around a bend. A drift of black swans watched their progress unruffled.

The sea was gone, though Ben could still half-hear, half-feel the vibration of the waves.

'How long till they miss us?' asked Guwara.

Higgins sat with his eyes closed, his forehead damp with sweat. 'Another half-hour maybe. They know we like the boy. They'll think we're helpin' him ashore, startin' a fire for him mebbe.' He opened his eyes and grinned sardonically at Ben. 'Think we'll be kind and light a fire for you, Sneezer?'

'Maybe,' said Ben cautiously.

'Find a spring of water for him too, maybe get a drink ourselves.' Higgins nodded at the spears. 'And some fresh meat would be good. They'll think you want to hunt for meat for the ship afore they sail.'

The world felt too bright, too strange. None of this could be happening, not his father's death, not the battle, not this strange and unexpected flight.

'Please, what is this about?' he asked, trying to keep his voice even.

'Told you,' said Higgins. He moved his legs. For the first time Ben saw the sack Higgins had with him during the battle. 'Couldn't take much without bein' noticed,' he added. 'But I got us a hatchet, a jug with a lid on it, a tinderbox and a good big knife.' He winked at Ben. 'Even got one of them plum puddins too. You should feel right at home with that.'

Higgins had planned all this, Ben realised. He'd known about the mutiny and guessed that Ben had won enough acceptance from the crew to save his life — with a bit of prompting. He must also have suspected that no one else would risk their life to take Ben ashore. And no one from the ship could have followed them to Rottnest without the ship's boat, or any of the other places Ben might have been left. But Higgins obviously hadn't planned to sail into the Black Swan River.

'I'm holdin' you to ransom, boy,' Higgins said, grinning. 'I couldn't never go back to Lunnon Town if I stayed on the ship. I'd be strung up as soon as I showed me mug. Danvers might think he can get away with mutiny, but men talk. Only needs a pot o' rum and a night's yarnin', and it's a hemp necklace for the lot of us.

An' I know how much dash your pa left with Mr Moore back in Sydney Town. It's a tidy sum, enough to see the two of us right.' He looked at Guwara and shrugged. 'Or maybe three of us, Sneezer lad, if you give us your word you'll share your coin.'

'You'd trust me?' Ben asked.

'Aye, I trust you, Sneezer. So what's it to be? Share and share alike?'

He had no choice. No, he corrected himself, I do have a choice. I could lie, and then have Higgins taken away in irons when we get back. But that wasn't a choice he'd ever make.

'Everything I have,' Ben said slowly, 'we share when we get back to Sydney Town.'

If they got back. The vast continent lay between them. But at least now he had a chance.

He looked over at Guwara. 'Why did you dive overboard?'

'To go home,' said Guwara shortly. He met Ben's eyes. 'I didn't understand "mutiny" at first when I heard the men talking. Then it was too late to leave the ship. They would have killed me.'

He looked back to where the waves muttered at the entrance to the river. 'I love the sea,' he said softly. 'I love the ships. But if I stayed on board, I could never go back to my own country. And I have ... duty there.' He cast

Ben and Higgins a brief look each. 'Duty you wouldn't understand.'

'Now all you need to do is sail through the heads into Sydney Town, matey, and you're a hero who refused to sail with mutineers. An' so am I,' said Higgins, grinning.

Another mutiny, thought Ben. A small one, against the mutineers. The *Golden Girl* could not follow them down this river. Captain Danvers couldn't even be sure where the boat had gone. They might have hauled it up out of sight on Rottnest, or on a section of one of the long beaches on the coast, hiding it in the scrub.

'Told you I look after me own, Sneezer,' said Higgins, leaning back as the boat rounded another curve of the river, with more dry scrubby land on either side. 'I've never let one of me lads down, and I ain't goin' to start now.'

Ben stared at him. He had misunderstood, right from the beginning. Yes, this man had run a gang of children, trained them to steal, to pick pockets ... But it was to survive, just as Higgins had, on the filthy dangerous streets of London. Ben had trusted the wrong man — the father who had risked his son in the Southern Ocean gales, who had sent him up the rigging — when all the time it had been this thief who was looking out for him.

'I'm sorry,' he said.

'Well, so you oughta be,' said Higgins, panting a little. His face was paler. 'It's goin' to be you an' me now. When we get back to Sydney Town, you're goin' to say how Billy-Boy and me rescued you bravely from the mutineers. I'm assigned to you, remember. Well, to yer pa, may the sharks nibble at him forever, but I don't think no one's goin' to quibble about you inheritin' a convict from your pa. I think you and me is goin' to buy ourselves a tavern.' His breath caught, and he grimaced and pressed his hand to the top of his leg.

'What is it?' asked Ben.

'A scratch,' said Higgins dismissively. 'I've had worse when a rat bit me.'

'Let me see.'

Higgins pulled his jacket away to show a rag binding the top of his thigh. It was weeping blood. He managed another grin. 'Looks like you'll have to be my servant for a while now, Sneezer. Look after me, like.'

The world seemed to suddenly become real again. A different world.

'I'll look after you,' Ben said, and met Higgins's eyes. 'But my name isn't Sneezer. It's Ben.'

'Pleased to meet you, Ben,' said Higgins, and he held out a twisted claw of a hand. 'But you know somethin'?'

'What?' asked Ben.

Higgins managed a pale grin. 'You'll always be Sneezer to me.'

CHAPTER 18

An hour later Guwara bent over the side of the boat, cupped his hands and tasted the water. 'Fresh,' he said.

Ben looked around. The country had changed; it was less sandy, with tall trees instead of scrub, though the land still looked barren. There was no grass between the trees, just strange low shrubs that grew down to the water's edge on one side of the river. The other side was edged with wide mudflats. Birds trod carefully in the ooze, bobbing and pecking, while above them flew gulls and the strange coal-black birds that gave hoarse cries as they flapped between the treetops.

Guwara changed tack, guiding the boat towards the flats. He jumped out, the mud rising to his ankles. Ben followed him, his feet still bare. The mud felt cold and smooth. Higgins lay in the boat, his face pale and sweaty.

Ben helped Guwara pull the boat over the shallow mud. Ducks flew off complaining. A small furred creature, not quite like any hopper Ben had seen before, gazed at them from behind a twiggy bush, then bounded off with a motion no civilised animal would employ. Ben shut his eyes briefly. If only this were England. There'd be berries to eat, hawthorns and hazelnuts, and rabbits or hares to snare. They could roast hedgehogs, like the gypsies did each year when they camped on the lower meadow.

This land begrudged its people even fresh water. How can we survive here? Ben wondered, suddenly desperate. How can we get back to Sydney Town with only a jug to carry fresh water in? Crossing the Thames was no preparation for a voyage like this. It would be impossible for a boy and an untrained man to sail back to Sydney Town with no knowledge of weather or navigation, or the hundred other things a ship's master needed. But with Guwara they had a chance. Just a chance.

Could this tiny boat with its single mast even reach Sydney Town? It certainly wouldn't survive the southern route taken by larger ships. Ben thought of the map Mr Appleby had given him. Flinders had hugged the coastline to create it, and even marked where he'd stopped, though not where he had found water — unless the map was incomplete. Perhaps Fred hadn't bothered to add all the details of the west or southern coast, assuming Ben would never go there. The Black Swan River was the only river marked on the western part of the map.

Guwara gestured to a pile of grey-white shells under one of the trees. 'Good camp.'

Ben looked around the clearing. How could they camp without a tent? The wind wasn't as strong as it had been at sea but it still shivered itself into his bones. He thought about Flinders's voyage — his boat had dried food, spare sails, tools, barrels to store water ...

'We need wood,' said Guwara, interrupting Ben's thoughts.

Ben nodded numbly. At least they'd have a fire.

Higgins saw his look. 'Gimme a hand out, Sneezer lad. You get the wood and I'll light the fire.'

Ben managed a smile. 'Yes, Mr Higgins.'

Higgins pulled the tinderbox and axe out of his sack, then pushed the bag under the seat again. He looked at Ben thoughtfully, then said at last, 'Your pa was a fool.'

'To lose his ships? His life?' asked Ben quietly. He tried not to remember the final sight of his father's face.

'To never know his son. You go get that wood, lad.' Higgins turned to Guwara. 'What d'you say, Billy-Boy? How long should we stay here?'

'The ship can't get past the sandbar,' said Guwara, still evaluating the land around them. 'They will look for us, but they need to put ashore for repairs. One month maybe. We stay here till then.'

Higgins lowered himself carefully onto the sandy ground. 'Right you are, Billy-Boy.'

'His name is Guwara,' said Ben.

'Guwara.' Higgins tasted the word. 'Why can't you have a proper name like Ebenezer or Murgatroyd?'

Guwara didn't answer. 'Wood,' he ordered again.

It would take days to cut down a tree, then chop it into firewood, thought Ben. But he took the axe from Higgins, thrust it into his belt and headed towards the stand of trees above the river.

Ten minutes later he had an armful of wood without any need to use the axe. Trees here dropped their branches freely he had discovered. Whatever else they lacked, it would not be firewood.

By the time he'd lugged back a fourth armload, Higgins had a blaze going within an old circle of blackened stones — another sign that others had camped here before. Higgins sat before the fire plucking the feathers from a swan. Another, already plucked, was suspended from a stick to one side of the blaze. Guwara had hunted fast and well.

Higgins grinned at Ben. 'Told you we'd be eatin' like kings soon,' he said. 'Billy-Boy here even found some roots that might be potatoes if you was a man on a gallopin' horse what didn't look too close.'

Ben drew nearer to the fire, shivering. Kings had beds, and a roof to cover them, walls to protect them from the sharp teeth of the wind. He blinked, realising he was shaking from hunger, fear, shock.

'Sit,' ordered Higgins. 'You'll feel better when you've got some grub into you.'

Ben sat. He stared at the fire, the flames. I am alive, he thought. It would be so easy to be dead today. And he had fire and food, and friends too.

Three days later they had built a hut of sorts: four tree-trunk posts with three walls of bark between them, stripped from the largest trees, and partially roofed with more lengths of bark. The fourth side was left open facing the fire, to capture its heat at night but with the smoke blowing away from them.

As Guwara had predicted, there had been no signs of pursuit from the *Golden Girl*. Now Ben's shock had worn away he realised that Captain Danvers had probably changed whatever his earlier plans had been. With Ben free, and Guwara and Higgins having deserted the ship and perhaps able to sail towards passing ships to tell the authorities about the mutiny, there was a greater danger of being caught. Mutiny was a worse crime even than murder. Captain Danvers would assume that eventually the three of them would try to make their way south, then east. He might linger a few weeks to try to capture them at sea, but after that he would take the *Golden Girl* far to the north before he ordered her ashore for repairs.

To Ben's surprise, their camp quickly grew more comfortable. Furs, roughly dried and still smelling of dead animal, made rough but warm cloaks and blankets. Guwara showed Ben how to use the sap from a spiny plant to glue sheets of flaking bark together to make a kind of cup to carry water. A morning spent lugging rocks miraculously made a fish trap in the shallows further up the river. The fish swam into the trap at high tide and were left stranded when the water receded, so that even Ben could catch them with his hands. Mussel shells became fish hooks — a matter of scraping out the bits of shell around the pinkish hook shape in the middle — to use later on their way back east. Strings of inner bark, plaited then let sizzle in the flame, became thin but tough string. Each night Guwara wove more of it into fishing nets.

The mussels tasted almost like the ones from home. The roots Guwara showed Ben how to dig were too sweet and fibrous to really be like potatoes, but they were satisfying. There was more than plenty at each meal with baked fish, swan, duck or the hoppers Guwara speared, as well as the berries he showed Ben were safe to pick. He even had him collect particular flowers to soak in water for a sweet drink.

Guwara hadn't offered to let Ben use his spears again, but did give him more lessons on how to creep up to the windward side of an animal so it couldn't smell them, practising standing on one leg, swaying gently like a tree, looking sideways rather than directly at an animal. Ben's body ached after an hour of standing still, but it was worth it to see hoppers begin to graze about them — and to have their meat to eat and their rough dried furs for warmth.

It was hard work. It was good work. It meant he slept well, too tired for bad dreams. And using his body this way meant that he didn't think; didn't remember the look on his father's face the moment before his death, all the words he had never said to the boy who was his son.

Higgins didn't work. His wound had stopped bleeding, but infection seemed to have set in, making him weak and feverish by sundown. He spent most of the day leaning against a cushion made from tussock and feathers stuffed into a roughly dried, crackly hopper skin. It was hardly a pillow to a boy who had grown up with sun-softened linen sheets scented with lavender, but possibly no worse than Higgins was accustomed to.

This morning, he sat with a half-dried hopper skin about his shoulders, sucking listlessly on a leg of swan Guwara had speared the previous night, then wrapped in mud and baked in the coals. Baked swan was softer than meat cooked above the fire and easier to eat for an almost toothless convict.

The wind spat rain; hard, fierce drops that made the tree leaves droop and dribble, but not thick enough to be true rain.

'Kings must have good grinders if they like eatin' swan,' Higgins said, and spat a mangled mess onto the ground. 'How about some fish, Sneezer boy?'

Ben glanced at Guwara.

'We hunt today,' Guwara said.

'An' I want some bleedin' fish,' snapped Higgins.

Guwara was silent. Ben was beginning to realise that despite his correct English accent and grammar, there were many words and concepts he didn't know.

At last he seemed to have assembled the words he needed. 'We have to carry water. We must hunt for that.'

Higgins snorted. 'You plannin' to find some water barrels hoppin' about the bushes, Billy-Boy?'

Guwara stared at him.

'My mistake,' Higgins said. 'You plannin' to find us some hoppin' barrels, Guwara?'

'Yes,' said Guwara.

They began the hunt by pushing sharp sticks into the sandy ground to create a small stockade with a yard doorway open to the clear ground by the river.

Guwara stepped back and nodded. 'Good.'

'But the fence will fall down if any animal leans on it,' objected Ben. He thought of the stone walls back at Badger's Hill, or the solid woven willow fences that even a bullock couldn't push through.

'You'll see,' said Guwara, and he beckoned Ben to follow him.

They waited in the scrub. The wind lessened as the afternoon drew on, and the rain thickened, more like the wet air Ben was familiar with from home. A drizzle filled the air till shapes grew vague. Finally Guwara touched his arm. A signal.

Ben stood as silently as he could, even his breathing shallow. I am a tree, he thought, waving slightly in the wind.

A thud, and then another. Five of the hopping animals approached, much bigger than the ones they had hunted before. A giant one that must be a male, two smaller, and two juveniles.

Guwara yelled and rushed from the cover, holding a spear horizontally in each hand, pushing the hoppers towards the stockade. Ben yelled too, following him.

The big male faltered, giving the does and youngsters a chance to get away. Two dashed around on opposite sides, but Guwara was there before them, driving them back together. As a group they leaped, terrified, into the stockade, then stopped, startled by what was obviously the first fence they had ever seen.

And that was the trick, Ben realised. The animals back home knew fences, knew they could push down a poor one. But these creatures thought this flimsy creation was solid.

Guwara stepped forward and stabbed his smallest spear into the throat of the big male. It made a clawing motion with its two front feet. It tried to leap over the sticks, then fell back. The does managed to leap out, but the young ones were too small. Guwara dealt with them swiftly.

Ben peered into the mist. The does had vanished, but the big male lay twitching on the ground.

Guwara pointed to the giant hopper and grinned. 'Water barrels. Spear points. Rope.' He gestured at the young ones. 'Dinner.'

Guwara worked on the hopper carcasses that night and all the next day. First he carefully skinned the small ones, removed their insides through the smallest of holes at top and bottom, turned the skins inside out, scraped them hard with the teeth from the big male, then hung them high in a tree to dry, with a small roof of bark above them. Their meat became dinner. The brains and liver were kept for Higgins, as well as the marrow from the bones heated by the side of the fire. Soft food, thought Ben, watching Higgins suck at the cracked bones with enjoyment. He still looked feverish, but surely good food would help him recover.

The meat of the big male was roasted on a spit over the coals the next day. Hopper meat was strongly flavoured, a bit like roast ox at home. Strangely Ben found he was starting to think of Badger's Hill without pain. Was it because the man who had betrayed it was gone? He suspected Mama would have liked Higgins and admired Guwara. She'd enjoyed dining with the tenant farmers and had chatted for hours with Foster, the gamekeeper. One could not ask such people to dine at the house, of course, but they were interesting, and more closely entwined in his and Mama's lives than the socially acceptable neighbours were.

Ben wondered suddenly what Mama would think of Sally.

By evening the next day, the hopper tail had yielded long, tough sinews, which Guwara rubbed with sap, then tied onto the mussel-shell hooks. The sinews became fishing lines too, as well as string to tie up the top and bottom holes of the juveniles' skins, suddenly turned into waterbags.

A line of fish fillets hung on string next to the fire, slowly smoking till they were hard-dried enough to preserve them. A line of strips of hopper meat hung next to them.

Ben sat with Higgins in the rough bark shelter, watching Guwara as he sat by the fire carving the nose bone of the male hopper's skull into a new barb for one of his spears. Higgins's leg seemed to be paining him even more, though he had made no complaint. But he didn't move far or often from the shelter, and then only with a stick for a crutch.

'You know what them waterbags mean, Sneezer?' he said softly.

'What?' asked Ben.

'Gettin' back to Sydney Town ain't just a dream, nor gettin' our tavern neither. The Indian is goin' to get us home, boy. Just look at him.'

Ben stared. 'You ... you didn't think we'd really make it?'

Higgins laughed. 'We had a chance is all. Apart from leavin' you to go mad on some poxy little island till you was old and bent, or feedin' the fishes down in Davy Jones's locker.'

'Then you'd have been safer staying on the ship,' said Ben slowly.

'It was a gamble, boy. If we won, it was life for you and riches for me, all respectable like. Worth a toss of the dice, I reckon.'

Ben watched as Guwara melted sap on one of the hot rocks by the fire to fix the new barb from the hopper skull bone to his spear.

'It was worth it,' he said.

CHAPTER 19

Days passed, then weeks. By the time Ben had thought to mark out the days of the week or month, he had lost track. But daylight lingered longer now. Spring would come soon, if this sandy land had a spring.

Higgins slept most of the day, still restless with pain. Ben brought him food and water, even a makeshift chamberpot that he emptied far from their camp so it didn't attract the flies. He didn't mind. For the first time he was finding the adventure he had dreamed of back in England.

It was fun to tether a duck to a tree so it called down other ducks and Guwara could swim underwater and grab their legs as they landed. So was hunting out the nesting places of the smaller hoppers and jumping on them while they slept instead of spearing them. Their skins became more waterbags.

The softest fur came from the creatures like overgrown squirrels that lived in hollow trees. Guwara stuffed their fur into their body cavity before roasting the meat on hot stones, then showed Ben and Higgins how to suck the meat juices from the fur, leaving the long strands to be skilfully woven into yet another kind of string. Finding the squirrels was easy — their claws left scratches on the trees they lived in. You only had to reach into the hollow and drag them out as they slept — as long as you were sure a snake didn't live in the hole instead. Guwara showed Ben how to scatter sand or mud about the tree, and then look for telltale slither marks.

This land was rich in snakes. Ben suspected some were deadly, for Guwara wouldn't let him try to catch them. Guwara trapped snakes behind the head with a forked stick, then quickly crushed the head so the snake couldn't bite its own body and poison its flesh. Once skinned and gutted, they tasted a bit like eel, which Higgins relished.

'Almost like what they sell in Spital Street back in Lunnon Town,' he said, spitting out the tiny bones. 'Me'n the lads would have jellied eel Friday nights for a treat, if the pickin's had been good. And a hot potato each too,' he added wistfully.

Ben was growing used to the birds' hoarse cries and chattering when he woke, the high blue arc that was their ceiling, the whisper of the trees about them. How did I ever think this land was ungenerous? he wondered, scooping up yet another netful of fish to add to the growing lines of them that smoked about the fire, and dipping each one briefly in tussock ash before stringing them up, to keep the flies away.

There were so many birds to trap too, by scattering grass seed on the ground, then waiting up in a tree to cast the net that, it turned out, caught birds as well as fish. They wrapped the birds in mud so there was no need to pluck or gut them, and baked them in the fire. The feathers fell off with the hard-crusted mud and the innards shrank away to nothing.

There were giant lizards that slept in hollow logs, so soundly that they didn't wake even when pulled out. Guwara gutted and roasted them too.

'Tastes like chicken,' said Higgins, smacking his lips. 'Only ever tasted chicken once, but it were good. Any chance of another one o' these?'

It became almost a game to find food that made Higgins grin, or furs to warm him. How long had it been since Ben had been able to make another person happy?

Ben lay back on his pillow of 'squirrel' skin filled with dried tussock. The night stretched above him, lit by a thousand tiny fires. Guwara had laughed at his need for a pillow, but had shown him how to punch holes in the skins with a bone, then poke the string through to sew the skins together. A year ago, Ben had been learning Greek and Latin at the rectory. Now he could skin a hopper, spear a fish sometimes, make a fish trap or a net, soak flowers in a rough bark bowl so they could drink the strange sweet nectar ...

'Gar-ooom!' The sound echoed down the river. Ben sat up, startled.

Closer to the fire, Guwara jerked upright too, listening. Higgins kept on snoring, muttering restlessly.

'Gar-ooom! Gar-oom!'

Was it cannon fire? Had the *Golden Girl* lingered to hunt down another Dutch ship? But she'd have needed to restock with cannon balls and shot, and take on more crew to replace those lost in the previous battle. Surely she couldn't have made it to port and back again by now?

'Gar-oooom!'

'What is it?' he asked Guwara urgently.

But Guwara was grinning. 'Murawang,' he said.

'I don't understand.'

'Tomorrow,' said Guwara, lying back down. Within seconds he was asleep.

Ben lay down too. Whatever the sound was, it was evidently nothing to worry about. There it was again, but from another direction. An owl? But owls weren't as loud as that. Or perhaps they were in this strange land. Except, he thought, it was no longer strange. He had grown used to seeing olive foliage instead of a hundred shades of bright green. A sky without clouds no longer looked bare and naked, nor did the wide horizon scare him.

What would they be doing back at Badger's Hill? It would be nearly harvest time, he realised. Would Mr Nattisville give the Harvest Home feast, as Mama had done? Ben hoped so. He hadn't seemed a hard man. Was Filkinghorn still the butler? A year ago Ben had hoped to buy back Badger's Hill. Now?

He looked over at Higgins; his toothless mouth was open as he slept and he was drooling slightly. Higgins could stay free in the colony, but it would be another six years before he could legally return to England. Higgins could buy respectability in Sydney Town, Ben realised, just as Mrs Moore had done. He needed only money and the manners he already knew how to assume.

Higgins muttered something, moving his leg as if in pain, though he didn't wake. Even if the money invested with Mr Moore was enough to buy back Badger's Hill, Ben realised he couldn't abandon the convict now. Nor would he risk hurting the man who had saved his life by suggesting that he might like to.

Higgins would have his second chance in the colony of New South Wales, just like Mr and Mrs Appleby had.

He wondered what Sally was doing now.

And what was a murawang?

Ben woke as Guwara threw more branches on the fire. The sun was still low behind the eastern hills, though a pale grey lit the sky.

Guwara picked up his spears, hesitated, then handed one to Ben. 'Quiet,' he said.

Ben walked the way Guwara had shown him: each footfall placed gently on the land, using the sides of his feet so the bark and twigs didn't crackle below. Along the river bank they went ...

'Gar-oom!'

Guwara stopped, then made a slight change of direction. Inland now ... And once more he stopped. Ben halted too, and peered through the twiggy bushes.

He saw a sandy clearing with thin ground covers that were able to wriggle their roots deep into the soil to survive. A giant bird sat in the middle of the clearing on what might be a vast, messy nest, its edges marked by large dead branches. Ben had never seen such a nest, or a bird as massive either.

If they stepped any closer, the bird would see them.

Guwara raised his spear. So did Ben, sighting in the way Guwara had shown him. The spears flew together ... The bird's head dropped.

Guwara ran forward, withdrew his spear from the bird's neck and checked it was dead. Ben followed and saw that his own spear had hit the bird's body. It had penetrated the feathers, but he doubted that it had been a killing blow.

He watched as Guwara dragged the carcass off the nest, which was mostly dried tussock and strips of bark laid on the sandy ground inside the larger outside branches, without even a depression for the eggs to sit in. There were fourteen of them, twice or three times the size of a goose egg, ranging in colour from pale green to a darker grey-green.

'Murawang,' said Guwara again, as if that was all the explanation needed.

They gutted the bird by the nest. Guwara stuffed the eggs into the cavity, handling each with care so as not to break the shell, then replaced some of the guts to cushion them. They took turns dragging the bird by its legs back to camp.

I couldn't have done this a month ago, thought Ben. I wouldn't have had the strength nor the skill to send a spear so deep. He laughed suddenly, for the sheer joy of striding across the sandy flats and carrying a spear too. For the first time Guwara hadn't asked for it back.

Guwara glanced at him and began to laugh as well.

It was so deeply good to be alive.

Higgins was crouching by the fire as they dragged the bird into camp. 'Wondered where you'd got to,' he muttered. He looked even more flushed this morning, the shadows under his eyes deeper.

'Hunting!' said Ben.

'Think I'm blind?' Higgins blinked at the giant dead bird. 'What do you call that, then?'

'Murawang,' said Guwara.

'That an Indian word?' asked Higgins suspiciously.

'I don't know. I suppose so,' said Ben as Guwara sat with the bird spread on the ground between his legs and carefully hauled out the eggs.

He took a chip of hopper tooth and pierced each egg with a tiny hole, then motioned for Ben to put them carefully next to the fire. Then he began to wriggle his fingers under the bird's skin, still with its feathers in place.

By the time the sun was at its midday height, the empty murawang skin hung from a tree. Guwara had placed wide seashells below it.

Hunks of the bird's meat were roasting on sticks, while Guwara used a knife to carefully cut away the leg meat, pulling out the tough sinews. More string and fishing line, thought Ben.

Higgins cut off a hunk of roasted murawang meat, gummed the juice from it, then spat the rest out. 'Tough,' he muttered. He heaved himself to his feet again, limped back into the shelter and lay down. 'Go get me some water, Sneezer.'

Ben looked at Guwara uncertainly. Higgins's fever was worsening, but he had no idea what to do about it.

Guwara crossed over to the shelter and motioned to Higgins to lift up his trouser leg.

'That's private, that is,' mumbled Higgins.

'He needs to see your wound,' said Ben quietly.

He remembered how Harry Trimble's leg had festered after he'd cut it deeply three years before at Badger's Hill. The surgeon had bled him, but the swelling grew worse, till Mama had fed Harry half a bottle of brandy, cut the leg open to let out the pus, and packed the wound with mouldy bread. She and Mrs Trimble had placed hot bran poultices on it every two hours. Harry had lived.

Higgins drew up his trouser leg. Ben bit his lip. The cut stretched from the top of his leg almost to his knee. The top part had healed over, but below the skin was shiny, red and puffed, and oozed yellow.

Ben looked helplessly at Guwara. They had no brandy. No mouldy bread. Even the pudding in its oilcloth covering in Higgins's sack wouldn't be mouldy. They didn't have bran to make a hot poultice.

Guwara looked at the leg impassively, then crouched and took his knife from his belt.

'No!' said Higgins sharply. 'I ain't havin' no ignorant heathen cuttin' me up.' He pulled down his trouser leg as if hiding the wound would make it vanish.

Guwara stood and vanished into the short tree shadows without a word.

Ben sat next to Higgins. 'You need to let him help you.'

'He's just an Indian.'

'And he knows how to sail and spear hoppers and catch murawang. He knows more than anyone on the ship. I don't have anything here to help you, but Guwara might. You'll die if we do nothing. I ... I don't want you to die.'

'I don't want me to die neither,' said Higgins. He lay back without speaking for a while. At last he said, 'I should've had Harry One-Eye put the iron on it soon as it was cut. But if they'd known it was this bad, old Danvers wouldn't have let me take the boat.'

And I'd be dead, thought Ben. 'Let Guwara help,' he said quietly.

'Don't have much choice, do I, Sneezer? Don't s'pose you know how to cut off a leg gone bad neither.'

'No,' said Ben.

'You just keep a watch on him. I trusts you, Sneezer. Don't let me down.'

'I won't,' said Ben.

The shadows had grown half as long as the trees when Guwara returned. He was carrying something in a length of bark.

He squatted down beside Higgins and looked at him questioningly. Higgins slowly pulled up the leg of his trousers. Guwara put down the bark container, then pulled out his knife.

Ben looked down and gasped, 'No!' Maggots wriggled in a hunk of putrid meat. Was Guwara going to put the rotten meat on the wound? It would be deadly!

Ben reached for it to throw it away, then found Higgins's hand on his.

'We agreed, Sneezer.' Higgins looked up at Guwara. 'You know what you're doin', don't you, Billy-Boy?'

'Perhaps,' said Guwara, showing none of the certainty he had with a spear.

'Old Gladys back in Lunnon Town put maggots on wounds,' said Higgins. 'She said the maggots eat dead meat an' clean the wound right out. Saw her cure two coves like that.'

'Were there some she didn't cure?' asked Ben.

Higgins shrugged. 'Always are. Hold me hand, Sneezer.' He shut his eyes.

An hour later Higgins, in agony, lay too exhausted to speak. Ben, too, was shaking.

Guwara had vanished, to swim, to fish or hunt, or whatever he needed to do to wipe away the memory of cutting open the leg, draining out the pus and carefully picking the maggots out of the chunk of rotten meat to place on the red flesh of Higgins's wound. As soon as the maggots had burrowed in, Guwara had taken one of the shells from below the dead murawang. A small puddle of oil had dripped into it during the day. He applied the oil liberally to the wound, then dipped a small sheet of paperbark in the oil and placed that on top, sealing in both oil and maggots. And then he left.

Ben fed the fire. Time passed. Guwara did not return. Higgins still lay with his eyes closed, though Ben didn't think he slept.

At last Ben walked down to the river with one of the hopper waterbags, squished through the mud, washed himself, then filled the bag and came back to Higgins.

He put his hand on the man's thin shoulder. 'Mr Higgins?'

'I'm not asleep.'

'Could you drink something?'

Higgins raised his head and drank.

'There are some eggs by the fire,' Ben said. 'You don't need teeth to eat an egg. You'll feel better after some food.'

'I'd feel better if some Dutchie hadn't slashed me with his sword.' But he raised himself up on his elbows and let Ben put another cushion behind him.

'I … I don't want to lose you too,' said Ben.

'Who? Me?' said Higgins scornfully. 'You gimme that egg, Sneezer. Don't you worry about me.'

The egg was hard-boiled or, rather, baked. Ben shelled it, sniffed, then tasted it. It was remarkably like a hen's egg. He broke off the top half of the shell and handed a mix of white and yolk to Higgins.

When Guwara returned carrying a large fish, the egg was half-eaten and Higgins was steadier than he had been for days.

'Hurts like billy-o,' he said conversationally. Then added grudgingly, 'Thank you.'

Guwara made no reply.

Guwara replaced the maggots with new ones every day, washing the wound with oil from the murawang. By the third day, it had obviously begun to heal. Higgins could even hobble around on his stick again.

Five days after that, Guwara lifted his face into the wind. He seemed to smell it, then gazed at the stars.

'Tomorrow,' he said at last. 'We sail tomorrow.'

CHAPTER 20

The wind blew strongly from the west as Guwara and Ben packed the boat the next morning. They had four small and one large hopper hide containers, sealed with sap and tied with twine, holding fresh water; smoked fish and strips of hopper meat wrapped in papery bark; roughly sewn cloaks and blankets of 'squirrel' hide; and a murawang egg filled with oil carefully stowed in a nest of dried tussock. They had fishing lines, nets and hooks they'd made, as well as the knives, axe, jug, flint and iron to make fire brought from the *Golden Girl.* They even had Higgins's plum pudding, still stored in the sack under the seat.

They had no map to show the hidden rocks or landmarks along the coast, but each night Ben had forced himself to recall every detail on the piece of paper Mr Appleby had given him. He hoped Guwara remembered their route along the west and southern coasts far better than he did, as well as any reefs the *Golden Girl* had avoided. But even though Guwara had travelled the Southern Ocean before, he had never hugged the southern coast of the continent. Still, they had no choice about their route. This boat was much too small to survive the gales and the giant, ice-frothed waves further south. Nor, without a compass and sextant or even a ship's log to follow, would they know when to sail north to find land again.

There was so much they needed and didn't have: spare sails, or even canvas to repair the ones they had; hammers, nails or wood to repair the boat. They were just a boy who had managed a sail on the calm lake at home in England, a feeble London convict whose longest voyage had been in the darkness of a hold, and a dark-skinned sailor — the only one of them with any experience of wind and tides and sailing on the ocean.

Ben looked at Guwara carefully rolling up the lengths of twine that he'd been making, the fishing net he'd fashioned, the two long spears and one short one, the extra spear points. If anyone could do this, it would be Guwara. And Ben and Higgins would survive with him.

The westerly wind dropped by mid-morning, just as Guwara had predicted. 'Buruwan,' he said softly. 'Wind from the north.'

'Is that your language?' Ben asked.

'Yes. You must learn it too.'

'To speak to the Indians here?' They had seen smoke far inland a few times, but no people yet.

'No. We leave before they come.'

Is that in case the people here attack us? Ben wondered. They would probably be friendly to Guwara, but how would they react to two white-skinned strangers?

Guwara headed over to the racks that held their dried fish and packed them into a rough bark basket. Then he and Ben helped Higgins into the boat, and pushed it across the mud and into the water. Guwara trimmed the sails and took the rudder. Ben leaned down for a final drink of fresh river water, then scooped more up in his hands for Higgins.

'You know what I'm goin' to do first thing back at Sydney Town?' muttered Higgins.

Ben shook his head.

'Drink me a whole barrel of fresh ale. And then a pint of rum.' He closed his eyes, leaning back on his rough pillow.

The river curved, and Ben glanced back as their camp vanished. He'd been happy there, he realised, happier than he had been since leaving Badger's Hill. But Guwara was right. It was time to leave. Life waited for them. Or death.

'We need to name the boat,' he said.

Higgins grinned and muttered a word Ben didn't recognise. He suspected it was rude.

'Mulgu,' said Guwara.

'An' what's a "mulgu" when it's at home?' demanded Higgins.

Guwara pointed to a pair of black swans paddling serenely in the reedy shallows, as if unaware that the strange object on the river carried humans who might spear them.

Higgins shrugged. 'All square with me, Billy-Boy.'

Ben grinned. 'I hereby name this craft the *Mulgu*,' he said and laughed, because suddenly they seemed invincible, the wind in their sails, their waterbags full, and Guwara guiding them back across to the east coast of New Holland.

Why had he ever doubted they'd succeed?

Eight days later the *Mulgu* tossed in the surges of the westerlies. The northerly had lasted less than a day. Travel south was possible, but only with constant attention to the tiller and sails, tacking, coming about or jibing, and with sharp eyes always searching for any reefs hidden below the swell that might wreck them.

How far had they come? Ben had no idea. Nor did he know how long it might take to reach the southerly coast, where they could turn east and ride the winds.

Night was the worst. The surging surf along the glaring white beaches or the crashing waves against rocky cliffs made it too dangerous to go ashore, and they didn't dare sail on in the dark. They had no anchor to keep them from drifting so they couldn't just lay up for the night. Guwara kept up only enough sail to keep them upright, but still he or Ben had to peer into the darkness, watching, listening for a change in the crash of waves that might indicate a reef, rocks, cliffs or an island ahead.

They rigged up a shelter of partly cured hopper skin to keep off the sun. Its top surface collected fresh water too in the brief scatters of rain, which was welcome as they had only one hopper skin of water left. Ben recalled one of the *Golden Girl*'s sailors saying a man could only survive three days without water.

They hadn't tried fishing yet. Simply keeping the *Mulgu* sailing required all their attention, one at the tiller, the other tending the sail. Even Higgins, pale as he was, worked hard bailing out water from the bottom of the boat as the waves slopped around them, or which seeped in between the planks. The *Mulgu* hadn't been built for a long voyage. Higgins hadn't realised this when he hatched his plan — his role on the *Golden Girl* had been as a servant not a sailor. But Guwara must have accepted the risk when he made that impulsive dive to join them. He had chosen this, instead of the comparative safety, and possible wealth, of staying with the mutineers.

Ben looked at him as he adjusted the sail yet again, his eyes sharp and careful as he watched the sky, the waves, the current, and listened to the wind.

Ben took out a fillet of smoked fish, tore at it, chewed and swallowed, then offered one to Higgins.

He shook his head. 'Too tough.'

'There's not enough fresh water spare to soak it in. How about you eat a piece of that plum pudding instead?'

The pudding still sat under the seat, wrapped in oilcloth.

'Keep yer dabs off that puddin',' Higgins said. 'We're keepin' it for somethin' special. Couldn't eat nothin' anyway.'

Ben looked at the shiver of cloud on the horizon. 'Maybe it'll rain again.'

'No,' said Guwara, his hearing keen even over the noise of the wind and water. He dropped to his knees, then thrust his arm, elbow deep, into the water.

'You tryin' to catch a shark, Billy-Boy?' demanded Higgins.

Guwara shook his head, obviously searching for the words. 'The water is changing.'

'You mean the current?' asked Ben. 'You think the coast might be going to turn east?' Surely we must be nearly there, he thought.

Guwara didn't answer, but watched the shore.

They sailed. They bailed. The sun rose, hot and baking. The sea reflected it back at them, almost as sharp on their eyes and skin as the sun itself. Ben's clothes, his hair, even his skin, were sticky with salt. His cracked lips tasted of salt. His skin was raw with sunburn, windburn, saltburn. He was scared too, and hungry, and thirst was becoming a source of desperation ... and yet in a strange way he was happy. For the first time in his life he was with companions who had chosen to be with him, not because he was the son of the mistress or the master.

Except for Sally ... He smiled as he composed a letter to her in his mind.

Dear Sally,

We are sailing in a small, leaky, open boat with no map, sextant or even a lead line to tell us the depth of water below. My companions are a convict, a member of the crew who mutinied and killed my father, and Guwara, an Indian. They are the best companions I could have.

I know that I may die, just as the men who fought on the Dutch ship that we attacked died, and many of our crew. Even if we survive, I do not know what will happen when we get back to Sydney Town, if we ever do.

Our journey is impossible. Yet somehow, deep within me, I am sure I will survive, just as your father told me to. I wish I could thank him for that advice. Maybe one day I will be able to.

I also wish I could put a letter in a bottle in the hope that one day it might reach you, but we don't have a bottle, paper or pen. Nor, I fear, would the currents here ever reach Port Jackson or your Hawkesbury River. But I am thinking of you.

Love,

Ben

He smiled again. It was safe to put 'love' as she would never see it. And even if she did ...

They took it in turns to trim the sails at night and tend the rudder, as well as keeping a lookout and bailing, one sleeping while the other two worked. The breeze still blew from the west the next morning, but by the time the sun was a handspan above the treed horizon, it had swung around and was blowing from the northwest in great heaving gusts, as if a giant had been holding his breath and finally let it out.

At last the *Mulgu*'s sails filled. She sped southwards.

They stayed as far out to sea as they could while still being able to see the coastline. Hills, trees, a white glimpse that must have been a beach, more hills, rising to almost mountains. Every few hours Guwara dipped his arm into the sea, testing the strength and direction of the current. At last he grinned and pointed eastward.

Now, at last, Ben's sharp eyes could see what Guwara had worked out from feeling the currents. The land had stopped. There were no headlands interrupting the endless sea to the south or east of them. It was time to head east, across the empty vastness of the sea below the southern coast of New Holland, then up towards Sydney Town.

But for now, Ben prayed desperately they would soon reach the harbour Mr Flinders had marked on his map, with safe shores and fresh water.

They sailed on. Days were marked only by the rise and setting of the sun, the endless waves and bailing, nights where the stars rolled in their eternal dance, then sunrise once again. The light glared from the sea and sky, as if trying to drain all life from them. They rarely talked now, grunting instructions to each other, mouths too dry to waste on speech. They had drunk the last of the fresh water, expecting to soon see the entrance to the harbour. Had they missed it? Ben thought of the narrow heads of Port Jackson. Captain Cook had never dreamed a vast harbour lay behind that narrow gap. Was King George the Third's Sound hidden too?

Guwara was at the tiller this afternoon, half-dozing, half-alert, his body feeling the wind and currents even with his eyes shut. Higgins lay asleep under the awning, gasping slightly. Ben felt his eyes close too.

Suddenly the boom swung across wildly as the *Mulgu* changed course, leaving the sails flapping. Ben rushed to set the sails for their new course.

'What is it?' he demanded.

Guwara pointed. There, along the seemingly endless coastline, was a blue gap. Now he knew what to look for,

Ben could see the way the colour of the water changed around it. King George the Third's Sound!

And if Mr Flinders was correct — and of course that master mariner must be right — there would be fresh water and game to catch, and natives who, if not exactly friendly, at least had not attacked Flinders and his crew. And a respite, at last, from the lashing and crashing of the sea, the burning sun and the buffet of the wind.

King George the Third's Sound seemed even bigger than Port Jackson but a lot less protected. The wind and swell still tore at them as Ben tended the sail and Guwara steered, swinging the *Mulgu* sharply away from inlets that showed the teeth of rocks, or the crash of surf, or, even more deadly, the pale green and white of rocks below the surface.

The sun hovered on the ocean, sending pink rays across the grey blue, as Guwara at last steered the boat to what looked like a safe spot on the shoreline: a narrow stretch of muddy sand in front of dense scrub.

A thin spire of smoke rose nearby. Indians. Would they help them, wondered Ben, or attack?

The *Mulgu* drew closer to shore more slowly now, all of them scanning the inlet for rocks or sandbars. Guwara turned the boat until the wind spilled from her sails, then he and Ben scrambled to lower and furl them. Then they began to row in towards the beach. At last they felt and heard the sand beneath the hull.

Guwara jumped out into the shallows. Ben took off his boots and followed him; then Higgins, limping and weak but unwilling to be seen as an invalid, also let himself over the side into the shallow water. With all three of them in the water the *Mulgu* rode a little higher and they were able to haul her up onto the shell-strewn sand. She wasn't secure yet as she was still below the piles of seaweed that marked high tide, but they were standing on land again.

Ben looked around as Guwara tethered the boat to a tree. Despite the trails of smoke there was no one on the beach. Two rough bark huts stood a short way from the shoreline, little more than shelters from the rain and wind. A fireplace sat close to them, its coals still red.

'Coo-yah!' yelled Guwara. The cry echoed along the beach, but nothing moved except the lapping waves and branches in the wind.

'Mebbe they'll attack at night,' suggested Higgins. He looked speculatively at Guwara. 'Better give me one of them spears of yours.'

Guwara laughed.

Higgins shrugged. 'Worth a try.'

'We are safe,' said Guwara.

'How do you know that then?'

'Why attack?' replied Guwara simply. 'If they want us to go, they ask. If they ask, we go.'

It sounded … civilised, thought Ben. Except civilisation didn't work that way. Civilisation meant that those with the muskets stayed. The ships that had the cannons with the longest range won the battle. The armies with the best generals prevailed …

'Wood,' Guwara ordered, before picking up his spears and the two empty waterbags and heading up the beach.

'Who does he think he is — blinkin' Napoleon?' muttered Higgins. 'Better do what he says though, Sneezer. Goin' to be cold tonight.'

It had been cold every night. Even though the days were hot, the wind from the west always seemed to be cold.

Ben made his way through the brush gathering branches, careful not to reach down to pick up a snake by mistake. By the time he got back, Higgins had added tinder to the hot coals. The fire flared as Ben threw on more wood.

'Where's his lordship?' began Higgins, just as Guwara appeared, a darker shadow in the growing night. He carried a fish almost half as long as he was and one of the waterbags, now bulging.

'You found a stream?' asked Ben excitedly. It would feel so good to wash off the salt.

'No. Water comes up from the ground.'

Guwara handed him the waterbag. Ben drank. It tasted a bit like mud, a little like shellfish, but good.

And because there was plenty, there was no need to stint. He drank his fill then passed the bag to Higgins.

'Good catch,' he said to Guwara, nodding to the fish.

'Not me. The people left it for us on the rock.'

'A gift?'

'We must leave a gift too. Your …' He pointed to Ben's woollen stockings, still in the boat with his boots.

'I can't wear boots without stockings!' Ben said.

Guwara looked at his own bare feet, at Higgins's, then at Ben's.

'My feet aren't as tough as yours.' Ben considered. 'How about I cut the stocking tops off. Would that do for a gift?' He couldn't think what else they could spare.

'Yes,' said Guwara. He pushed a stick through the fish to hold it over the fire to roast, then pointed to a basket in one of the shelters that was filled with brown knobbly things, a bit like the roots he'd shown Ben how to dig up at Black Swan River. 'Cook those too.'

'How?' They had wrapped the other roots in wet papery bark, but there was none here.

Guwara gave a short laugh at Ben's ignorance. He grabbed a nearby stick and dug a long hole in the hot soil next to the fire, shoved in the roots, then covered them with coals.

Ben flushed, embarrassed. It was so obvious, so easy, once you had been shown how.

*

The next morning Ben followed Guwara to the fresh waterhole or, rather, holes — muddy sandy areas where almost white water welled up. He scooped some up to wash the salt from his face, hair and arms, before holding the waterbags down till they slowly filled.

'I hunt,' said Guwara, and he vanished into the scrubby bushes.

Higgins had the fire well built up when Ben returned, and a pile of oysters sitting on a length of bark.

'Found these just round the bend,' he told Ben. 'Always been fond of oysters. Where's His Nibs?'

'Hunting, I think.' Ben took a couple of oysters and swallowed. They looked and tasted like snot. He passed the platter back to Higgins.

'Keep eatin',' said Higgins. 'Took me a long time to prise them shells open.' He patted the knife at his belt.

'I'm not really hungry.' And hopefully Guwara would be back soon with meat.

Higgins regarded him sternly. 'You're goin' to eat everythin' we find here, young Sneezer, and keep eatin'. That's how you survive at sea. You eat when you can, and the fat keeps you alive when the food runs out.'

Ben sighed and reached for another oyster.

CHAPTER 21

They stayed at King George the Third's Sound for another three days, gathering wood and fresh water, hunting and eating, while they waited for a favourable wind. Ben parted with the tops of his stockings, which vanished the next day from the rock where Guwara had found the fish, but he discovered them again near their camp the next day, abandoned.

Once he heard Guwara's voice, talking in a strange tongue to a man in the trees behind their camp. But no native appeared.

'Was that an Indian? What did he want?' Ben demanded, when Guwara returned carrying a hopper already skinned and gutted.

'They want us to leave. I tried to ask about fresh water to the east, but we do not have the same words.'

'Then how did he ask you to leave?' Higgins replied.

Guwara laughed and made a shooing gesture. 'I told

him this.' He held up his hand to the wind, as if to say, 'We will go when the wind is right.'

The wind changed at dawn. They'd already stocked the *Mulgu* with fresh water, adding another two freshly made — and smelly — water bladders. Guwara had tried to seal the gaps in the boat's planking with sap from the local trees. But even though it seemed to hold when he applied it, the thick ooze cracked off as it dried overnight.

The northerly coming off the land was just a breeze smelling of hot sand and gum trees. But it was enough for them to launch the boat, raise the sails and sail out of the sound and beyond the most obvious rocks into the open sea again. And there they stayed, unable to make progress in the strong current till the wind gusted and then began to blow, fierce and unrelenting, carrying them east.

'Binyang,' said Guwara, pointing at a seagull, its wings outstretched to let the wind carry it across the waves. For some reason he had decided it was time for Ben to learn the language of the Cadigal.

Ben bailed out another bark bowl of water and tried to copy the sound. Guwara's language had sounds he had never tried to make before. He suspected he wasn't even hearing some of them properly, much less able to repeat them. 'Bungyon ...'

'Binyang,' said Guwara patiently. He glanced up at the way the wind filled the sails and moved to adjust the tiller again.

Learning the new language at least filled in the time. There was little else to do — or rather, too much to do, but so much of it the same. Follow Guwara's instructions to tension or loosen the sails, or take his turn at the tiller, or cast out the fishing net, or bail and keep bailing as the cracks in the planking remained and water continually seeped in. There was no respite. On this small boat, someone had to be at the tiller and another adjusting the sails all the time. Ben was already tired of the featureless blue on three sides of them, and the brown land to their left, too far away to make out details.

'Gadjal,' said Guwara, pointing to the land.

'Gadjal,' Ben repeated carefully. Was 'gadjal' beach, or land, or maybe that spire of smoke?

Guwara grinned. At last Ben had spoken a word correctly, even if he wasn't sure what it meant.

Was Cadigal really going to be of any use to him? Guwara had told him that the Indians on this side of the vast land didn't speak Cadigal; and if they got back to Sydney Town — *when* they got back — Ben would probably never speak to another Indian, except those who spoke English like Guwara. He supposed that Guwara assumed he would stay in the colony forever, just as Higgins did.

Ben couldn't bring himself to tell the convict that he didn't want to run a tavern, especially the kind Higgins probably imagined — a refuge for pickpockets or worse. But what sort of life could he have in Sydney Town with its criminals and shanties? He wondered how much of his father's money was left. Perhaps it had already been claimed to pay his father's debts in England. Maybe Ben could find work with Mr Moore? He built ships, as well as his other businesses. Perhaps Ben would know enough about boats by the time they got back. Or would Governor Macquarie give him a land grant, and convicts and rations for them to clear the land and build a house?

Guwara held his hand up as if testing the strength or changing direction of the wind. 'Baninmaree.'

Was that wind, or west wind, or testing the wind? 'Baninmaree,' Ben said absently.

What was Sally's farm like? Did the Indians there speak Cadigal or another language?

'Cheese it, long shanks,' Higgins said amiably to Guwara. 'We just caught somethin' in the net.'

Ben peered over the side as Guwara's strong arms hauled the net out of the water, a bundle of heaving silver scales and gasping mouths.

'Narrami,' said Guwara, glancing at Ben.

Did that mean fish or net? Ben didn't know, but he was sure of three things. Their journey east would take much longer than he had thought, for the winds here were far more variable than those further south. He would give anything to see green fields of soft lush grass and fat sheep instead of endless brown. And he was getting very tired of eating raw fish.

Ben lay under the skin roof of the *Mulgu*'s shelter amidships. He had been awake almost constantly, but was still too alert to sleep now. Three weeks had passed since they had left King George the Third's Sound; three weeks of rationing the water further and further till now they took only three gulps each twice a day. Three weeks of gazing at the sky, hoping for the mare's tail wisps that might mean a storm approaching. Storms meant danger for their rickety craft, but they also brought fresh water to catch in their spare sail.

None of them had any real idea how far they had come. The land kept changing — cliffs, beaches, then more cliffs — but with no map to guide them it was impossible to tell if they were almost across the long, fresh-waterless Bight or still just at the beginning.

If this was the beginning, they would never make it to the next source of fresh water: the island Mr Flinders had called Kangaruh. Nor could they turn back, as the westerly winds meant the return journey to King George the Third's Sound would take far longer than it had taken them to get here, wherever here might be.

Guwara had stopped giving Ben language lessons. He saved his strength for steering, instructing Ben on trimming the sails and watching out for waves or white froth or the water changing colour that might indicate rocks ahead.

They rarely spoke at all now. Their lips were dry and cracked, their skin swollen and peeling with too much sun, not just from the sky but also reflecting from the water. Higgins was almost skeletal again, grimly bailing night and day, catching short naps then waking to bail again.

Dear Sally,

We are sailing along what is called the Great Australian Bight on the map your father gave me, though I don't know if it was Mr Flinders who gave it that name. When I say we are sailing, it only means that we are in the Mulgu. *Too often in the past weeks we have not sailed at all. Guwara and I thought it would be easy to sail east, with the strong westerly winds to speed us. But we had only known the strong winds far to the south, where we dare not go to face the storms in our little boat. Some days we have not even travelled a league.*

Our voyage started easily, with a good wind. The coast was hazy, but we could see giant cliffs. Within a day the cliffs were behind us, with sandy beaches marking the shore instead, rising up to dead and barren hills. Their bareness was frightening, but at least we were going in the right direction, and speeding along well, till Guwara pointed out white breakers on one side of us, about two miles away, at almost the same time as I saw waves on the other. We were between two vast reefs, about four or five miles from shore. For long desperate hours we travelled between them, bailing all the time, terrified that wind or current would drive us onto them.

At last they were gone. But the risk of hugging the shore was too great, especially as the wind had dropped again. We hung between land and sea, hardly moving, for two long days and nights, before the wind rose and we moved further out to sea, the land now only a dim line on the horizon.

Since then ...

No, even in an imaginary letter Ben could not describe what had happened then. The days had merged into each other: waves and wind and salt, and increasingly desperate thirst, wondering whether the explorers who had passed this way might, by some miracle, have missed a harbour or a river; knowing, from the colour of the water, the currents and the bird life about them, that they had not.

If his memory of Mr Flinders's map was correct, Kangaruh Island would be too big to miss when they did come upon it. Flinders had said it was a paradise, with no people and vast numbers of animals and birds that had never learned to be scared of hunters. And water, wonderful fresh water. To be able to drink as much as his body craved, to wash off the salt, to rest under trees or in a bark shelter ...

Ben peered towards the east yet again. That paradise was there, somewhere, just like Port Jackson was there, and Sally and Badger's Hill. But every day a little more hope that he would ever see them drained away.

Higgins lifted the last waterbag to his lips, then offered it to Ben.

Ben shook his head. 'You didn't swallow,' he said. It hurt to talk.

'Drink,' said Higgins sharply.

'Drink,' said Guwara.

It was the most any of them had said all day. Above, the sails filled and emptied with gusts of wind, enough to keep them heading east. But strong enough to save their lives? Ben didn't know. They lived at the mercy of the wind and currents.

He drank, two slow swallows, letting the water slide around his parched mouth, then tied the waterbag firmly. They no longer put out the fishing net; its weight slowed them down. The dried food was almost gone too, but without water none of them could eat.

He felt Higgins sit down beside him, his bad leg outstretched. 'Sneezer! Sneezer lad, look at me.'

'We're going to die,' whispered Ben.

'Course we're goin' to die.'

Ben looked at him, shocked. He had expected Higgins to say that all would be well.

Higgins gave him a crumb of cracked smile. 'But *when* are we goin' to die? Just keep sayin' "not today" and keep on livin'. How d'you think I kept on livin' in the poorhouse, eh? Two bowls of gruel a day and every young'un but me dead of the fever. Every day I said, "I'm goin' to live." That's how I survived the streets, and the prison, and the hold of your pa's ship too, with all the dead about me.'

'I thought you stole other people's food and water,' whispered Ben.

Higgins shrugged. 'I got me share. An' those that couldn't, died.' He nodded towards Guwara, still sitting erect in the stern, his hand on the tiller, watching, watching. 'Ever think what he's gone through? You hear tales back in the colony. Nearly all the Indians died of the smallpox twenty year ago. He'd have been just a whippersnapper then. Must have seen his family die, his whole village, if the Indians have villages. Maybe that's why he goes to sea, so he doesn't always have to see the empty places.'

Ben shut his eyes. He was tired. Just too tired.

'You want to live?' demanded Higgins sharply.

'Yes,' breathed Ben.

'Then stop bein' a flea-bitten pup and keep bailin' and stand your watch.'

Night: the wind dropping; straining eyes and ears for reefs or islands. Day: the ever-present light. Ben had grown so used to the pain in his eyes he hardly noticed it. Every bone, every muscle ached. Water all around them, wave after wave, but none that they could drink. Day after day …

A shower, so brief the clouds sped past almost too fast to see. But a quarter of an inch of water caught in the skins of the roof of their shelter and it was enough to keep them going for another two days, giving them energy to tend the sails, eat a little dried fish, to bail and bail.

Dolphins played about the boat, laughing at them. Whales pursued their long leisurely courses, rounded black shapes on the horizon; or playful, rearing up and crashing back down in a splash of foam, as if the giant animals were curious about this tiny battered craft trying to cross the sea that belonged to them. Sunsets blazed in orange and yellows; dawns in shades of pink and red.

None of that mattered. Ben lived for the mouthfuls of water, the hope on the horizon that might be land, the end of the Bight, the paradise of Kangaruh Island.

Day after day, hour after hour, he took his turn at the tiller, staring into the distance. Time after time he was sure he could see a faint bulge that would mean land. But each time it was heat haze or a cloud; clouds that never seemed to send down rain to lend them life for just a little longer.

The days swam into each other. His eyes crusted with salt. It took an effort of will now even to lift the bark container and bail. How long had it been since they had spoken to each other? Yet, somehow, Guwara still had the strength to tend the sails.

Ben closed his eyes.

'Sneezer.'

Ben ignored the whisper. He had no strength now. No hope. His body seemed to float away, back to the green of Badger's Hill.

'Sneezer. Pox on the lad! Sneezer!'

'No,' he whispered.

'Land,' croaked Higgins. 'Sneezer, we've reached land.'

CHAPTER 22

Ben opened his eyes and saw a small carpet of golden white sand between the teeth of rounded rocks; blue sky and green trees. Birds balanced on the wind above him.

Water stung his lips. Fresh water that didn't taste of salt or decayed hopper skin, but of the bark basin they had used for bailing and the faint taste of grass. He drank, then drank some more, and sat up.

Guwara sat beside him, emaciated and hollow-eyed. He must have navigated here while Ben was unconscious, rowed the heavy boat into the shallows of the cove and tied a rope around a tree to stop her drifting off. Guwara must have carried him here, onto the sand, and maybe Higgins too.

Higgins lay on Ben's other side. For a heart-wrenching second Ben thought he was dead. Then he heard him groan.

Guwara pushed himself to his feet, walked away and returned, the basin full of water again. Ben drank, then watched as Higgins drank as well.

They were going to live.

They slept on the beach that night, too exhausted to clamber across the rocks that bordered their small cove, wrapped in the heat the sand had stored during the day.

The tide was out when the chill of morning woke Ben. Guwara had vanished. Higgins sat above a small pile of dead tussock and driftwood, the axe and tinderbox beside him, trying to light a fire.

The bailing bucket next to Ben was full of water again. Guwara must have placed it there. Ben drank, then stared at the rocks on either side of the tied-up boat, the sharper-toothed rocks lurking just below the water. It had been a miracle — and Guwara's superb seamanship — that had brought the *Mulgu* safely to this beach. The tiny craft had carried them so far, yet from here Ben could see the gaps in her planking, far larger than he'd realised during the last few days of bailing, bailing, bailing.

If this was Kangaruh Island, the most dangerous part of their journey was done. The southern edge of the continent should be within a few days' sail. From there they could make their way along the coast, a coast with streams and rivers they could sail into and find fresh water to drink and shellfish to eat. It would not be easy — any sea journey could be deadly — but the winds would be more reliable, and there would be harbours to shelter from storms. Ben could even remember most of the landmarks they had passed on the *Golden Girl*, first on the way to Port Jackson, and then on their route south.

But could the *Mulgu* make it? They had been lucky in their voyage across the Bight, he realised wearily. The lack of wind that had almost killed them with thirst had also meant calm seas. One storm, even a high wind dashing waves hard against her sides, and the *Mulgu* would break up. And only Guwara could swim.

Was there any way to repair the boat without nails or pitch? Perhaps some of the tree saps here would stick, unlike the ones at King George the Third's Sound. They had to try. They had no choice if they wanted to get home.

When had he begun to think of the colony as home?

He turned to look at the rounded rocks and dapple of green trees behind them. An arrow of black swans flew overhead, their distant honks bitten off by the wind. He looked back at the turquoise water, the pure white sand, the birds soaring, darting. That grey shape must be a seal ... It was as if someone had suddenly washed the window through which he saw the world. This place was beautiful.

He should hate this land whose harshness had so nearly killed him, might still kill him. But all at once he knew he didn't want to exchange the hot harsh blue sky for the softer light of England. He had grown used to distance. To this land that called upon all his strength of mind and body, till he found he had more courage than he'd dreamed of. How could he go back to England and live there tamely, harvest to harvest, among the same faces and the same routines year after year?

Ben could never be his father, chasing wealth at any cost to others. But he needed challenges too.

'Poxy blaggard of a beggar,' cursed Higgins nearby.

The driftwood must be too damp to flare easily, Ben thought. Then suddenly it did; the tinder sparking, the flame rising. Should they eat the plum pudding now, he wondered, to celebrate their arrival? But Mr Flinders had described the island as a paradise where you hardly had to hunt to catch game to eat, he remembered — just as Guwara appeared above the rocks, wearily carrying a hopper carcass.

Guwara hadn't skinned or gutted the animal. He just draped it next to the fire and watched the flames eat at the skin while he sat there in exhaustion. His face was gaunt under his beard, but he still had the strength and determination to hunt, thought Ben, and to care for them.

They hacked off pieces of the still half-raw meat with their knives, pulling away the burnt skin. It hurt to eat, their lips chapped bloody by sun and salt and wind.

Higgins's hands trembled too much to mince his meat into pieces, so Ben chopped it for him.

His skin burned, and his hands were almost as weak as the convict's, but he could think more clearly now his body had water and food. They needed to find shade where they could rest today, then, when their strength had returned a little, they'd build a shelter to live in while they tried to repair the *Mulgu* and recovered their health. But just now it seemed too far to walk even to the trees behind them.

The smoke rose from their fire. The meat sizzled. They ate more, forcing it down. They drank, then drank again, their bodies slowly learning to absorb water again.

More birds flapped above them: ducks, pelicans, seagulls and others Ben couldn't recognise, shrieking and colourful against the deep blue sky. He tried to recover his earlier joy in the beauty of the world around him. But all he felt was bone-deep tiredness and a longing to rest, to escape the ever-burning sun and glare of sea, for a bed, and other hands to tend him, spooning up toast soaked in creamy milk, the invalid food Mama had brought him when he was ill …

'Well, what lollpoops are lyin' on my beach, eh?'

Ben turned. For a moment the light was too bright to see the figure outlined in front of the rising sun. Then he saw it was a man.

A man holding a musket.

*

The man stepped down across the rocks. He was short, grey-bearded, his hair long and straggly, barefoot and wearing faded convict-issue pants with a seaman's knitted jersey. He held the musket higher.

'Any one of youse moves an' I'll have your head off. Except for you,' he added to Guwara. 'You step away from them spears. Now what you doin' here?'

Higgins rose shakily to his feet. 'Sir,' he said, using the not-quite-right accent of an upper-level servant he'd used to Ben's father, 'you are speaking to young Master Ebenezer Huntsmore, only son of shipowner Branwell Huntsmore, of Badger's Hill estate in England. I am Higgins, his manservant, and this is our trusty companion, Billy-Boy.'

The man looked suspiciously at Ben. 'This true? You don't look like a nob to me.'

'Play the toff,' muttered Higgins out of the corner of his mouth.

Ben managed to scramble to his feet. He gave a short bow. 'It is. Please excuse our shabby attire, sir. We have been sailing for months. My father's ship, the *Golden Girl*, was sadly attacked by mutineers who stole her,' which was the truth, he thought, 'but we managed to escape in the ship's boat.' He gestured at the *Mulgu*.

'So where's this rich pa of yours?'

Higgins laid a sympathetic hand on Ben's shoulder. 'The young man's father was foully murdered by the scoundrels who attacked us. But if you can help him reach Port Jackson, his uncle, Sir Thomas Mudskin, will pay you handsomely for restoring him to his family. Master Ebenezer here is his uncle's heir, as well as inheriting his father's estate.'

Surely Higgins could have thought of a better name than Mudskin, Ben thought. And his father's estate amounted to the worn out planks of the *Mulga*, two tattered sails and whatever monies his father had left invested at Sydney Town, which they would need when — and if — they made it back. Exactly how much of a reward would this man expect?

'This shandygaff, boy?' demanded the man.

What did 'shandygaff' mean? That Higgins was feeding him lies — as indeed he was? Ben tried to look aristocratic. 'I can promise you a rich reward if you will help us return to Sydney Town, sir. Will you help us?'

'I might.'

Hope flared. Was there a ship anchored on the other side of the island?

'You have a ship?' Ben asked.

The man grinned, showing yellow teeth. 'I got more'n that. I got a whole kingdom of me own!'

He put his fingers to his mouth and gave a loud whistle.

Two young Indian women appeared over the rocks. They wore hopper skins shaped into an attempt at short dresses that reached below their knees. The first woman's face was bruised and swollen. And Ben realised with a shock that the second woman must have recently lost an ear, for blood still caked where it had been.

'I'm Bucky Morris,' the man said. 'This is my island, and these are my women. An' if you are who you say you are, just maybe I can help you. You got summat to say against any o' that?'

'No, sir,' said Ben. 'We will appreciate any help you can give us.'

'And Master Huntsmore's uncle will surely reward you richly,' added Higgins.

Bucky Morris glanced at the *Mulgu*. 'Anythin' worth bringin' from that?'

'No,' said Higgins quickly. 'As you can see, it is falling apart. We have only what you see before you.'

Bucky grunted. 'Fetch me them spears,' he said to the woman with the swollen face. He gave her a quick shove when she didn't understand.

Guwara moved to pick them up.

'Try it, boy, and I shoot,' said Bucky.

Guwara stayed where he was.

The woman picked up the spears, and Guwara said something to her, speaking quickly. She must have understood for she answered him briefly, darting anxious glances at Bucky.

'No yabberin'!' ordered Bucky. 'You bring them spears to me, Elsie.'

Elsie handed the spears over, then moved quickly away from him.

'Now bring me them knives and the axe. May as well have that tinderbox too.'

The other woman stepped towards them. Ben held out his knife. She took it without meeting his eyes, then moved to Higgins and then Guwara.

'Better get you fed and rested if there's goin' to be a reward,' said Bucky to Ben. He nodded to the two women and ordered, 'Help 'em walk,' then he strode back across the rocks.

Ben stumbled as he tried to follow. Elsie helped him.

The woman without an ear lent her shoulder to Higgins. Guwara walked alone, his expression impossible to read.

CHAPTER 23

Bucky's hut sat above a small river winding through the sand to the sea. Ben glimpsed green carpeted headlands and what might be a big lagoon or harbour, and the shapes of swans drifting slowly across the water. Above them ducks and birds he didn't recognise swept and swooped across the sky, as unconcerned by the humans as the grazing herds of hoppers — he could not think of them as 'kangaruhs', as Mr Flinders had called them — that merely lifted their heads and stared at them as they walked among them, or the mobs of vigilant long-legged murawang birds that stalked across their path giving them no more than a few contemptuous glances.

It was the paradise Mr Flinders had described — the tall trees, the grasslands, the low bushes and ground covers, even a mob of pelicans, their beaks drooping full of fish. But Flinders had also said that no one lived on Kangaruh Island, not even the Indians. He certainly hadn't mentioned anyone like Bucky.

The hut had a framework of freshly hewn logs, the walls filled in with thin branches twisted together and daubed with clay, like so many in the colony. A giant metal pot dangled on a tripod above glowing coals in the campfire outside. Two longer, rougher huts, possibly storerooms, faced the sea further down the hill. Long driftwood fences had reddish-furred sealskins draped over them, flapping in the wind. The wind smelled of smoke and drying sealskin.

To Ben's surprise, an extensive garden had been roughly fenced off with driftwood. He recognised potato plants, onion tops, Indian corn, still a long way from bearing, turnips and other greens. Six young Indian women worked among the plants, hoeing, digging and picking. Unlike the two women who accompanied Bucky, they were almost naked, wearing string belts and animal pelts over a shoulder or around their waist. They glanced up nervously, then quickly bent back to their work.

Elsie helped Ben to the hut door. He was about to enter when he realised Bucky was gesturing with his musket to push Higgins and Guwara towards one of the longer buildings.

Ben stumbled towards them. 'We stay together.'

Bucky casually aimed his musket at Ben. 'Them's the seamen's quarters. If youse really are a gentleman, you'll stay with me.'

'Seamen?' Ben asked. He longed for the shelter of the hut. To lie down, away from the sun. To rest. But they should not be separated.

'From the ships I supply,' said Bucky. 'Sealers, whalers.'

That explained the vegetable garden, the drying skins.

'Do what the big huff says,' Higgins said quietly to Ben. His sunburnt face was swollen and shiny, his eyes shadowed, his body almost skeletal again. 'We can't do nothin' till we've recovered. You just keep playin' the gentry cove, Sneezer lad.'

Ben hesitated. But Guwara and Higgins were already heading for the larger building without protest. He stepped into the hut.

It was finished more comfortably than he'd expected from the outside. Hopper fur lined the walls, blocking off draughts; sealskin blinds were rolled up above three windows, two looking seawards and one towards the garden and hill. A table made from four poles dug into the dirt floor with rough planks on top stood in the middle of the room; rough shelves held tin mugs, pannikins, slushy lamps and piles of what looked like well-cured skins sewn to become blankets, cloaks or clothes. A wide bed with a bulging feather mattress sat at the far end of the hut, with fur rugs rolled up neatly at one end. Three narrower beds with mattresses abutted the walls at the other end.

The two women led Ben to one of them. They looked at his shoes with curiosity as he slowly took them off, then wordlessly fetched pillows — soft skins filled with feathers — and a fur rug to cover him. The fur was soft, the leather perfectly cured, the pillow was soft too, and the bed surprisingly comfortable.

The woman who had lost an ear went outside and came back with a wooden bowl and a spoon. Ben tasted the food. Stew. Meat cooked till soft with potatoes and onions, soft on his raw lips and mouth. Real food, for the first time in months. He finished it all, then another when the bowl was filled again.

His body craved rest. He knew that if he tried to get up now he wouldn't even be able to walk back to the beach. But he was wary too.

For he had seen something red and shrivelled on the doorjamb. The woman's ear.

Ben was back on the *Mulgu*, bailing, watching, the sun's heat eating him, the planks buffeted by the waves and wind, even as he knew he was lying restless on a feather mattress. Time vanished or shivered about him. Women's hands held water to his lips and spoonfuls of stew. He drank, he ate.

Badger's Hill appeared, cold and green, and then became a damp cloth, washing his face. In brief moments he wondered if he had typhoid fever again, then remembered the blazing relentless sun. This illness came from that, from thirst, exhaustion and starvation.

And then he woke. He tried to sit up, but the world quivered. He blinked and it grew steadier.

'Master Huntsmore?' The voice was almost respectful. 'You feelin' better?'

Ben saw Bucky sitting at the table, cleaning a musket. Two more were propped up by his chair.

'Yes.' Ben managed to sit up and swung his legs off the bed. He was still dressed in the salt-encrusted clothes he had worn ever since they'd left the *Golden Girl*. 'How long have I been sleeping for?'

'Five days,' said Bucky.

'Five days!'

'Gave you laudanum to make you sleep,' said Bucky shortly. 'That way I didn't have to keep checkin' on you.'

So that was why he had slept so long and soundly, and felt so odd.

'Why would you have to check on me?'

'Like I said, this is my island. Don't want no strangers gettin' their dabs on what's mine.' Bucky returned to cleaning his musket. 'Your servant was worried about you. Told him I'd had Elsie and Mary shove some food down your gob and send you off to nod again.'

Mary must be the woman without an ear. He glanced at the doorjamb. The shrivelled skin was still there, not part of his fevered dreams.

'You own the whole island?' Ben asked. Surely the

Governor wouldn't have granted an island to a man like Bucky.

Bucky laughed, showing gaps in his long yellow teeth. 'This island is Bucky's kingdom, that's what it is.'

'I think Mr Flinders called it Kangaruh Island.'

Bucky shrugged. 'Who cares what some flash cove called it. I took it and I'm keepin' it.'

'How are Higgins and Guwara ... I mean, Billy-Boy?'

'What does a nob like you care about coves like them?'

'A gentleman always cares about his men,' said Ben. It sounded priggish, but Higgins had told him to behave like a toff. And anyway, it was true. 'Where are they, if you please, Mr Bucky?'

'Havin' a nice kip, that's what they're doin'. That man of yours ain't feelin' none too flash, but Elsie and Mary have been tendin' to him. I've been thinkin' he might teach them a bit o' servantin'.' Bucky grinned again. He put down his musket and took up another one. 'A king should have proper servantin', I reckon.'

'What do you do here, sir?'

'Whatever I like. Got the girls to hunt for me, grow the vegetables, scrape the salt for me to sell to the sealin' crews. Mostly I just sit and watch 'em work for me, just like a proper toff.'

'Do lots of ships come here?'

'More every year. Best sealin' in the world on these islands. I sells the crews meat and vegetables, sells them me skins too.' Bucky grinned again. 'And women. They always wants women.'

Ben tried to keep the horror from his face. 'Women?' he asked carefully.

'Every few months I goes over to the mainland to get me some more. I trains 'em up a bit, then sells them to the ships.' The matter-of-factness in his voice was more frightening than gloating.

'What if the women don't want to come?'

Bucky laughed. 'What's that got to do with anything, eh?' He held up one of the muskets. 'This makes me boss. Look out there.'

Ben gazed out the window. Women hoed between the vegetables, their heads down. A small barrow was loaded with potatoes and cabbages. There was no sign of Higgins or Guwara, but a boat was pulled up on the bank of the river. It was smaller than the *Mulgu*, but still a good size and looked sturdy.

Bucky inspected his musket more closely. 'Got two more girls out huntin'. Told 'em to bring back ducks. I've had me fill of hopper meat.'

'Do you give them muskets? Or spears?'

Ben saw that Guwara's spears hung on the wall above the fireplace.

'What do you think I am? A sapskull? The girls dig a pit an' drive the hoppers into it. Sometimes them big birds too, but they're greasy in a stew an' too tough roasted. The girls know how to catch ducks and swans by swimmin' under 'em — they're good swimmers, them Indians.' He shook his head. 'One of 'em tried to swim for the mainland a while ago. Got halfway there afore I caught her.'

'What happened to her?' asked Ben without thinking.

Bucky grinned. 'What do you think, little master? Let's just say she won't be swimmin' no more. Me girls will be back soon, if they knows what's good for 'em.' He frowned at Ben. 'All that guff your servant was sayin' … you really got a lord in your family?'

The title had been extinguished when Mama's brother had died, but Ben spoke the truth when he answered, 'Yes.'

'An' your father's a shipowner?'

'He was,' said Ben shortly.

'An' so everythin' he had belongs to you now?'

Ben nodded.

Bucky smiled. 'Then I better see you're treated right, hadn't I?'

'Will you sail us back to Sydney Town?' The boat by the river was small, but looked sound enough to sail up the coast.

'I could,' admitted Bucky. 'But it might not be a healthy place for me, if you catch me drift.'

Was Bucky an absconded convict? Probably worse, thought Ben. And a second offence meant whipping or, more likely, the gallows.

'Which makes gettin' a reward for savin' your hide a bit difficult,' Bucky continued. 'But I got a plan. Now, don't you worry none — it'll work out pease pudding for you too. Next ship headin' north that calls here can take you with 'em. They can pay me a reward for you — not as much as your uncle'll give 'em, but a guinea in the hand is worth two in the bush. Safer for you on a big ship too — there can be bad storms around here.'

'I know,' said Ben briefly. Bucky's plan didn't sound like a reward but a ransom. And what would happen when the ship's captain found there was no rich uncle waiting for Ben in Sydney Town?

'My servant Higgins will come too, of course, and Guwara,' he added.

'You mean Billy-Boy?' Bucky glanced out the window. 'Had a bit of trouble with him, but nothin' a touch o' the lash didn't cure. He's quieted down now. Got to show them Indians who's boss.'

'You whipped him?' It was impossible not to let his anger show.

'Don't get in a twist, lad. He's your property, not mine, and I intends to let you keep him. You might even get a price for him from one of the ships as wants more crew, though I suppose a toff like you don't need more lolly.'

Ben stared at him. Slavery was illegal in England now, even if it wasn't in places like America — and on this island. For that was what the women were he realised. Slaves kept in check by this evil man and his muskets.

'Ah, the girls is back. Roast duck for dinner, lad.' Bucky got to his feet, stretched, picked up the muskets and strode outside.

CHAPTER 24

They dined formally; which was to say, Bucky and Ben sat at the table with battered tin plates, helping themselves from the platters of sliced roast duck, boiled potatoes and cabbage Higgins and Elsie carried around.

Higgins waited on the table as solemnly as he had served Mr Huntsmore. Bucky obviously enjoyed having a footman offer him a platter of potatoes. Elsie followed Higgins's movements, holding out the platter of duck, even dropping a short curtsey that he must have shown her how to do.

Higgins didn't try to speak to Ben; he didn't even meet his eyes. But he looked a little better, his skin no longer swollen though still red. His limp was worse, and his hands still trembled as he held the dishes, but he had obviously been well-fed and rested.

'Sure you don't want to leave him here?' asked Bucky, his mouth full of cabbage.

'I couldn't part with him,' said Ben truthfully.

'He better get the girls trained up fast afore you leaves then.' Bucky shook his head and glanced out the window at the women tending the fire. 'Indians. Don't know how to do nothin' proper. I'll need to be gettin' some more girls soon. The *Freelander*'s due back any day now.' He clicked his fingers. 'Here, footman, get me a rum, quick sticks!'

He chuckled as Higgins turned obediently to the shelves, then said to Ben, 'You ever seen the King, lad?'

'Only passing by in his carriage,' said Ben.

Bucky looked disappointed.

'My father used to play cards with the Prince of Wales,' Ben offered. And lost, he thought, thinking of his father's gambling debts still waiting unpaid in England.

'A prince? A real prince? Here's Bucky sittin' with a lad whose pa played cards with a prince! But then I'm a king here, ain't I? What's the prince like?'

'Fat,' said Ben.

Bucky laughed. 'I bet he is, right fat an' all. Eats from silver dishes, does he?'

Ben had never thought about it. 'Some would be silver. And some porcelain.'

'What's that when it's at home?'

'Thin crockery.'

Bucky had no interest in crockery. He grabbed the last piece of duck and wiped his greasy hands on his trousers.

'Your rum, sir,' said Higgins, offering the tin mug of rum and hot water on a plank of wood, like a tray.

Bucky grinned. 'Thank you, my man. Ain't you forgettin' your young master?' He nodded towards Ben.

'I don't want any. But thank you, sir,' Ben added quickly.

'Sir,' said Bucky thoughtfully. 'Maybe it should be "Your Majesty". What d'you say, eh?'

'Do the captains call you "Your Majesty"?' asked Ben.

Bucky sighed. 'You got a point there. Most of them is Yanks, and Yanks don't have much truck with kings. Best not push it. I got a good pitch here and I don't want to queer it.' He stood, draining the last of his rum. 'Time to lock up.'

Ben looked out the door. 'Where's Guwara ... Billy-Boy?' he ventured.

'Him? Shut up safe.'

Bucky whistled, and Elsie and Mary appeared. Both gave rough curtseys, then looked down at the ground.

'That's what I like to see,' said Bucky approvingly. 'Might even keep you two, eh? Come on.'

Ben and Higgins watched from the doorway as Bucky led the women to the larger storeroom and opened the door. The women obediently vanished inside. Bucky pulled the wooden bolt over the door, sealing them in. 'Come on!' he yelled to Higgins over the mutter of the island wind.

'Listen quick, Sneezer,' Higgins whispered. 'Come an' get me as soon as His Nibs is asleep.'

Ben nodded.

Higgins limped to the other storeroom. Ben watched as Bucky opened the door, waited for Higgins to enter, then bolted it securely. He strolled back to the hut, his face greasy in the firelight from the duck.

'Now, another rum for me and a nice mug o' cow juice for you, except it's goat juice, and you'll be sleepin' like a lamb. Got to get you fat and healthy afore the *Freelander* comes, eh?'

'Yes, sir,' said Ben.

Moonlight turned the island black and silver through the window. Bucky snored on his feather bed. The mug of milk sat on the floor by Ben's bed. He was fairly sure it contained laudanum, so had pretended to sip from it as Bucky fell asleep.

'Bucky?' he whispered. Then more loudly, 'Bucky?'

The snores didn't change.

Ben pulled on what was left of his stockings and boots — cracking now, after too much saltwater — then slipped silently out of the hut and over to the storeroom Higgins was locked in. He wrenched back the bolt and opened the door. The smell of stored potatoes and onions wafted out.

'Took yer time, didn't you?' whispered Higgins, limping out quickly. His face looked taut but determined. 'We got to get away from here,' he added softly. 'Tonight.'

'Why tonight?'

''Cause if we wait any longer, Billy-Boy'll be dead, that's why.'

'I don't understand.'

'Bucky shot him,' whispered Higgins. 'He whips the women, but Old King Bucky ain't goin' to whip a cove what might fight back. Bucky tried puttin' Billy-Boy to work, cuttin' down trees, but on the second night he dug through the wall.' Higgins gestured towards a recently repaired spot. 'I was too weak to go far, but I saw Billy-Boy about to open the bolt to the women's hut. Then old Bucky came out and shot him in the shoulder. Thought he was going to kill him, but I reckon he thought seein' Billy-Boy die slow would teach the rest of us a lesson. Except for you. You were to be kept nice and quiet with the laudanum till he could sell you.'

'Sell me?'

'He ain't likely to trust anyone to bring back a share of a reward, is he? No, he's goin' to sell you to one o' them ships, just like he sells the women here. An' then what do you think the captain'll do when there ain't no big toff uncle to pay him? Can't see no captain tryin' to get the Governor to give him your pa's money. He'll shanghai you as crew, most like.

'Now, come on. Billy-Boy's over by the gardens.' Higgins grinned in the moonlight. 'We're goin' to take Bucky's boat and get ourselves to Sydney Town.'

There was a bark lean-to at the bottom of the vegetable garden, the door a sheet of bark too. At least Guwara wasn't locked in, thought Ben in relief, pulling the bark away.

He stopped. Guwara lay on the dirt, shirtless, his arm black with dried blood. He was so motionless that Ben was afraid he was dead, but the noise and moonlight must have woken him. He slowly turned to look at them. Something clanked.

Ben saw chains at his wrist and ankle, bolted to an iron bar in the ground. Bucky wasn't taking any chances that Guwara might escape.

Higgins grunted in pain as he kneeled. 'Hell's bells, never knew he'd chained you, Billy-Boy. Go get the keys, Sneezer.'

'But I haven't seen any keys.'

'Then go and look for 'em!'

'No,' said Guwara, his voice wearier than Ben had ever heard it. 'The women say Bucky sleeps with the keys under his mattress. You'll never get them without waking him.' Slowly, carefully, he stood, lifting the chains and the iron bar with him.

'You can't escape in chains, man,' said Higgins.

'Have to,' said Guwara quietly. 'We must get the women away. The ship is coming soon.' He moved his chains and they clanked. 'He will hear me if I go too near the hut. You must open their door before he wakes.'

Higgins hesitated, then said, 'All right. Sneezer, you free the women, then get yourself down to the boat. I'm goin' to get our things from the *Mulgu*.'

'Bucky already has our knives and tinderbox and axe,' protested Ben. 'There's nothing left there. Higgins, you're not well enough to —'

But Higgins was already limping swiftly into the moonlit darkness. The shadows swallowed him. Has he gone to get that wretched plum pudding? Ben wondered. He needed to save his strength. And Bucky might wake up at any moment!

Ben ran to the biggest shed and lifted the bolt, then hesitated, unsure how to make the women understand. But Guwara must have told them what he planned — or hoped for — and they'd heard the sounds outside. A dozen or so of them were gathered at the door, Elsie and Mary at the front.

Most immediately ran down to the beach in the direction of the boat, but Elsie ran to Guwara and spoke to him urgently, lifting his chain to take as much of the weight as she could.

Someone moved behind Ben in the darkness. He turned just in time to see Mary run to Bucky's hut and slip inside. Was she going to warn him? There was no time to catch her. He hurried to Elsie and Guwara.

'Come on!' he hissed, and placed one of Guwara's arms over his shoulder. Elsie propped herself under Guwara's other shoulder.

Guwara drew in a sharp breath of pain, but made no other sound.

They stumbled down towards the boat, the chains clanking continuously. It was a strange sound on an island of wind and waves and bird calls, and the thud of hoppers in the night.

'Too much noise,' gasped Guwara. 'Go! Go now!'

'We're not leaving you,' said Ben.

Guwara said something urgently in his own language to Elsie. She replied, but didn't release his arm or the chain.

They staggered down the hill. The river's ripples gleamed a golden path in the moonlight. Ben felt his arm grow wet — Guwara's wound was bleeding. Where is Higgins? he thought desperately. Has he collapsed trying to run to the *Mulgu*? They couldn't leave him here. Ben wasn't sure that Guwara would be able to help him row the boat from the shore, or raise the sails once they were in deep enough water. But Ben was strong enough to row a short way at least on his own. If they could just get the boat out to sea, they could sail around the island to find Higgins.

They were nearly at the boat. The women had already pushed it into the water. Some sat inside it, while others held it close to the bank, waiting for them. Ben wondered briefly if any of them knew how to row or sail, if they were deliberately risking their lives so he and Guwara could escape too.

Where was Higgins?

A shot.

Ben staggered as Guwara sagged next to him.

Elsie gave a cry and stepped back.

Blood pumped from Guwara's back. Ben used all his strength to keep him upright. Elsie pulled her shoulder under Guwara's arm again and he muttered in pain, then whispered something urgently to her.

Then his eyes met Ben's. 'Go!' he breathed.

'No!' said Ben. But Guwara's eyes had dulled. His weight slumped in Ben's arms.

Ben lowered him gently to the rocky ground, then looked back up the hill. Bucky stood at the crest. He held a musket in his arms. The musket he had just used lay at his feet.

'Move away where I can see you,' he ordered. 'Thought you'd steal my women, did you? And my boat.'

He only has one more shot unless he reloads, Ben thought, looking at the musket. If he shoots me, the women can get away before he can get another musket, or powder and shot. If the women can sail or row …

But what if they couldn't?

His only hope was to get Bucky to shoot at him and miss. It would take precious minutes for him to get back to the hut and reload, and grab the third musket, assuming it was kept loaded. Ben glanced around. He could duck and roll in the tussocks as soon as Bucky aimed at him.

'All that talk about the prince and a reward!' yelled Bucky as Ben readied himself to run. 'Well, I'll show you a reward! This time you —'

Bucky fell at the same time as the sound of the shot reached them. Mary stood in the darkness, the musket in her arms. She dropped it and ran to Guwara.

She and Elsie kneeled beside him. Even in the moonlight Ben could see the red of Guwara's blood on the ground.

'What's goin' on?' puffed Higgins, limping out of the darkness, the sack that contained the pudding in his arms.

Ben couldn't reply. His friend was dead. The man who had brought them so far, who had protected them, and would now never see his home again. He wanted to yell at Higgins for leaving them just to get a plum pudding. But he knew Higgins's presence wouldn't have changed anything.

Higgins looked at Guwara's still body and the two women weeping over him. Then he put the pudding down and walked up the hill to Bucky. He prodded the body with his toe.

'Dead,' he called briefly, and added, 'I ain't buryin' him neither.'

'I wasn't going to suggest it.'

Ben looked at Mary and Elsie, then at the other women now hauling the boat back onto the shore. What had they endured in the last few months, or even years? But with Guwara dead he had no way of speaking to them, beyond a few words of Cadigal they might not understand.

Guwara. Dead.

Tears came then, the first he'd shed since he'd kept watch up in the lookout on the *Golden Girl*. Guwara was a brave man who had died saving his friends, his people — the bravest perhaps that Ben had ever met. He had been sailor, warrior, protector, teacher, friend. But they couldn't put that on his tombstone for the sealers who would come here to mock. There could be no tombstone. Yet.

One day I will come back, he promised his friend silently. *One day I will build a tomb for you.*

Higgins was still out of breath and standing unsteadily, clearly not well.

'You stay here,' Ben told him. 'Sit down for a while. I'll try to explain to the women that we'll leave tomorrow, not tonight.'

Somehow they must launch the boat without Guwara's help, and soon, before any sealing ships arrived.

He found himself striding through the moonlight. I am not a boy now, he thought. I am a man. My friend is dead, but I will see the women he wanted to protect back to their people. And then Higgins and I will sail back to Sydney Town, together.

CHAPTER 25

The soil was easiest to dig in the potato bed. Ben hoped Guwara would not mind being buried among potatoes. It wasn't fair that he should have travelled all this way, and left behind the treasure of the *Golden Girl*, to lie here among the vegetables, his grave unmarked. Ben and Higgins would have died without Guwara's care. His greatest gift, thought Ben, was to teach me to survive.

He dug the grave himself. Higgins retreated to the hut and the temporary luxury of a bed to lie in and Bucky's leftovers to eat. He wouldn't let Ben look at his leg wound, stubbornly insisting it had healed.

Ben hesitated over Guwara's spears. They should be buried with him. But Guwara had let Ben use them, and he might need them on the voyage up the coast, even though they would have Bucky's muskets and provisions. Muskets could only be used till the shot ran out, and might not work at all if the gunpowder became damp in the boat.

'I'm so sorry,' he said to Guwara. 'I'm not stealing your spears. One day I'll bring them back, or ...' He stopped as a breeze rustled the corn plants and the trees up on the hill, and smiled. 'No,' he said softly, 'I'll find a boy — a boy with black skin — who needs a friend, just as you found me. And when I know he can use spears well, I will give him these.'

The breeze dropped. It was just a coincidence. But Ben felt that Guwara was content.

The boat was sturdy, but small enough for Ben to sail her by himself as Bucky must have done. It was already provisioned with three full water barrels, a waterproof chest for food, spare sails and oars. Ben loaded everything else while Higgins rested: the muskets, shot, tinderboxes, knives, axes, smoked duck, swan and pelican and another dried meat that was probably hopper tail, as well as the fur blankets.

He roasted as many potatoes as he could too, for it would almost certainly be too dangerous to try to take the boat into the shore again, with the perils posed by rocks or hidden reefs that guarded the bays, and the fierce surf along the beaches.

Ben tried to make the women understand that they could take whatever they wanted from Bucky's hut or the storerooms. But they looked away from the hut, pretending not to see.

Ben and Mary helped Higgins limp down to the boat, still carrying his precious pudding in its sack. They settled him among cushions and fur rugs. Mary and Elsie had discarded their 'dresses', and Ben thought they would discard their slavery names too.

The boat was low in the water with the weight of so many people, but the sea looked calm and the wind was steady. After rowing out into the deeper water Ben was able to raise the sail himself. He felt the wind grasp the boat and begin to carry her and her cargo down the river and out to the channel separating the island from the sea. He felt no triumph, just sadness that Guwara could not see the boy he had taught to be a sailor during the hard months behind them.

The women sat silently, as if in shock that they were free. He wished he could speak to them, but though he tried various words that Guwara had taught him, they didn't respond. Perhaps he said the words incorrectly, or Guwara had spoken their own language to them, just as he could speak English as well as Cadigal. Or possibly, Ben thought, the women didn't want to speak to a white man, even a young one who had helped them escape.

He didn't look back as they sailed away from the island. Neither did Higgins nor any of the women. Mr Flinders had called it a paradise a few years earlier, and maybe one day it would be again. But just now Ben could not bear to see it.

It was only a few hours' sailing to the mainland, the women gesturing to show Ben where to go — a small greyish beach where the water lapped gently at the sand instead of raging in large waves. There was no sign of their people, except for a spire of smoke inland, but the women didn't seem worried. The people of this area had probably learned too well that those who came in boats like this one, with muskets, must be avoided. Ben assumed that when their boat left, the women's people would return, or the women knew where to find them.

They beached the boat for the night, not bothering with a fire. The women melted into the afternoon shadows. At first Ben thought that they'd all gone, but Elsie and Mary and another woman returned before he and Higgins had rolled themselves in the skin cloaks to sleep.

Elsie carried a big bark container of fresh water; Mary's bark platter held oysters mixed with something green that looked like a sort of seaweed, evidently to be eaten. The other woman carried some kind of vegetable cakes. They must have found their people, Ben thought.

The women put the containers on the ground, hesitated, then moved away.

'Please, stop!' called Ben. He couldn't let them go without something to mark all that they'd been through together. But he had no words, nor any gift to give them.

Except he did.

He bent down and took off his boots, then held them out.

The women didn't move. Then slowly Mary walked forward and took the boots from him. She spoke softly for a long time, the words guttural and song-like and impossible to understand.

Except he did understand, and so did she.

Guwara had saved them all and he was gone. And all of them were free.

The next day, Ben managed to push the little boat back into the water, row past the shoreline swell and raise the sail again. He even managed to tack into the onshore wind until it changed further out to sea, becoming a westerly that carried them briskly eastward, as if he and Higgins had given orders for exactly the wind they needed.

They didn't name the boat. The *Mulgu* and her fellowship was gone; and this would always be Bucky's boat, a slaver's boat. It might carry them to safety, but it still felt to Ben as if evil had settled into its timbers. He would be glad to see it gone.

They passed brown hills and thin gold sandy beaches, then green hills of tall trees and black cliffs. The waves looked too high for them to land easily along most of the coast, but even where there were streams or harbours that seemed free of rocks Ben sailed on. He didn't trust his seamanship to manoeuvre the boat in strong currents or high seas, and with the good wind they should have enough food and, hopefully, enough water to reach Sydney Town without landing.

Each night he lowered the sail, and during the darkness he and Higgins took turns watching and bailing out the spray. Higgins seemed even more feeble now, but he doggedly stood his watch, even managing to hold the tiller, peering for changes in water colour, or a dash of spray that might mean hidden rocks, and as always bailing out the water as the waves slapped spray against their faces.

Islands floated by as they sailed east. Ben was so used to the rocking of waves now that it seemed it was the land that moved, not them. Early one morning he glimpsed the entrance to the big southern harbour called Twofold Bay that Mr Flinders had mapped. There was fresh water there, but Flinders's boat had gone aground on the way in, and even though it had been easily refloated, Ben couldn't risk a shipwreck now.

At last, one sea-misted morning, his sharp eyes saw the high hummocky rise that marked the most southern part of the mainland. Vast clouds of gulls and other sea birds rose and balanced on the sky. Ben could just see the fat shapes of seals upon the rocks.

The wind changed. Waves slapped high against the boat, sending so much spray into the craft that both he and Higgins had to bail furiously to keep her afloat. The wind gusted this way and that, and Ben frantically hauled on the sails, swinging the boom and sails across as he tacked repeatedly. At last the wind steadied to a southeasterly gale that spat ice-cold froth onto their faces. Each breath seemed more salt than air.

No sleep that night. Higgins bailed in darkness, while Ben kept up only enough sail to hold the craft steady, desperately wishing for Guwara's knowledge and experience. Finally day crept in as a grey light over the horizon. As the sky turned blue, the wind dropped to a strong and steady southerly, carrying them north at last.

Higgins lay back under their rough shelter, exhausted, his lips blue against the shiny red of his skin. Both he and Ben were sunburnt again, even though the cooler air from the south, as well as a relative abundance of water, had made this journey far easier than crossing the Bight.

'Here.' Ben held out a flask of water.

Higgins gulped some down, then waved the rest away.

'We've still got a few potatoes,' Ben said, though they were slimy now. He realised the rest should probably be thrown away.

Higgins shook his head.

'You have to eat,' said Ben desperately. 'I could chew some dried fish for you. Or how about the plum pudding?' He tried to smile. 'We're on our way home now. It's time to eat that pudding.'

'All I want is sleep,' said Higgins hoarsely. He gave a grimace that might be a grin. 'Grand work, Sneezer. You done good.'

Ben looked at the land on their left and at the sky. It was a clear blue, with no looming clouds or sneaking mare's tails, and he felt the cool wind at their back.

'A couple more weeks with a good wind and we'll be in Sydney Town,' he said.

Higgins nodded, but didn't answer. A few minutes later Ben heard a snore

CHAPTER 26

Ben remembered this part of the *Golden Girl*'s route. If he could keep their boat the same distance from the shore, they should be safe from rocks and reefs. Even the islands they passed were close to the shore. And still the wind bore them steadily northwards, cold and gusty. Then it stopped.

The boat bobbed, her sails flapping only a little in the breeze from the land. Ben lowered them and sat back.

'The wind should rise again tomorrow,' he assured Higgins. As far as he remembered, it was a rare day when an afternoon southerly didn't gust up the coast.

Higgins nodded, gazing at the blue shore where mountains twisted with what might be mist or cloud obscuring their tops. 'Soon be home,' he said quietly.

Ben grinned, glad to see him looking hopeful again. 'We'll have that tavern yet,' he promised.

He still didn't want a tavern himself, but Higgins needed to return to the life he was used to.

Higgins said nothing.

'What do you think — should we buy one down by the docks or along the river?'

Higgins smiled. 'Which would you like, Sneezer lad?'

Ben hesitated. 'I don't suppose you'd like a farm instead? On the Hawkesbury maybe? I know more about farming than keeping a tavern.'

'And that girl you liked might be on that farm too?'

'Perhaps,' said Ben cautiously.

'Can't see me as a farmer,' said Higgins.

'You wouldn't have to farm. You could sit in an armchair and put your feet up.'

Higgins shook his head. 'You wouldn't want the likes of me in your parlour, Sneezer.'

'Yes, I would,' said Ben softly. 'You've been more of a father to me than anyone in the world. You'll sit in our parlour and ...' He tried to think what else Higgins might do.

'And be a grandpa one day?'

Ben flushed. 'Maybe.'

Higgins chuckled. 'Me, a grandfather. I'd like that, Sneezer. Wouldn't care if I could call the King me uncle if I could have grandpups playin' round my feet.'

'You said you'd look after me,' said Ben. 'And you have. And now it's my turn to look after you. We'll stay in Sydney Town till you get better. Then I'll ask Governor Macquarie for a land grant — I'm pretty sure he'll give me one, even if I am a bit young. You'll live like a gentleman, Mr Higgins.'

'An' the little'uns will call me Grandpa. I can just see it, Sneezer. You and me and yer wife and lots of little'uns. I'll watch me language too. No bear-garden talk with 'em. I'd make you proud of me, Sneezer.'

'I am proud of you,' said Ben.

'I know, lad. I think this might be the happiest day of me life, hearin' you say that and knowin' it's true.' Higgins looked at the blue line of the shore again. Or was he looking back to England? 'It's been a long way to come to find meself a son,' he said at last. 'But I got a good one. We'll share everythin', Sneezer, you an' me.'

'We'll soon be at Sydney Town,' Ben said eagerly. 'I recognised that river back there. Another few days of sailing. And we've only used one barrel of water too.'

'No,' said Higgins gently. 'No Sydney Town for me.'

'But …' Ben stopped and looked at him. How could a man be so pale under his sunburn? Higgins's eyes were sunk in dark shadows, and every breath seemed torn from him. Ben hadn't noticed he was so weak, perhaps because Higgins had stayed so still except when bailing and tending the tiller.

'Is it your leg?' he asked. 'We'll find a surgeon for you at Sydney Town.'

'No, you won't,' said Higgins calmly. 'I want you to promise me somethin', Sneezer lad.'

'Anything,' said Ben desperately. 'Higgins, you're all I have!'

'No, I ain't. You got a future. A fine future. You can be anythin' you want to be.'

'With you!'

'You promised you'd do whatever I asked. An' so I'm askin' this. Don't go ashore to bury me. It's too risky. Any place there's safe harbour might have whalin' ships that'll shanghai you to be their crew, or Indians who've met men like Bucky and think every white man is a slaver. When I die, send me down to Davy's deeps —'

'No! You're not going to die. And if you did —'

Higgins gave a chuckle. 'What, you'd pickle me in rum to get me to Sydney Town? We don't have rum on board, Sneezer. An' I don't want you riskin' goin' ashore neither.'

'You're not going to die,' said Ben stubbornly. 'We'll find a place where we can land for a few days and you can get better. You can rest in the shade and I'll hunt fresh food. Remember how much better you were after a few days on the island?'

'Well, we'll see,' said Higgins, lying back on his fur pillow. 'Maybe tomorrow, Sneezer lad. We'll talk about it then.'

At dawn the next morning, when Ben turned from adjusting the sail, Higgins was gone.

The wind had risen enough for Ben to tack back, to sail in circles, shouting, searching. But no one answered. No body floated on the waves.

Higgins must have slid overboard and let himself sink noiselessly into the sea.

Ben searched all that day, forcing his body from tiller to sail and back again, doing the work of two crew.

He kept searching, even after he knew there was no chance Higgins might be alive. He could not leave his friend's body drifting below.

And yet he had no choice.

At last, as the wind rose in the late afternoon, he set the sail and headed north.

CHAPTER 27

The shape of the land was familiar to him from those long days when the *Golden Girl* had swung at anchor outside the heads, waiting for a pilot to bring her in. That was Botany Bay, and those giant cliffs guarded the narrow passage that led to Port Jackson and Sydney Town. He was here at last.

It seemed so long ago that Ben had sailed into the harbour aboard the *Golden Girl*. He had been so afraid of Higgins then. Yet Higgins had never lied to him, unlike Ben's father. In his own way, Higgins was the most honest man Ben had ever met.

The boat slid through the heads. She was small enough not to need a pilot and the tide was high. Ben set course not for the wharf but one of the small beaches to the side. After the loneliness of the vast sea, it was strange to see fishing canoes and other boats, even two big ships at anchor.

He jumped out, his bare feet sinking into the mud, and pulled the boat up as high as he could. A few men working in a garden on shore looked at him curiously. Ben knew what they saw. A ragged lad, his breeches far too short for his legs, his shirt no longer able to be buttoned across his chest, barefoot, and in what they probably assumed was a fishing boat. He had nothing of value, yet he had everything he needed: his life, and the skills, loyalty and friendship given to him by two very different men from opposite ends of the world.

Ben looked at the boat. He didn't want to see it again; whoever found it here could have it. He would take Guwara's spears with him, as well as the knives, the axe and tinderbox. All but the spears would fit in the sack with Higgins's plum pudding. He pulled the sack from under the seat. That wretched pudding! Had Higgins kept it as a talisman of the toff's life he hoped for when they got back to Sydney Town?

Ben stopped, surprised at the bag's weight. He opened it and saw something gleam in the sunlight.

Gold.

The workmen stared at him as he laughed, and kept on laughing. Higgins — dear, cunning Higgins — hadn't just planned to save Ben's life. He had been waiting to take Ben *and* the gold he'd secreted onto the *Golden Girl*'s pinnace during the chaos of battle.

'I'll take care of you,' he'd said. 'Me and you, Sneezer.'

Ben had no doubt that Higgins had planned to share the gold with him, and with Guwara too. He stopped laughing. Sudden tears ran cold down his sunburnt face instead. How Higgins must have loved imagining Ben's shock when they arrived here. He'd probably planned to run the best tavern Sydney Town had ever seen, with him and Ben presiding over it. And after that, a grand farmhouse, with Higgins at the head of the table while servants served the family meal.

Ben stared at the gold again, then hurriedly shoved a hopper-skin rug on top of it, to hide it from idle glances. What would he do now?

'You need a hand carryin' somethin', mister?' an urchin asked Ben hopefully, obviously expecting a coin in return, or a few fish.

'You can show me the way to Government House,' said Ben, keeping hold of the sack.

He'd have to convince the Governor's staff that the ragged young man before them was indeed the boy who had left with his father on the *Golden Girl*. He must report the mutiny too, and the circumstances. Governor Macquarie needed to know that the Prince of Wales was giving permission for privateers to attack enemy ships near New Holland. The Governor also needed to deal with the sealers' slavery on Kangaruh Island. Bucky might be gone, but others could take his place. And Government House was possibly the only place in Sydney Town where so much gold would be safe.

Ben knew that gold wouldn't buy land in this colony where the Governor controlled all transactions, but it would buy sheep, horses, tools and whatever else he needed. He would keep only the treasure from his real father, Higgins, and give the Huntsmore money away to those who needed it far more than he did, both here and back at Badger's Hill. He did not even need the Huntsmore name now.

He hefted the sack and picked up Guwara's spears in his other hand.

'My name is Ben Higgins,' he said to the urchin. 'What's yours?'

EPILOGUE

BADGER'S HILL, LIMESTONE PLAINS, NEW SOUTH WALES, MARCH 1838

The land was gold as the autumn grass dried on the hills, but the fields of corn were green. Ben paused in the doorway of the sprawling house on the hill, tray of plates in hand, to watch as dark- and white-skinned workers moved between the rows of corn, picking cobs and throwing them into the sacks on their shoulders. Neighbours had come to help with the harvest: Tugger with his three sons, as well as Ted Filkinghorn, Ben's son-in-law, married to his oldest daughter, Margaret. Several of Ben's friends back in England had accepted his invitation, years ago, to join him in the colony, to become landowners, not tenants. Even Filkinghorn had made the journey, though the old man had stayed in a cottage in Sydney, while his nephew crossed the mountains with Ben and Sally.

The dark skins belonged to Annie's relatives, a Yuin woman who had married Ben's second oldest, Thomas. Ben was proud of his son's courage, and loved and admired his daughter-in-law, though he worried about the lives of his grandchildren. But here, in their close-knit community at least, they were accepted.

It was a good harvest, not just of corn but friendship too. Ben smiled and carried the plates out to the trestle tables under the plum trees. Their fruit was all picked now, and bottled or turned into jam; the jars sitting in the big stone storeroom next to the dairy, along with crocks of honey slowly dripping from the comb, sacks of apples, grapes withering into raisins in their tubs of dry sand, and ropes of onions hanging from the rafters. There'd be the pumpkins to pick next, along with the quinces and late pears.

This was a rich country. Every day Ben's eyes saw more beauty in it: the shape of the ancient hills, the twists of gumtree branches, the soft-furred bears that glared down at him as they chewed their gum leaves, the native badgers charging for their holes.

He and Sally had created a hint of England here, since they'd married, crossed the Blue Mountains and settled by the river. Ben had fields marked by hawthorn hedges, like a ghost of home every time they blossomed, and an English orchard. And Sally had planted English roses and wisteria along the veranda of the long low house that had grown year by year as their family had grown too, its terrace looking down upon the river. But the roses bloomed with brighter colours under a sky more vivid blue than any seen in England; and beyond the hedges, the sheep grazed in unfenced pasture, tended by shepherds who had once been thieves.

'Time to light the fires,' said Sally, carrying a vast platter of hearth cakes to the tables. Her younger children trailed behind her, Gwyneth, Anne and young Matthew bringing flagons of sarsaparilla tea to refresh those picking the corn.

Tonight the harvesters would feast on boiled maize with butter; mutton roasted on the spit; hearth cakes and apple pies and boiled puddings rich with dried fruit, the kind that Higgins had loved so much. Every ingredient had been grown on Badger's Hill — this new Badger's Hill, oceans away from the one where Ben was born.

But this one held his heart now. His home, his land, his friends, his family.

This was his gold now.

AUTHOR'S NOTES

This novel is entirely fiction. It is, however, based on true events. The piratical/privateer venture of the *Golden Girl* might not have been possible without a combination of circumstances: England was at war with France; Holland had been taken by Napoleon in 1795, and Napoleon put his younger brother, Louis Napoleon, on the throne of the Netherlands in 1806; and King George III had been declared insane, thus giving his son, the corrupt and corpulent Prince of Wales, the ability to grant privateering licences (letters of marque) to his friends and gambling cronies, like Mr Huntsmore in this book. These letters of marque permitted English merchant ships to attack French ships or those from any other country that Napoleon had conquered.

We don't think of Sydney as a pirate port, but for several years it did provision 'privateers' to such an extent that Governor Macquarie requested assistance from England to defend the colony from French attack in retaliation.

I have been unable to find any record, however, of which or how many ships were captured. The best estimate is 'some', as British ships wouldn't have persisted in the practice if none had succeeded. But neither would they have advertised what they'd captured or where, especially as they were expected to give a percentage to the Crown. It is possible that there are records in the Netherlands of ships that were taken by privateers off the Australian coast, but if they exist, I have been unable to track them down.

There was still great honour in 1810 in getting a naval 'prize' from a ship captured in war (see Jane Austen's novel *Persuasion*). But riches won as a privateer weren't quite so honourable, especially when it might turn out that the war had ceased a year before your plunder.

The armed forces of most nations today fight for wages, not plunder. This was not the case in 1810. The high risk of death and the appalling living conditions meant that rewards had to be high to entice men of quality to enlist. Crew, on the other hand, might be picked up drunk at a port and wake up at sea; and young criminals were often sent to sea instead of to the gallows.

In these days of radio, satellites and mobile phones, it is difficult to imagine a time when one in four ships would eventually be shipwrecked, often vanishing without trace. Unless they travelled in a fleet, or survivors were picked up by another ship — unlikely along the vast coast of Western Australia, where ships tried to keep well out to sea to avoid being wrecked — a ship might vanish and not be missed for months or even years, especially if no one expected it at the port it was heading to. Australia has many old wrecks along its coastlines, and probably far more are yet to be found.

THE DUTCH EAST INDIA COMPANY

There is another major factor that made privateering possible during these years. The Dutch East India Company (the VOC), which had been trading with various ports in the Netherlands East Indies, including Batavia (present-day Jakarta, the capital of Indonesia), was declared bankrupt and dissolved in 1800. The government of the Netherlands took over what the VOC had controlled, including Batavia.

In 1808, the Napoleonic regime of the Netherlands sent Marshal Herman Willem Daendels to be Governor-General of Batavia. He was there between 1808 and 1811, when he was replaced as Governor-General by Jan Willem Janssens. In August 1811, that command was taken over by the famous Sir Stamford Raffles, who went on to become the Lieutenant-Governor of Java,

Governor-General of Bencoolen and founder of modern-day Singapore.

This was a time of confusion both politically and commercially, with different trading patterns from those that had operated in the 1780s and 1790s.

THE ROUTE OF THE *GOLDEN GIRL*

I based this on voyages made by similar ships of the time. The passage east using the Roaring Forties — the strong, almost constant westerly winds at the fortieth parallel or latitude — had been for centuries a convenient way for sailing ships to quickly cross the Southern Ocean, and was used by the Portuguese and Dutch as well as the English to reach 'New Holland'. But these strong winds made it difficult, and usually impossible, to sail west on this route.

THE *MULGU*

Ship design has changed dramatically since 1810, but sailing techniques have not, except for modern and more automated watercraft. The *Mulgu* would have been a small open ship's boat: a fore-and-aft gaff-rigged, single-masted cutter. A cutter could be handled by a couple of men and rowed ashore when needed. Those sailing it could tack into the wind if need be, and wouldn't be caught on a lee shore quite as easily as in a square-rigged ship. The *Mulgu* wouldn't have had a keel, so couldn't point as high into the wind as a keeled boat, but it could be hauled up onto a beach — essential in a place and time with no wharves and an almost unknown coast.

In a craft like this, Guwara could tack and catch the wind even if there were local offshore winds. The winds close to the coast are much more variable than those in the open ocean as they are affected by features on the land as well as offshore islands.

The *Mulgu* almost certainly wouldn't have withstood a major storm; nor could Ben have sailed Bucky's boat by himself except in calm weather. The journey that Ben, Higgins and Guwara made in the *Mulgu* is possible, but only with Guwara's understanding of tides and winds, and a large amount of luck.

INDIGENOUS SAILORS

I've written before about Nanberry White, one of the first Indigenous sailors to serve as crew on ships sailing from Sydney. (There was already a long history of Indigenous sailors employed by various countries north of Australia.) By 1810, an unknown number of young Indigenous men were crewing on ships, from English merchant vessels to sealing or whaling boats based in the United States and elsewhere, or on voyages across the ocean in tiny (to our eyes) sailing ships. They braved the storms and vast waves of the Southern Ocean, and the mountainous seas by the Cape, sailed past ice floes and through the doldrums, where you could die of thirst when there was no wind to fill your ship's sails. These young men were respected and valued crew members, and were usually paid regular wages and given regular rations on the same basis as white sailors.

From a modern perspective, the question is: why on earth would they want to? Despite colonial incursion into the lands of the Indigenous nations, in 1810 a comfortable Indigenous life was still possible, though nowhere near as secure as it had been. Sea voyages were dangerous and often deadly, conditions were appalling, and scurvy almost inevitable. Wages might have been an incentive, but at that time in the colony Indigenous fishermen could make far more money, and with far less danger, selling fish to the colonists who didn't have their knowledge of when and where fish might be caught.

The answer is probably that these young men wanted adventure and a chance to see the world. This doesn't seem enough to someone like me, who gets seasick on a calm river and likes a comfortable bed and the least danger possible, but it's been a motive for many people in many places and of many races, so it is the only one I can give.

THE KANGARUH ISLAND SLAVE TRADE

Sealing and whaling ships often kidnapped Indigenous women, and in some places large numbers of people were slaughtered in the process. At other times and in other places, Indigenous women willingly married sailors, including those from sealing and whaling ships, and seem to have led happy and fulfilled lives, either on board the ships or in comfortable cottages, waiting, as wives did, for the times their husbands came home.

Kangaroo Island seems to have been a place where women were held for sealing ships to pick up — essentially, a slave trade. Governor Macquarie twice sent detachments to 'restore order' on the island, though gave no details in his reports back home. Slavery was by then illegal in England, and possibly he wanted to avoid a major outcry by abolitionists there. His second detachment to Kangaroo Island appears to have been successful.

Bucky and his 'kingdom' are fictitious, but based on rumours about conditions on the island at various times. Another word for 'rumour' can be oral history: no one wrote down what happened, but the stories were reliably passed down the generations. I don't have enough information, or knowledge of the people involved, to judge whether the stories I have heard are true, but given Macquarie's actions, at a time when he was also worried about the war with France, and the more certain histories of Indigenous women captured in other areas, the rumours almost certainly have at least a basis in fact. It is possible that the true history is far worse than I have described here.

INDIGENOUS LANGUAGES

At the time of the novel's setting, Australia had over three hundred Indigenous nations and at least two hundred languages. Most Indigenous people were at least bilingual, and some spoke between six and twenty languages and acted as translators. In places where there were regular trading routes, languages tended to have some words in common, or words that were similar enough to enable communication.

Guwara wouldn't have been able to speak to the Indigenous people of Western Australia, but there are records of Indigenous sailors from the Sydney region being able to talk to people in South Australia. There seems to be no record of whether they were using just a few terms or had a wider vocabulary in common, but it does mean that Guwara would have been able to communicate with the women held on Kangaruh Island.

GUWARA'S SPEARS

Guwara would have used several different kinds of spears: fighting spears, spears for hunting kangaroos, spears for fishing, two-metre-long spears for use from a canoe and shorter stumpy spears for animals like seals. He wouldn't necessarily have carried all types with him at the same time.

Spear-making was a difficult craft to learn; the spear had to be perfectly straight to be accurate. Some trees gave long, straight saplings and could be used as they were; others had to be straightened using a variety of techniques, including straightening green wood in hot damp sand or over a fire.

The shafts were bound by kangaroo sinews that tightened as they dried and were waterproof, and a variety of saps, such as that from the xanthorrhoea or grass tree.

The spearhead might be 'Darwin glass' or 'meteor glass', or other stones that could be chipped to a sharp point and were traded over thousands of kilometres; or the nasal bones of a kangaroo, certain fish bones and many other substances.

A woomera, or spear-thrower, was often used to make the spear travel faster, harder and more accurately. An axe or cutting blade could also be attached to the woomera, making it a multi-purpose tool, but as a sailor

Guwara would probably have had a metal knife and access to a metal axe, if not one of his own.

WATER CARRIERS

Many different forms of vessels to carry water were used by Indigenous Australians circa 1810. These included the waterbags described in this book: the skin from the leg of a large kangaroo would be carefully removed and tanned, and made waterproof by oiling, then the ends would be sealed with cords made of kangaroo sinew.

ENGLISH AND AUSTRALIAN 'BADGERS'

While Ben would have called his new home after the one in England, wombats were commonly called badgers back then, and his farm would have had many wombats.

ACKNOWLEDGEMENTS

I would never have attempted *Pirate Boy of Sydney Town* if I hadn't had the assistance and advice of Angela Marshall. Angela not only turns my scribbles into readable text, but has a wide, rich and eclectic knowledge of history. For much of our lives, both of us have relied on the skills of our forebears to build our own houses, create gardens, fences, water and power systems, and much else, from homemade paint to home-grown string.

Angela and her partner, Pete, are also experienced sailors. (I get seasick even on a pontoon waiting to board.) This book would have been impossible without them, and once again I owe them more thanks than I can say.

Titles by Jackie French

Australian Historical

Somewhere Around the Corner • Dancing with Ben Hall
Daughter of the Regiment • Soldier on the Hill • Valley of Gold
Tom Appleby, Convict Boy • A Rose for the Anzac Boys
The Night They Stormed Eureka • Nanberry: Black Brother White
Pennies for Hitler • Pirate Boy of Sydney Town

General Historical

Hitler's Daughter • Lady Dance • How the Finnegans Saved the Ship
The White Ship • They Came on Viking Ships • Macbeth and Son
Pharaoh • Oracle • Goodbye, Mr Hitler • Just a Girl

Fiction

Rain Stones • Walking the Boundaries • The Secret Beach
Summerland • A Wombat Named Bosco • Beyond the Boundaries
The Warrior: The Story of a Wombat • The Book of Unicorns
Tajore Arkle • Missing You, Love Sara • Dark Wind Blowing
Ride the Wild Wind: The Golden Pony and Other Stories
Refuge • The Book of Horses and Unicorns

Non-Fiction

A Year in the Valley • How the Aliens from Alpha Centauri
Invaded My Maths Class and Turned Me into a Writer
How to Guzzle Your Garden • The Book of Challenges
The Fascinating History of Your Lunch • To the Moon and Back
The Secret World of Wombats • How High Can a Kangaroo Hop?
Let the Land Speak: How the Land Created Our Nation
I Spy a Great Reader

Miss Lily Series

1. Miss Lily's Lovely Ladies • 1.5. With Love from Miss Lily: A Christmas Story
2. The Lily and the Rose • 2.5. Christmas Lilies • 3. The Lily in the Snow

The Matilda Saga

1. A Waltz for Matilda • 2. The Girl from Snowy River
3. The Road to Gundagai • 4. To Love a Sunburnt Country
5. The Ghost by the Billabong • 6. If Blood Should Stain the Wattle
7. Facing the Flame • 8. The Last Dingo Summer

Shakespeare Series

I am Juliet • Ophelia: Queen of Denmark
The Diary of William Shakespeare, Gentleman • Third Witch

The Animal Stars Series

The Goat Who Sailed the World • The Dog Who Loved a Queen
The Camel Who Crossed Australia • The Donkey Who Carried the Wounded
The Horse Who Bit a Bushranger
Dingo: The Dog Who Conquered a Continent